If he kissed her, he was surely lost

Yet kissing her was as necessary as breathing. His lips touched hers, and a feeling of homecoming flowed through him. How had he lived without this? Without her?

She tasted of everything and nothing. Femininity, passion, warmth, strength and softness—all lay in the sweetness of her kiss. It was like nothing he'd ever experienced before. It was magical.

Magical. The word stayed in his mind. *Magical*. His hands loosened slowly. *Magical*. Sheri's fingers drifted down to rest against his shirt. *Magical*. He broke the kiss slowly, reluctance in his every movement. *Magical*.

Their eyes met, and Sheri saw the question in his, read the thought in his expression. Her fingers touched his mouth, feather-light.

"No, Jack. What is between us is not of magic." A smile flickered over her mouth. "It's more of dreams. But not magic. Never magic."

ABOUT THE AUTHOR

Dallas Schulze is a full-time writer who lives in Southern California with her husband and their Persian cats. An avid reader, she devours books by the boxful. In what little spare time she has she enjoys doll collecting, old radio shows, classic and current movies, doll making, sewing, quilting and baking.

Books by Dallas Schulze

HARLEQUIN AMERICAN ROMANCE

Don't miss any of our special offers. Write to us at the following address for information on our newest releases.

Harlequin Reader Service
901 Fuhrmann Blvd., P.O. Box 1397, Buffalo, NY 14240
Canadian address: P.O. Box 603,
Fort Erie, Ont. L2A 5X3

OF DREAMS AND MAGIC

DALLAS SCHULZE

Harlequin Books

TORONTO • NEW YORK • LONDON
AMSTERDAM • PARIS • SYDNEY • HAMBURG
STOCKHOLM • ATHENS • TOKYO • MILAN

To Barbara...
thanks for the samovar,
the sanity, the insanity
and the friendship

Published November 1989

First printing September 1989

ISBN 0-373-16317-7

Prologue

The flowers were a vibrant contrast to the mound of dirt on which they lay. White daisies and bright California poppies, the pale shades of columbines—a mixture at once wild and soft. The hand that arranged the delicate blossoms was slim and graceful, the fingers gentle.

"I would have brought roses, but you always said they looked better on the bush than cut."

The girl's voice was soft, with a lilting intonation and an accent impossible to place. As she knelt beside the grave, hair of a color somewhere between gold and silver spilled over her shoulder, down her back, and stopped just short of touching the ground.

Around her, the Sierra foothills spread out in endless vistas of beauty. The sky was a bright clear blue and the air was so clean it almost hurt to breathe it. A chickadee settled in a huge oak tree just above the girl's head. He cocked his head as if listening.

"I miss you." She moved a columbine a few inches before reaching out to touch the solid tombstone that marked the head of the grave. "In town they say he should be here soon." Her breath caught a moment and her teeth worried her lower lip. She continued in a rush, her fingers trembling as they traced the name on the marker. "I know you said that everything would be all right. You said he needed me more than you ever had. But does he *know* he needs me?"

There was no answer to the urgent question and she sighed.

"Can you really know him so well? I wish you'd told me more about him. If he doesn't want me..." Her voice trailed off and she stared out at the hills, seeing something else. "Do you know what that means, my friend? Did you truly understand?"

A quiet breeze brushed over the small graveyard. It tangled in the girl's pale hair, lifting it in a soft caress. She looked at the gravestone, her smile quivering around the edges.

"I know you did your best for me. I will be all right. Whatever happens, I will be all right. Perhaps you should have told him about me. It's not for everyone to accept such things. You could have explained." She sighed again. "But perhaps some things can't be explained."

She stood up, dusting her hands against the legs of her jeans. "I will always remember your kindness to me."

The breeze stirred the leaves above her and she smiled, her eyes lighting with a bright spark of blue that rivaled the sky. She lifted her head, looking at the chickadee. "Such a cheerful fellow you are."

Her hands came up, palm out, a crust of bread offered. The chickadee tilted its head first this way, then that before opening its wings and sailing across the short distance to light on her fingers and peck daintily at the offered crust. Her smile grew into a soft laugh of pleasure, stirring the deep quiet.

"Perhaps everything will be all right, after all."

Chapter One

"I simply don't understand why you have to make this trip, Jack. Can't you send someone else? Or hire someone from the area to take a look at the house and decide what to do with it?"

Jack set his suitcase down next to the front door and turned to look at his fiancée. Did Eleanor's mouth always have that pinched look?

"I told you why I'm going to see to the cabin myself." He struggled to keep the impatience out of his voice. It wasn't Eleanor's fault she didn't understand his reasons for going. He didn't fully understand them himself.

"You can't do anything for your uncle, Jack."

"I'm not trying to do anything for him." He heard the snap in his tone and stopped, drawing a deep breath before continuing. "I'm doing this for myself."

"I fail to see just what this is going to do for you. A long drive to some tumbledown little house in the back of beyond. That's hardly restful. And once you get there, the place probably won't be habitable."

"Uncle Jack lived there."

"I hardly think that qualifies as a recommendation. Your mother has told me about him."

Eleanor didn't do anything so inelegant as sniff. She didn't have to. The faint tilt of one patrician brow said it all.

"Don't believe everything Mother tells you about Uncle Jack," he said dryly. "He was the black sheep of the family and he was a bit eccentric, but I'm sure he lived in relatively civilized surroundings. He always appreciated the creature comforts. Besides, in the letter his lawyer forwarded he asked me to see to the place myself."

"Well, I think that's very inconsiderate of him."

"Eleanor, the man is dead. I hadn't seen him in almost two years." Guilt made his voice sharper than he'd intended. In the two weeks since he'd received word of his uncle Jack's death, guilt had become a familiar companion. How was it that he'd lost touch with someone who'd been so important to him? Uncle Jack, who'd encouraged his dreams, listened to his fantasies.

He swallowed the anger that was mostly self-directed. How could he blame Eleanor for not understanding how important Jack Ryan had been to his namesake? She'd certainly not seen any evidence of it before this.

His voice was calm when he continued. "It seems a small enough thing for him to ask. He left the property to me."

"Fine. I can see your mind is made up, but do you have to go now?"

From another woman the tone might have been coaxing, but coaxing was not Eleanor's style. The question came out more as a demand, and Jack swallowed his annoyance. Eleanor hadn't changed. He was the one who was suddenly chafing under her tone.

"Yes, I have to go now. I *want* to go now. I need a few days away."

She smoothed the collar of her tailored shirt, her wide brow puckered with annoyance. It wasn't that she was annoyed because her fiancé had announced he needed some time away from her. No, she was annoyed because he was being unreasonable.

It was at moments like this that Jack considered he was planning to spend the rest of his life with this woman. The prospect didn't bring him the satisfaction it once had. In fact, he was having a hard time remembering just why he and Eleanor had decided to marry. He rubbed at the ache gathering at his temple and tried to focus on what she was saying.

"You know the Smith-Byrneses' party is the day after tomorrow. I accepted for both of us almost a month ago. Will you be back in time for it?"

"No, I won't." He should have softened the flat refusal. The way Eleanor's mouth tightened told him she felt the same, but he didn't add anything more. He was sick of being polite, sick of going to dinner parties given by people he didn't know and wouldn't like even if he did know. He rubbed his forehead again. It seemed as if lately it was unusual *not* to have a headache.

"They're going to think it very odd if you don't show up."

"I'm sure they'll understand when you tell them there was a death in the family. Even in the best of families these things can't always be planned."

"I just don't understand you, Jack. You're being very flip about this whole matter. We have several important dinner engagements in the next week. Do you plan to simply miss all of them?"

"Yes, I do," he said bluntly.

"Good for you Jackson. Stick to your guns."

The new voice came from the doorway. Jack turned, grateful for the interruption.

"Roger! When did you get back from the Bahamas?" Jack strode across the room toward the other man.

Roger Bendon straightened from his slouched position against the doorjamb and took his best friend's hand. "Just this morning. You should have come with me, Jack. The weather was fantastic. The beaches were gorgeous and so were the women. Oops. Sorry, Eleanor." He nodded in her direction, his dark eyes holding a wicked glint that said he wasn't in the least sorry.

"Hello, Roger. I saw your mother yesterday." Her tone was accusing."

"Really? How is she these days?"

"She's well. She was surprised to hear you were out of the country."

"That's probably because I didn't tell her I was going," he admitted cheerfully.

Eleanor's mouth tightened, and her gaze took on an iciness. "Don't you think you should have let her know? After all, she *is* your mother."

"I can't be blamed for that." His tone was baiting and he watched her for the expected reaction, but Jack stepped in before she could reply.

"Stop it, you two. Why is it you can't be in the same room for more than twenty seconds without one or the other of you picking a fight?"

Roger shrugged, grinning innocently. "I didn't say a thing."

Eleanor stood up, smoothing one slim hand over her silk skirt, carefully ignoring Roger. "I think I'll be going now, Jack. I'll make your excuses where necessary. Call me when you return."

Jack bent to kiss the cheek she proffered. Her skin was smooth and soft, smelling vaguely of lavender. The scent reminded him of his great-aunt Alice, who'd died when he was ten. It occurred to him that his fiancée probably shouldn't remind him of his great-aunt Alice, but he pushed the thought away and forced a smile.

"I'll call you as soon as I know when I'll be back. I hope my absence doesn't cause you too many problems."

"I'm sure I'll be able to manage anything that comes up," she told him briskly.

She walked past Roger, according him a nod in farewell. He responded with a low bow, mocking her formality. Her stride was just a little tight as she crossed the wide hallway and pulled open the huge door.

"I'd frown if I was engaged to her, too."

Jack hadn't been aware of his expression until Roger's flippant comment. He rubbed his fingers over his forehead as if to erase the creases. "Lay off, Roger. I'm engaged to Eleanor. The least you can do is be polite."

"You're absolutely right. And I am polite. It's not my fault she doesn't like me." Roger perched on the arm of a Chippendale chair, his worn jeans a vivid contrast to the chair's ornate style.

The look Jack threw him made it clear his innocent pose wasn't fooling anybody. He had the grace to appear ashamed. "Sorry. I'll try harder."

"I'd appreciate that. Otherwise the wedding is likely to end up a war zone."

"Don't even mention the wedding. I can't believe you're actually going to marry—" He caught the warning in Jack's eyes and threw up his hands. "Okay, okay. Not another word. You know what I think of this engagement."

"Yes, I do."

The conversation lagged until Roger broke the awkward silence.

"So, tell me, where are you going? It's about time you took a vacation. You've been working like a dog at that bank for too long. Tahiti is nice this time of year."

Jack sat down opposite Roger. He'd planned to be on the road half an hour ago, but there was no set time he had to leave—a novel experience for him. In the ten years since he'd left college, he could barely remember an instance when he didn't need to be somewhere at a specific time. He wasn't entirely comfortable with this new freedom.

"I'm not going to Tahiti."

"How about Europe? I'll go with you. We could paint Paris red. I know this great little bistro. The food is out of this world and the waitresses—" Roger kissed his fingertips, his expression ecstatic.

Jack laughed, feeling some of his tension fade. Roger never failed to make people smile. It was one of his best qualities.

"Sorry. Paris is out. I'm on my way north."

"North? Alaska? No, really, Jack. I know things look bleak, but I'm sure they're not that bad."

"Northern California, you fool."

"Northern California? Land of latent Communists and ecologically minded citizens? No wonder Eleanor was so concerned."

"That's the place. I don't think Eleanor is concerned with *where* I'm going. It's the timing that bothers her."

"Ah, yes. How could you go in the middle of the season? Inconsiderate scoundrel."

The look Jack threw him was enough to make him raise his hands in apology.

"Sorry. Couldn't resist," he continued. "So, what's in the northern portion of our fair state? A local bank that

Smith, Smith and Ryan Fiduciary, Inc. plans to swallow whole?"

"No. This has nothing to do with business."

Roger arched one dark brow, his face expressing amazement. "Nothing to do with business? I didn't think you knew how to do anything else anymore."

"Thanks," Jack told him dryly. Roger's comment had too much truth in it for him to be truly annoyed.

"You're welcome. So if it's not business, what's prying you away from your charming fiancée and your beloved desk?"

"My uncle Jack died and I'm going up to take a look at the place he left me."

"I'm sorry to hear that. I remember the summer he came to visit. We were what? Fifteen, sixteen? He smuggled us into that strip joint. I thought your mother was going to have a coronary when she found out."

Jack grinned. "I was grounded for a month. And Uncle Jack was forbidden to come near me for almost a year. I don't think Mother ever entirely forgave him for that."

"He was a great guy. What happened?"

Jack shrugged, his smile fading. It hurt to remember those good times. "Heart attack."

"Well, at least it was quick."

"Yeah. He wouldn't have wanted a lingering illness. Anyway, I'm going to drive up and take a look at the house and decide what to do with it. I shouldn't be gone more than a few days." He glanced at his watch. "I ought to get along."

Roger followed him out to the car, watching as he loaded his overnight case into the trunk of the gray Jaguar.

"You know, one of the best things about traveling is that it gives you a chance to think," Roger said casually.

Jack glanced at him. There was nothing in his friend's expression that hinted at deeper meaning, but he'd known Roger a long time. If anyone could understand the way he'd been feeling lately—the sensation of falling deeper into some dark hole—it would be Roger.

"Rog, I—" He stopped.

"What is it?"

Jack shook his head. "Nothing. Just a stray thought I had, but it's not important."

Roger wanted to press the issue, but didn't. "Have a good trip" was all he said. "I hope you find what you're looking for."

Jack was still pondering Roger's last remark a few minutes later as he drove onto the Ventura Freeway and joined the stream of cars heading west.

Find what he was looking for? Just what was he looking for? He had to admit there was something. There was a gap in his life. Something missing, an incompleteness he couldn't quite put his finger on. He shoved a hand through his hair, trying to shake the odd mood that had been with him ever since he'd gotten the letter telling him his uncle had died.

Though, if he were honest, the mood had been with him longer than that. It was just that Uncle Jack's death had sharpened the vague discontent, making it more real, more vivid. Just pointing the Jag's nose away from Pasadena, Los Angeles and Southern California as a whole made him feel he'd left a ball and chain behind.

But there was nothing in his life that justified that feeling. He wasn't being held prisoner or forced to do anything he didn't want to. Perhaps when his father had died his last year in college, he hadn't had much choice about jumping into the banking business. There'd been no one else to hold things together. But he'd stayed in the business because he enjoyed it. Didn't he?

He reached out and snapped on the radio, looking for something to fill the echoing silence left by that question. The soothing strains of Brahms filled the car, reminding him of concerts with Eleanor at his side, perfectly coiffed and immaculately dressed.

He punched a button and the rhythmic blast of the Beach Boys harmonizing "Little Deuce Coupe" effectively banished any concert-hall atmosphere. Tina must have set the station last time she'd borrowed the Jag. His little sister was not known for her sophisticated tastes in music.

He reached out to change the station again, then stopped. God, he hadn't heard the Beach Boys in years. They hardly suited his corporate image, but the song brought back memories of other times. He and Roger taking surfboards down into the Pacific, girls in bikinis, beach parties that lasted all summer. Life had been so much simpler then.

He left the station on, acknowledging a foolish feeling of defiance. Maybe Roger was right. Maybe he had forgotten how to play. It had been much too long since he'd taken time off just to relax.

Uncle Jack had wanted him to have a look at the property before deciding what to do with it and he was going to take his time, make sure that whatever he decided was what his uncle would have wanted. It wouldn't surprise him if that was exactly what the old scoundrel had had in mind when he'd made that will. He'd been pretty outspoken about his namesake's life. Maybe this was his final effort to get his nephew to break out of the corporate life-style he believed was just about the lowest way of living.

Jack grinned and reached out to turn the radio up another notch.

He made the long drive without stopping, except to get gas and have a late lunch—a thick hamburger and a mound of French fries, which he ate at a tiny café in a town so small he hadn't even noticed if it had a name. The napkins were paper, the booths were cracked vinyl and he could feel his arteries growing harder with every bite he took. Still, he couldn't remember the last time food had tasted quite so good.

As the sun began to set, he debated the wisdom of finding a place to stay the night, then continuing in the morning. From the instructions he'd been given, he suspected his uncle's home was easier to miss than find. But he didn't feel like stopping before he reached the end of the journey, so he went on, switching the high beams when he turned onto a winding country road.

It was almost midnight when he found the narrow dirt lane that led to the house. The road was just as he'd expected—unkempt, unmarked, barely usable. He found it more by instinct than sight, though he'd slowed to a crawl the last five miles, peering into the darkness for the shallow indentation in the overgrowth that was all the marker Uncle Jack had felt necessary.

The Jag grumbled in protest as it inched its way onto the rutted surface. Jack had the fanciful thought that it was complaining because the accommodations were hardly what it was accustomed to.

Now that he was nearly there, he felt a stirring excitement. He'd been right to make this trip himself. Not only did he owe his uncle this much, but he needed the time away himself. Time with no one making demands, no one expecting anything from him.

He stopped in front of the house and stared at the dark bulk of it. Funny, he thought he'd glimpsed lights when the lane curved and the house had been visible for a moment. But there were no lights now. He shrugged. It must have been an illusion. Maybe moonlight catching in the windows.

He opened the car door and stepped onto the coarse gravel that functioned as a parking area. Around him the night was still. No traffic noises, no distant wail of a siren. Just the rhythmic creak of a cricket and, in the distance, the mournful hoot of an owl. He took a deep breath, wondering if his lungs were up to handling air without smog.

This was exactly what he'd been craving. Total peace and quiet. He could spend a week up here and get a little perspective on his life. The only real problem was that he'd been too pressured lately. A small vacation was just the thing to shake everything back into its proper place.

He drew in another deep breath. This was exactly what he needed. No problems, no worries.

Chapter Two

The inside of the house did not live up to his expectations, considering the rather ramshackle look of the exterior. Or did he mean it didn't live *down* to his expectations? Whatever, it didn't match the outside, which even in the moonlight, showed signs of neglect and age. The sagging porch was sturdy enough, but in desperate need of a few coats of paint. In contrast, the hallway he stepped into was immaculately clean and had to have been painted within the past year or so.

So, the place was not the hut Eleanor had imagined and it wasn't exactly the shabby little building he'd been expecting. Uncle Jack had obviously kept it in good shape.

The hardwood floors were old and worn, but they were clean. In fact, they were much cleaner than he would have expected, considering the house had been empty for a month. He moved into the kitchen, and found it equally spotless. An ancient refrigerator hummed in one corner and Jack tugged open the door. He was only slightly surprised to find the shelves full of food.

He reached in and pulled out a bottle of beer, his mouth relaxing in a smile. Coors. Well, that told him Eleanor hadn't arranged this. She thought his taste in beer appalling. If he had to drink such a disgusting brew, at the very least couldn't he drink something imported? He twisted the cap off and took a long pull directly from the bottle, another action that would have made Eleanor's patrician nose wrinkle.

He left the kitchen, wandering toward the stairs that led upward from the front hall. The upstairs was as clean as the rest of the house. There were only three rooms on the second floor. A small but immaculately clean bathroom, a bedroom not much bigger than the bathroom, which his uncle had apparently used for storage, and another bedroom.

The larger bedroom was clean, which he had come to expect. The surfaces of the ancient oak furniture had that subtle glow that comes from generations of elbow grease. The bedspread—hand-crocheted, if he didn't miss his guess—was spotlessly white. When he flipped back the corner, he found the bed neatly made with linen sheets and a thick wool blanket.

He went back down the stairs and out to his car. The night was clear, the sky full of stars whose light never reached the city. The quiet *pop* of the trunk opening sounded loud in the thick stillness. He lifted his suitcase out and shut the trunk, wincing as the heavy *thunk* seemed to echo much too sharply.

When he stepped inside again, he had an odd sense of welcome, as if the old house were glad to see him. Jack smiled at the whimsical thought. Must be all this country air. It was bringing out a side of him he'd lost touch with so long ago he hadn't even remembered it existed. Shutting the front door behind him, he felt as if he'd come home. Not the way he felt about the huge house in Pasadena where he'd been born. That was home, but this was something more. This was— Just what was it?

He shook his head and carried his suitcase upstairs, setting it down in the old-fashioned bedroom. The stairs creaked as he walked back down. Maybe it was just that he was overtired from the long drive or the stresses of the past few months, but he couldn't shake the feeling that the house welcomed him. That it *liked* him.

He picked up his beer and carried it into the living room. There was firewood neatly laid in the fireplace and Jack hesitated only a moment before setting a match to it. The flames licked upward, burning through the crumpled newspaper before catching at the neatly stacked twigs, then licking up around the pile of small logs.

He hadn't even been sure his message to Mr. Jenkins had gotten through. The letter from the lawyer had said that Jenkins would be taking care of his uncle's property until Jack arrived or forwarded instructions. Jack had sent word he was coming up, but he hadn't asked Jenkins to get the place ready for him. He hadn't even known exactly when he'd be arriving. But apparently Jenkins had received the letter and had gone out of his way to get everything ready for his arrival.

The house had been cleaned, the kitchen stocked, even a fire laid. Maybe there really was something to the stories about country hospitality. Jack was going to have to make it a point to thank the man. He could go into the little town tomorrow and see about locating him. In a place this small, someone was bound to know where he lived.

The grandfather clock in the hall creaked like an old man going up a steep flight of stairs, then began to bong—a deep, dignified sound. Jack leaned his head against the back of the chair, counting the notes. It was late. If he had any sense at all, he'd go straight to bed, instead of lighting a fire he couldn't possibly stay awake to watch burn out. But he was tired of being sensible. Tired of doing the reasonable thing.

He'd been doing the reasonable thing since college. In this one small thing he was going to be unreasonable, unsensible. Unsensible? He smiled, taking another drink of beer. Even his command of the language was going to pot. It felt surprisingly good.

He stood up and adjusted the screen in front of the crackling flames, then turned to study the rest of the room. He'd barely glanced in here earlier, but his first impression had been accurate. Like the bedroom upstairs, this room had a vaguely Victorian flavor. The furniture was on the heavy side and looked as if it had remained in exactly the same place for decades.

But the room didn't feel like a museum. Jack settled back into the chair and took another sip. Oddly enough, the room looked just as he might have expected Uncle Jack's place to look. It suited him. It was not quite of this time, and that was exactly what Uncle Jack had been. A man in the wrong time. He should have been born a century ago, when he could have gone adventuring.

Jack's mouth twisted in a wry grin, and he lifted his bottle in salute. "To you, Uncle Jack. I hope that wherever you are now, it offers more excitement than this world had to give."

He took a long drink, angling his head back as the bottle emptied. As he lowered the bottle, a golden gleam in one corner caught his eye. He tilted his head, but all he could make out was something fairly large sitting on a low table in one corner of the room.

He got up and moved to investigate. The light appeared to shift as he approached, illuminating the corner. Then the firelight caught on gleaming brass. Settled on a low mahogany table was an enormous samovar. The slightly squat urn shape seemed to hunker in the corner as if trying to avoid being noticed.

"What on earth were you doing with something like this, Uncle Jack?" Jack asked the question out loud as he lowered himself to his heels to get a better view of the object.

It was exquisite. Nearly three feet high, with curving lines that flowed in an almost sensuous pattern. The brass glowed as if lit from within. Every flicker of firelight caught on the shining sides and Jack wondered how it was possible he hadn't noticed the samovar the minute he walked into the room.

He reached out to stroke the shining surface. It felt warm to the touch, warmer than he might have expected, given the temperature of the room. It must be a sensory illusion. The golden brass *looked* warm, therefore it *felt* warm. Still, the illusion was so strong he had the odd thought that the exquisite samovar was alive.

Jack drew his hand away, still staring at the urn. It was made in a pattern of overlapping leaves, each one intricately carved to match its mates so that the pattern appeared continuous. It was so bright. Not a spot of tarnish marred the perfect surface. No dust settled on the gleaming sides.

Jack reached out to touch it again, wanting to feel that warmth, but he drew back before his fingers contacted its surface. *If he touched it, he'd be lost.*

He shook his head as the bizarre thought flitted across his mind. Lost? Lost to what? In what? He shook his head, standing up and moving away from the low table. Maybe Eleanor was right. Maybe he should stay away from Coors. Would one bottle of a more respectable imported brew have had this effect?

He picked up the empty beer bottle and left the living room, refusing to acknowledge the uneasy itch between his shoulder blades when he turned his back on the samovar. Once he was in the kitchen the uneasiness slipped away, and he laughed at his strange fancies.

It must be the lateness of the hour and all this clean, healthy air. They were having a deleterious effect on his imagination. And speaking of healthy air, he was suddenly starving.

He rummaged through the refrigerator, finding a thick package of sliced ham and the rest of what he needed to construct a sandwich of truly mammoth proportions. He devoured his concoction hungrily, unable to remember the last time his appetite had been so sharp.

Once the snack was finished, tiredness rolled over him in a wave. He set his dishes in the sink and switched off the lights as he left the kitchen. He glanced into the living room to make sure the screen was in place around the fire. The samovar shone from its corner. Now that he knew it was there, it was impossible to ignore. In fact, he had the odd fancy it was watching him. He shook his head, turning away from it to climb the stairs.

He was tired and his imagination was working overtime. He'd been working too hard lately and he needed a rest. A long rest.

The mattress yielded beneath his tired body and Jack let out a long sigh. The bed felt like heaven. He could sleep as late as he wanted and tomorrow this place would look like an ordinary, slightly tumbledown house. He'd realize that this strange feeling of welcome, of homecoming, had been the result of too many hours on the road. And too many months of twelve-hour days before that.

He'd spend a few days here, get some rest, then go back to the real world. He drifted off to sleep on the thought, aware that the real world seemed very far away indeed.

Moonlight shone in through the open curtains, gilding the room in cool silvery light, catching the gilt of the watch lying on the dresser, the heavy brass latches of his suitcase, which he hadn't bothered to unpack. Outside, the owl hooted, the sound closer now. It hunted and some small creature would soon provide it with dinner, part of the cycle of nature.

Jack slept deeply, his breathing slow and shallow, his long body totally relaxed. He slept more soundly than he had in years. So soundly he was unaware of no longer being alone.

He didn't stir when a slim figure crept out of the shadows to stand beside the bed. Moonlight tangled in hair as pale as a moonbeam, shadowing more than revealing the delicate oval of a face and the slender hands clasped anxiously together.

She studied his face, all planes and angles. There was no softness there, but still . . . something drew her. A deep response she didn't fight. It wasn't in her to fight what her instincts told her was right.

He was handsome. And strong. She could read strength in the set of his jaw. She reached out, her fingers hovering over the lock of thick black hair that drifted across his forehead. She drew back without touching him, wondering at the odd tingling she felt. It was as if the air itself were alive.

He was her future, if a future she was to have. How would he react? She pressed her hand to her chest, feeling the slight acceleration of her heartbeat. She was nervous, but there was something more. Something she'd never felt before and couldn't quite define.

She watched Jack a few moments longer, tracing the strong lines of his face in the moonlight, wondering about a future she could only guess at. The future could never be predicted. Whatever was meant to be would be.

She slid back into the shadows, disappearing as silently as she'd come, like a wraith of smoke dispersed on a summer breeze.

Jack sighed and frowned slightly in his sleep, but he didn't awaken.

RIVERBEND, CALIFORNIA, was hardly a booming metropolis. It was, in fact, little more than a wide spot in the road—a narrow road at that. It had a gas station, a tiny post office, a café, two bars and a general store that carried everything from aspirin to videotapes. The two bars gave Jack a fair idea of what the residents of Riverbend probably did on a Saturday night.

Jack pulled the Jaguar into the narrow dirt parking area next to the general store. Overhead the sky was blue, a blue so bright it almost hurt to look at it. There was no traffic noise, there being no traffic to speak of in Riverbend. The mountains rose up on all sides, vivid reminders of the fact that so far man was only a visitor to this particular part of nature. Jack rather hoped it stayed that way. It was nice to know there were places where concrete and steel didn't reign supreme.

Entering the general store was like taking a step back in time. The aisles were packed with an assortment of items in no visible order. He assumed that the people who shopped there must simply memorize the position of any item they were likely to want. There was a single counter in front. Behind that was a display of rifles and shotguns and, in jarring contrast, a huge display of the latest movies on videotape.

Jack wandered up and down the aisles, picking up a Swiss army knife with enough gadgets to satisfy even the most avid of campers. He had no intention of going camping, but he remembered having wanted one when he was a boy. He bought a few groceries, thinking he should have given a more thorough check to the contents of the kitchen, since he wasn't sure if he was duplicating what was already there.

When he moved up to the counter, the man behind it gave him a measured look, as if trying to decide what he was doing in this sleepy little town.

"Find what you needed?"

"Yes, thanks." Jack nodded to the store behind him. "It would be pretty hard not to find what you needed. You've got a bit of everything, haven't you?"

The man's lean face softened into what could have been a smile.

"We try to keep most things on hand. It's a far drive to the next town and farther than that to a big city. Folks like to be able to get most things local."

"Well, you've certainly done a good job of choosing your stock."

"Thanks. You stayin' around here?"

The question was casual, but the look that accompanied it was sharp.

"I'm Jack Ryan." He held out his hand and the other man took it, his eyes sparked with interest.

"You must be old Jack's nephew. Knew you were supposed to come up and take a look at the place. I'm Burt Jenkins. When did you get here?"

"Late last night. I guess I have you to thank for taking care of the place. I appreciate the work you've done."

Jenkins shrugged. "Not much to do. We don't have any real crime up here, so I just looked in on the place once a week or so to make sure no animals had broken in. If I'd known exactly when you were going to get here, I'd have taken some lamps over. How'd you manage in the dark?''

Jack's smile took on a puzzled edge. ''Lamps? The electricity was on.''

It was Jenkins's turn to look puzzled. ''Electricity on? You must have gone to the wrong place. Jack had the electric cut off years ago. Said they charged too damn much, and besides, he preferred oil lamps. Bought all his oil here. You'll be wanting to get a supply for yourself, I reckon.''

''Yeah. Yeah, I guess I'd better. Are you sure about the electricity?''

''Sure as can be.'' Jenkins set two bottles of lamp oil on the counter.

''But I had lights last night. The refrigerator was working.''

Jenkins shrugged. ''Maybe the electric company heard the place was getting a new owner and figured he wouldn't be as stubborn as old Jack was. Maybe they turned it back on.''

He started ringing up Jack's purchases, obviously losing interest in the puzzle.

''Yeah. Maybe.'' Jack paid for his groceries.

''You going to be here long?''

Jack shrugged. ''I don't really know yet. A few days at least. There are a lot of decisions to make.''

''Well, if you need anything, let me know. I'm here most of the time.''

''Thanks. I'll keep that in mind. And thanks again for keeping an eye on the place.''

Jack loaded the sacks into the passenger seat of the car and started back toward his uncle's house. He drove automatically, a heavy frown drawing his dark brows together. He didn't know a whole lot about utility companies, but one thing he was willing to bet on was that they didn't just reconnect electricity in the hopes that a new owner was going to pay for it.

There *had* been electricity last night. He hadn't imagined it. But Jenkins had been so sure and having the electricity disconnected sounded exactly like something Uncle Jack would have done.

Jack pulled up in front of the house and studied it for a moment. This was definitely his uncle's house. The key he'd been sent fit the lock. He went inside and flicked lights on and off. They all worked, just as they had the night before. He went back outside, loosening the top few buttons of his shirt in response to the heat. It wasn't hard to find what he was looking for. The electric meter was on the side of the house, firmly nailed to the wood siding. The glass door hung drunkenly on one hinge. The meter inside was badly rusted and obviously hadn't worked in years. Squinting upward, Jack could see where the connecting line had once been hooked up to the house, but the line was long gone.

Curiouser and curiouser. He had electricity, but there was no way for it to be getting to the house. A quick check assured him there was no generator on the place. So where was the power to run the lights and the refrigerator coming from?

He stood in front of the house, his hands on his hips, and stared at the old building. A huge old rosebush rambled over the front of the porch. Big fat blooms the color of palest apricot covered the canes, filling the air with scent. It was a scene of domestic peace. Jack frowned. Roses were a passion of his mother's. Wasn't this awfully early in the year for them to be in bloom, especially at this altitude?

Now that he thought about it, there were other things about the place that were odd. The dishes he'd left in the sink the night before had been put away this morning. And the ones he'd used at breakfast were gone just now when he'd checked the power in the kitchen. He'd noticed it peripherally, but it hadn't registered that there was anything unusual about that. At home the housekeeper dealt with things like dishes. But this wasn't L.A. and there was no housekeeper.

And his car. Damn! Why hadn't he realized it before? The Jag had been in the garage this morning. Nothing odd about that, except that he'd left it in the driveway last night. And he'd had the keys with him. So someone or something had moved it into the garage. It was a measure of just how much he needed this time off that he was just now noticing things that should have hit him right away.

Despite the heat of the day Jack felt a shiver run up his spine. The sun didn't seem quite so bright. This whole thing was beginning to feel like something out of the *Twilight Zone*. He dismissed the thought as soon as it appeared. There was a perfectly logical explanation for all of this. At the moment he couldn't imagine what it was, but there was one.

He shivered again, and reached up to rub the back of his neck. It was stupid, but he suddenly felt as if he were being watched. Ridiculous. Yet the feeling persisted. Scanning the scruffy area around the house, he could see no signs of anyone, but the feeling grew stronger. He could feel eyes on him, watching, waiting. Waiting for what?

Every eerie story he'd ever heard flitted through his mind. According to childhood lore, there could be anything from a ghost to a banshee lurking in the underbrush.

"Right, Jack. In broad daylight." The sound of his own voice seemed too loud. A scrub jay started from the roof of the porch, his raucus cry making Jack jump.

"Don't be an idiot," he muttered to himself, but the feeling of unseen eyes persisted, until he had to believe someone was out there. Watching him.

He took a deep breath, squelching the urge to get in the car and drive away from this place. *If* there was someone out there, doing his dishes and moving his car and pulling electricity out of thin air, they'd already proved they weren't malevolent. There was a logical explanation for this, and whoever was out there could provide it.

"I think I'll go for a walk." He tried to sound casual, as if just talking to himself. Feeling like a total fool, he began to walk toward the thin forest of oaks that blanketed one side of the mountain.

The sky was still a brilliant blue. Another scrub jay called loudly, the harsh sound shattering the quiet air, leaving a thick silence behind. The dry grass crackled under his shoes. Ahead of him, a white butterfly flitted from one weed to another, pausing an instant before skipping to the next.

Jack noticed everything with senses that seemed more acute than they had just a few short hours ago. He walked into the woods until he judged that he was out of sight of the house, then turned and crept back, not sure if he really wanted to catch whoever—or whatever—had been watching him.

More than anything, he wanted to believe that the feeling had been nothing more than his imagination. That might leave him without an explanation for the odd occurrences, but it was better than what he was afraid he might find.

"Don't be an idiot," he mumbled. "*If* there's someone out there, it's probably just some local kid who's curious about a stranger in the area."

Sure. A local kid who just happened to know how to generate electricity from nothing. Who stocks refrigerators that shouldn't be working, does dishes without a sound and can move a ton and a half of car without a key. Sure. Just your average country bumpkin.

The mental argument continued, drawing Jack's nerves thinner and tighter. He moved carefully from tree to tree until he was within a few yards of the house, then waited. Around him, nature went about her business, oblivious of the little drama being played out. As he waited, Jack felt like more of a fool with each passing second.

He'd almost managed to convince himself that the only mystery was why he wasn't in a straitjacket, when he caught a glimpse of movement. Adrenaline surged through him. Someone was stepping out of the house onto the sagging porch. The sun was in his eyes, making it impossible to see more than just that it was a human shape. Jack felt a ridiculous flood of relief and he chided himself.

"What are you expecting, you idiot? A three-headed Martian?" The muttered comment made him feel a little better. All he had to do was talk to whoever this was and he'd have all the logical explanations he'd need. Then he'd see just how completely ridiculous this whole thing was.

He stepped out from behind the tree and started toward the house. "Excuse me."

Startled, the figure stiffened, then rushed off the porch and started to run. Jack saw all his logical explanations disappearing. Reacting instinctively, he gave chase. He hadn't spent four years on the UCLA track team for nothing. The distance between the figure and him shortened rapidly. He judged the space and threw himself forward in a flying tackle that caught his quarry behind the knees. The two hit the ground with a thud. Jack consolidated his grasp, his hands catching a pair of surprisingly slim shoulders and pinning them to the dirt as he straddled the stranger. He had a brief glimpse of masses of pale blond hair, so light it was almost white, and a pair of frightened blue eyes.

In the space between one second and the next, she was gone and he was suddenly flat on his face on the ground. He spit dirt out of his mouth as he pushed himself upright. She must have punched him when he wasn't looking. Though how such a fragile-looking creature could pack such a wallop he couldn't imagine.

"Are you all right? You aren't hurt, are you?"

The voice was soft, with the lilt of some accent he couldn't quite place. He turned his head to look at the speaker. He'd expected her to run, but she was still there, hovering a few feet away, her expression uncertain.

"Who are you?" He'd meant the words to come out as a demand, with a hint of righteous indignation, but the sheer beauty of her softened his tone. Never in his life had he seen a woman so exquisite. From the thick mass of pale hair to the tips of slender feet, she was like a painting of a fantasy.

"I'm Sheri." She reached up to coil a strand of hair around her fingers.

"I'm Jack." He stared at her, searching for some flaw but finding none.

"I know. Your uncle told me you'd be coming."

"You knew Uncle Jack?"

A smile flickered on the perfect oval of her face.

"He was my friend."

Jack moved closer, drawn toward her beauty, not believing the reality of it. Sheri shifted uneasily, watching him with a sort of nervous anticipation that Jack didn't understand.

"Are you the one who put the food in the house and cleaned the place up?"

"Yes. Was everything all right?" She twisted a lock of hair around her finger before releasing it to fall against the shoulder of her blue cotton shirt.

"Everything was fine," Jack replied, forgetting about all his questions, about the strange occurrences that had seemed so important a few minutes ago.

"Good. I wasn't sure what you'd like."

Jack was standing next to her now, and she tilted her head back to meet his eyes. My God, when had he ever seen eyes that color? Blue, yes, but more than blue. There was a touch of green in their depths. It was like looking into the heart of a pure sapphire and seeing a hint of emerald beneath.

She wasn't tall—not an inch over five feet—and she was slender. She looked as if a puff of wind would blow her over. But something told him she might be stronger than she appeared.

"Would you like to come in and have a cup of coffee or some iced tea or something? I guess iced tea would probably be better on a day like this. We could talk."

Unconsciously he'd lowered his voice, gentled the tone. She seemed so skittish, as if she might disappear in a wisp of smoke if he startled her. Maybe she hadn't seen many strangers.

She hesitated a moment, and he found himself wanting to know what she was thinking behind that wide blue gaze.

She nodded. "That would be nice."

As Jack led the way into the house, he had the feeling that nothing in his life was ever going to be quite the same again.

Chapter Three

"Shall I get the tea?"

Jack waved Sheri to a seat, shaking his head. "I'm the host. I'll get it. You just sit down and relax. It will have to be instant, I'm afraid."

"Oh, I think there's a pitcher of brewed in the refrigerator."

Jack glanced at her. "I don't remember seeing it."

"I think I put one in there. Your uncle was very fond of tea." She opened the refrigerator and reached in to pull out a tall white pitcher. "See? I was sure I'd left some in there."

Jack stared at the pitcher. It hadn't been in there last night. Had it? It was certainly possible he'd overlooked it. He'd been looking for sandwich makings, not tea. Still, he didn't remember seeing that pitcher.

Sheri poured tea into two glasses and set them on the table before looking up at him. Jack was still standing next to the cupboard, staring at the pitcher. Her eyes followed his and she seemed uneasy, but perhaps it was his imagination. Her voice was normal enough.

"It was way in the back. That's probably why you didn't notice it."

"Probably." He shook off the fruitless questions assailing him and sat down across the table from her. It took a conscious effort to keep from staring at her.

"Did you know my uncle long?"

"A few years. He was a very nice man."

"Yes, he was. A bit rasty but nice."

"'Rasty'?" Her forehead wrinkled as she tried out what was obviously a new word to her. "What's that?"

"Rasty. Ornery. Rough around the edges. Hard to get along with."

"Oh. Yes, he could be that, but underneath he was a very sweet man. A little lonely, you know."

Jack felt a surge of guilt. "I should have come up to see him years ago. Why is it that it always seems like there's plenty of time to do something, so you put it off, and suddenly there's no time left."

"That's the way things always are. But your uncle understood. He didn't mind. I think he was glad. He wasn't well the last few months, you know, and I don't think he would have wanted you to remember him that way."

"I didn't know he'd been ill." Guilt washed over him in a fresh wave. Why hadn't he made it up to see the old man?

Sheri's hand covered his on the table, her touch cool and soothing.

"Truly, he didn't want you to know. I suggested you should be called, but he said there would be time enough for you to visit when he was gone."

"Time enough for what?"

Her eyes shifted, flickering away from his, and she withdrew her hand. Jack found himself missing the light touch.

"I don't know. He didn't always tell me things."

"It sounds as if you spent quite a bit of time with him."

"I did. He was a good man."

Jack's eyes sharpened as a thought occurred to him. "Did you take care of him the last few months?"

She seemed to consider the question as if debating an answer, then she nodded slowly. "I did. He'd helped me when I needed help."

"My God. I had no idea." He shook his head, staring down at the scarred oak table, wondering how it was possible to lose touch so completely with someone so important to him. "You must have been very fond of him."

"I was," she answered simply.

"What about your family? Didn't they mind?"

"I . . . have no family."

He looked at her, another thought forming in the back of his mind. "Did you stay here with my uncle?"

She looked uncomfortable but answered quietly. "Yes, I did. He was quite ill and I preferred that he not be alone."

"Oh, God. I feel like a total scum. He didn't even feel as if he could come to me. I would have helped him."

Again she reached out to touch his hand. "He knew that. Please. He did not want you to feel this way. He wanted it this way. He said, 'I don't want the boy comin' up here and seein' me lookin' like a horned toad scared out of half a year's growth by a hoot owl.'"

Her soft voice had dropped into an uncanny imitation of Uncle Jack's gruff tone, and Jack had to chuckle. Yes, he could see the old buzzard saying that. "Uncle Jack always did go his own way," he murmured, remembering.

They were quiet for a while as they sipped the chilled tea.

Jack shook himself out of his memories and looked at her. "If you were living here with Uncle Jack, where did you stay last night?"

She reached up to twist her hair, a gesture he was already beginning to associate with her being nervous.

"There are a lot of places around here to stay."

He didn't press for a more precise answer, sensing she didn't want to say anything more, but he suspected he knew where she'd slept. He'd noticed that the old barn had a fairly good supply of straw. It wasn't hard to imagine her having spent the night there.

Maybe she didn't have the money to stay elsewhere. She'd said she had no family. She was so slim. Had she been living alone up here since Jack died? Maybe not eating enough? But she'd stocked the house with food. She must have had some money to do that. Still, she looked so waiflike.

"Are you hungry?"

"Not really."

But Jack didn't believe her. He could see that she had a fair share of pride. She wouldn't want him to know she was hungry. It was silly, really. If she'd taken care of his uncle in his last few months, a meal was the least Jack owed her.

"Well, I'm hungry. You'll stay for dinner, won't you?" Outside, the sun was beginning to lower. One of the disadvantages of having slept until almost noon was that the day was gone very quickly.

"I— Yes, that would be nice. May I cook for you?"

"I can manage."

"I'm sure you can, but I like to cook."

She gave him that shy smile he found so enchanting.

"Uncle Jack liked my cooking."

"'Uncle Jack'?" He raised one dark brow in teasing question. "Is that what you called him?"

"Yes. You don't mind, do you?"

"I don't mind. But I'm certain I don't have any cousins as beautiful as you."

Sheri flushed, dropping her eyes away from his, and Jack realized the remark had been unmistakably flirtatious. Not his usual style at all. He was an engaged man. Even without Eleanor to consider, flirting had never been his style. But, then, he wasn't feeling much like himself these days, anyway.

Sheri was so insistent about cooking the meal that Jack gave in, letting her shoo him out of the kitchen. He retreated to the living room and turned on a couple of lamps, dispelling the encroaching gloom. There was a fresh laid fire in the fireplace. Sheri's doing, no doubt. Her presence explained a lot of things, but it didn't explain the power that couldn't be on but was. Maybe she knew something about that.

He looked at the samovar. The last of the dying sunlight splashed across the table, casting golden rays onto the brass. It looked just as out of place now as it had the night before. Amid the worn, dated furnishings, the gleaming brass urn stood out, blatantly unsuited to its surroundings.

Jack moved closer. In better light the workmanship was even more remarkable. It really was a stunning piece of work. What on earth had Uncle Jack been doing with what looked like a museum piece? As far as he knew, the old man hadn't been a collector of anything except tall tales.

He reached out to lift the lid and his fingers had just settled on it, when Sheri spoke behind him.

"Dinner is ready."

Jack turned, startled, his hand dropping away from the samovar. She was standing in the doorway, her blue eyes on him, their expression wary. Wary? Now what made him think that? He shook his head slightly and smiled at her. He was getting paranoid in his old age.

"So soon? You must be a very fast cook."

Her smiled flickered. "It's nothing fancy."

Her eyes shifted to the samovar for an instant and Jack wondered if it was his imagination that her expression seemed distressed. He glanced over his shoulder at the gleaming urn. "It's beautiful, isn't it?"

"Yes."

"Do you have any idea where Uncle Jack got it? It doesn't seem like the kind of thing he'd have just had lying around the attic."

This time there could be no mistaking her expression. She looked almost frightened, and Jack's curiosity sharpened. Yet her tone was level, making him wonder if he was imagining the whole thing.

"I believe he said he found it in a shop in Hollywood. It amused him."

"Hollywood, huh? Land of dreams and magic." Jack looked at the samovar again, wondering what it was about it that drew him so. "Well, it seems a suitable place to find something like that. Odd that Uncle Jack would have bought it and hauled it all the way up here, though. Did he ever have it appraised that you know of?"

"He said it wasn't terribly valuable. Just something that amused him. Dinner will be getting cold."

She appeared anxious to change the subject, and Jack didn't object. He could find out more about the intriguing pot later. Maybe he'd take it home with him and have it appraised himself. He'd love to know where it came from, how old it was.

Dinner was perfectly cooked fried chicken, with mashed potatoes, gravy and fresh corn on the cob. Jack was halfway through the meal before it occurred to him that he didn't remember seeing chicken or corn in the refrigerator, but when he mentioned it to Sheri, she just looked at him with wide blue eyes and said he must have missed them.

He pushed his chair back from the table with an exaggerated groan of contentment.

"Did you get enough to eat?"

Sheri's anxious question brought another groan.

"If I ate one more bite I'd probably explode. It was wonderful. I haven't had a meal like that in years."

She flushed, her eyes sparkling with pleasure, and Jack found it was all he could do to keep from staring. She seemed completely unaware of her beauty, though that was hardly possible. In all his life he'd never met a woman so absolutely exquisite. She had to know how beautiful she was. But if she did, it didn't show in her mannerisms. She seemed eager to be liked, uncertain of being accepted.

"Would you like some coffee? It's fresh ground."

"Sounds good." He watched her pour a cup of the fragrant brew. "Fresh ground, huh? I thought Uncle Jack was more of a tea drinker."

Her hand froze over the cup for a moment. "He was. I drink coffee myself and your uncle insisted on buying a small grinder for me."

She poured herself a cup and carried both cups to the table, then sat down across from him. Jack sipped the coffee. It was perfectly brewed, smooth and rich.

"I hope it's as you like it."

"It's perfect. Don't you think so?"

Sheri lifted the cup and took a tiny swallow before smiling at him. "Perfect."

Now why did he have the feeling she didn't like coffee at all?

"You know, there's one thing that's been driving me crazy."

She started nervously, slopping coffee onto the table. "What?"

"The electricity."

"Electricity?"

"The lights, the refrigerator. I can't figure out where the power is coming from." He motioned at the lights.

Sheri's eyes followed his gesture. "The power?" she repeated uncertainly.

"The meter box is rusted out. There are no wires coming into the house, no generator. Jenkins down at the general store says that Uncle Jack used oil lamps for years. But all the lights work. So where is the power coming from?"

There was a long silence while Sheri stared at him wide-eyed. She finally shrugged, dropping her eyes to the table.

"I do not know. Your uncle never mentioned it to me."

Jack nodded and took another swallow of his coffee. He hadn't really expected her to say anything else. There had to be a logical explanation for everything else that had seemed so peculiar.

Except for the car being in the garage, when he'd left it outside. He frowned into his cup. Maybe he'd been mistaken. Maybe he really had put the car in the garage and he just didn't remember it.

"Is something wrong?"

Sheri's question broke into his thoughts. Jack shook his head. "I was just thinking about something."

"Something that disturbs you? May I help?"

"No. It's just something a little odd. No big deal." He finished his coffee and waved away her offer of more. "Tell me about yourself?"

"Myself?"

She seemed startled by the request, and her hand rose automatically to grasp a lock of silvery hair. Jack found himself wondering if it could possibly feel as soft as it looked. He dragged his eyes away, hoping she couldn't read his mind. "Yes. Yourself."

"What would you like to know?"

"I don't know. Anything. We've talked about me quite a bit. It's only fair that we spend a little time on you."

"There is very little to tell."

"Where were you born?" Jack felt like an interviewer with a nervous job candidate. "I can tell from your accent that you're not from around here."

"No, I'm not from around here."

The idea seemed to amuse her.

"So where are you from?"

"Europe. I was born in Europe. My parents traveled a great deal, so I'm afraid my accent is a mixture of many things."

"Well, it's very pretty."

"Thank you."

She flushed and changed the subject, obviously uncomfortable talking about herself.

Jack lost track of time as they sat around the old table, talking. He'd never met anyone quite so easy to talk to. They talked about Uncle Jack. Sheri seemed interested in his memories of the old man and she laughed aloud at some of old Jack's more risqué exploits. Jack found himself searching his memory for stories that might amuse her just for the pleasure of watching her laugh.

She was so natural, yet there was a fey quality about her that made him want to shelter her, keep her safe. She appeared fragile, a delicate porcelain figurine in need of protection.

He smiled at the thought. He sounded like some knight in shining armor looking for a damsel in distress. Like something out of a fairy tale. If there was one thing he'd learned, it was that fairy tales didn't exist. Damsels in distress were as rare as leprechauns and fairies.

The thought brought a twinge of regret. The world had seemed a much nicer place when he was young enough to believe in fantasies. Maybe that was the problem with life these days. There wasn't time for fairy tales. He shook his head, drawing in a deep breath, aware that the conversation had lagged and Sheri was watching him, her head tilted in question.

Jack shook his head, laughing at his own foolish thoughts. "I was just thinking about fairy tales and fantasies and how it's a shame we don't have more of them."

Something sparked in Sheri's eyes, but it was gone too quickly for him to identify. She looked down at the table, her lashes dark against her cheeks.

"Perhaps there are more fantasies and fairy tales alive than most people realize," she said softly.

"It's certainly a nice thought." Jack stifled a yawn. "Sorry. I guess this fresh air is taking its toll on me. I think my body misses the smog."

"It is late. Perhaps you would like to go to bed."

Jack's eyes sharpened. Was she aware that her words could be taken as an invitation? But her eyes were clear of anything more than concern. He shook his head. God, his imagination was working overtime lately.

"I am tired."

Sheri stood up and set their coffee cups in the sink. "I will just tidy up here and then I will leave."

"Why don't you stay here tonight?" She looked at him over her shoulder and Jack raised his hands. "I'm not making a pass. Look, you said you were living here when Uncle Jack was alive. I assume you've been staying here since he died. I suspect you slept in the barn last night rather than tell me you were here. I can't bear to have that on my conscience again tonight.''

"I was not uncomfortable last night." She ran water in the sink.

"Well, I'll be uncomfortable tonight if you don't agree to stay here. That couch in there is big enough for a football team. I can sleep there and you can have the bedroom upstairs. There's even a lock on the door, if it will make you feel better.''

"I do not need a lock. I know you would not hurt me."

Such total faith took Jack a moment to absorb. He wasn't sure if he should be insulted that she didn't see him as a threat or complimented that she believed in his integrity.

"Then stay here tonight."

She nodded slowly. "Yes. But I will sleep on the couch and you will keep your bed."

Jack didn't argue, afraid that she might change her mind if he pushed the issue. Why it should be so important to him, he couldn't have said.

Within a few minutes, the lights were off—lights that shouldn't have been on in the first place—and the front door was locked, though Jack doubted the necessity of that. The two of them stood in the living room doorway a little awkwardly, not quite looking at each other.

"Well, good night," Jack said.

"Good night."

"I've enjoyed this evening."

"So have I." She looked up at him, her eyes shy. "I am glad to meet you. Your uncle told me much about you."

"I wish he'd told me about you. I would have made it up here sooner." Was it possible to fall into someone's eyes. Hers were so blue, so clear. It was like drowning in a sea of sapphires, warm and cool at the same time. Sheri blushed, ducking her head. Jack tried to shake off the spell threatening to take hold of him, making him forget duty, family, fiancée and common sense. He cleared his throat.

"I'll see you in the morning."

"Yes, in the morning."

But Jack lingered, reluctant to give up the feeling of peace that seemed to surround her. He'd never felt anything quite like it. There was a gentle calm, as if the cares of the everyday world didn't affect her.

It took a conscious exercise of willpower for Jack to turn and climb the stairs. He had to force himself not to turn and look back down at her. He had the feeling he wouldn't be able to stop with just looking.

He shut the bedroom door behind him and leaned back against it for a moment, trying to remember that he was a man known for his cool logical mind.

When he crawled into the big bed a little while later, he found himself wondering how Sheri was settling in, found himself looking for an excuse to check on her.

Willpower kept him from going downstairs. Willpower and the memory of those trusting blue eyes. It it hadn't been for her trust in him, nothing could have kept him up there alone. Not duty, family, fiancée or common sense.

DOWNSTAIRS, Sheri stared into space. It had gone well. Not the way she'd hoped they'd meet, but perhaps best, after all. There'd been only a few awkward moments, fewer than she'd feared. Perhaps the old man had been right when he'd said his nephew needed her. She sensed a deep loneliness inside him, a yearning. And something inside her responded to that yearning, that need.

She frowned. He hadn't asked too many questions tonight, but he would. He wasn't like his uncle, who'd accepted so easily. No, the younger Jack was not the kind of human who accepted without question. Already he was questioning things. Probing, wanting answers she couldn't provide.

Still, if this was meant to be—and she believed with all her heart that it was—it would work out in the end. It had to work out. For as sure as she sensed his need, her own was just as strong, just as real.

THE SUN WAS JUST SLIPPING over the horizon, spilling warmth over the mountainside when Jack awoke. He slipped on jeans and a pale blue T-shirt, not bothering with shoes. He couldn't remember the last time he'd been quite so eager to start a day. He refused to speculate, even to himself, just how much his unexpected houseguest had to do with his anticipation.

The house was quiet as he opened the door and stepped into the hall, and he made a conscious effort to avoid the squeaky board at the top of the stairs. If Sheri was still sleeping, there was no reason to wake her. Maybe he'd make a cup of coffee and take it out onto the porch to enjoy the new morning, a bucolic pleasure he never had time for at home.

When he reached the hallway, he couldn't quite resist the urge to glance into the living room. Just to make sure she was all right, he told himself. He'd only intended a quick glance at the sofa to see if she was still asleep.

What caught his attention was the samovar. The squat urn stood stolidly on its table near the fireplace. The room was on the west side of the house, so it had yet to catch the rays of the sun. Yet the samovar seemed to glow as if lit with its own light. The brass didn't shine—it gleamed, it glittered, it drew his eye like a brilliant jewel.

Jack took a step closer. He was only peripherally aware that there was no sleeping form on the sofa. All his attention was on the samovar. The shining urn was mesmerizing, a warm golden pool of light. Gathering above the samovar was a vague misty cloud, gossamer thin at first, then slowly thickening.

Jack stared, aware of each separate beat of his heart, each shallow breath he took. He blinked and then blinked again, unable to drag his eyes from the gleaming samovar.

The smoke swirled lazily, growing thicker until it was impossible to see the wall behind it. It twisted as if guided by some intelligent hand, swirling and turning, coalescing into a solid, impossible shape.

Jack swallowed hard, feeling his pulse pounding in his ears, his heart threatening to push its way past his breastbone with the force of its beating.

The smoke wasn't smoke anymore. It had a shape, a form.

A woman's body, her back to him, her slender frame draped in a gossamer robe that revealed yet concealed, made of some glittering fabric that seemed to have no substance at all. A fall of pale, pale hair spilled down her back to the waist. It lifted as if with a will of its own, shifting in some unfelt breeze, seeming to beckon him closer. Slim hips and long slender legs ended in delicate ankles and bare feet.

She stretched, raising her arms over her head, her spine arching in a graceful gesture that was pure femininity. Jack felt beads of sweat rise on his forehead.

It wasn't the fact that she was stretching that bothered him.

It was the fact that she was floating in midair. Those slender little feet were at least two feet off the ground.

He'd obviously gone completely mad. He was probably not really here at all but locked in a padded cell in Camarillo State Hospital.

She drifted slowly to the floor, a leisurely descent that showed she was in complete control. He must have made some sound—possibly a murmur of disbelief—or maybe she'd heard the screaming denial in his mind. She turned suddenly, aware that she was longer alone, and her eyes met his.

Jack stared at Sheri, his tongue glued to the roof of his mouth. There was a logical explanation for this. He seemed to have been telling himself that ever since he arrived here. Their eyes held, hers frightened, his dazed.

"You were just floating." His tone said that he'd really appreciate a denial. He was amazed that he had a voice at all.

She didn't say anything, only stared at him with those wide frightened eyes. Jack waited, his mind working frantically, seeking the logical answer that just had to be there somewhere. But nothing came to mind.

"Who— What are you?" The question emerged on a whisper.

Sheri hesitated, lifting her hand to twist her fingers in that incredible mass of hair. A smile flickered uncertainly, then was gone.

"I am what I told you. A friend of your uncle's."

"Sure, and I'm Elvis Presley." The puzzled look in her eyes told him she hadn't the faintest idea whom he was talking about. That one silly thing was the final straw. The fact that the name meant nothing to her put the last touch of unreality on the moment.

"What are you?"

"I was your uncle's friend," she insisted.

"But that's not all, is it?"

"No." She dropped her eyes, her fingers twisted tightly in her hair.

"What else?" Jack felt almost calm as he waited for her answer. He was either dreaming or he was insane. Either way he didn't have anything to worry about. If he was dreaming, he'd soon wake up, and if he was insane, they'd probably come in to feed him anytime now.

"What else are you?"

Her voice was low, but not so low that he couldn't hear her. Every word came through clearly. Much more clearly than he would have liked.

"I am a genie."

Chapter Four

"I beg your pardon?" Jack groped behind him for a place to sit, beyond being surprised to find a chair where there shouldn't have been anything but floor.

"Are you all right?"

"No, actually. I'm not. I'm obviously insane," Jack said conversationally. "Or I'm dreaming. That's it. I'm not having this conversation at all. I didn't just see you form in a puff of smoke. You didn't just say that you were a genie. In fact, none of this is happening. I'm still lying upstairs asleep, and any minute now, I'm going to wake up and you won't be there."

Jack waited, but he didn't show any signs of waking. Sheri was still standing in front of him, her brow puckered in a frown. He closed his eyes, willing himself to wake up, willing himself to be somewhere else. When he opened his eyes, he was still sitting in the chair that shouldn't be where it was, looking at someone who shouldn't exist.

"Oh, God. You're still here."

"Yes. You would like me to go away?"

"Yes—no. Don't move. And don't do anything." He rubbed the bridge of his nose, aware of Sheri's anxious eyes on him. Did she have to look so eager to please?

Didn't she know that her very existence was an impossibility, that what she claimed to be didn't—couldn't exist?

And yet it explained so much. The food, the car, the electricity. So many things that had defied logic were suddenly explained. Only the explanation was more impossible than the original puzzles.

"Good God! What am I doing?" He shot to his feet so suddenly that Sheri took a nervous step back. "I'm actually considering this."

"It is the truth."

"No. No, it's not." Jack put the chair between them, staring at her. "I don't know what the truth is, but you are not a genie. Genies don't exist."

"But I am here."

The simple statement left him momentarily speechless. It was undeniably true. She was there. No matter how much he wished she wasn't, she was right there in front of him. And he'd seen her materialize. Only he couldn't have seen it, because it was impossible. Wasn't it?

He laughed abruptly, a sound that held little humor. "I can't believe this. I must be more stressed out than I thought. I'm actually considering the idea that you really could be a genie. Since that's obviously not possible, there must be some reasonable explanation for what I think I've seen."

Sheri's puzzled expression mirrored his own. "I've given you an explanation."

Jack laughed again, a little more uneasily. She sounded so sincere. "Look, I don't know who put you up to this. Was it Roger? It sounds like exactly the kind of demented joke he'd love to play. I don't know how you did the tricks, but—"

"Tricks?"

She tilted her head looking confused. She was really an incredible actress. At least, he hoped that's what she was.

He waved his hand in the direction of the samovar, avoiding actually looking at it. "Tricks. You know, the puff-of-smoke routine."

"It is not a routine." She put the accent on the wrong syllable, giving the word a peculiar sound.

Jack stared at her, feeling desperation creeping around the edges of his control. Looking into those wide blue eyes, it was difficult to believe she was part of some elaborate trick. On the other hand, it was impossible to believe what she was telling him.

"You can't be a genie," he told her firmly.

"Why not?"

The simple question left him without words for the space of several slow heartbeats.

"Why not? Why not?" He heard the barely restrained bellow of his own voice and stopped to take a deep breath. When he continued, his voice was painfully calm. "Why not? I'll tell you why not. Because there is no such thing. Genies are like elves and fairies and hobbits. They're all imaginary. Pretend. Things to tell little kids. They aren't real. They're fantasies. Dreams." He threw his arms out, emphasizing his point.

"And you don't think dreams are real?"

"No. Not that kind of dream," Jack told her firmly.

She nodded. "I think I understand."

While he watched, her figure seemed to blur around the edges, like a photograph just out of focus. The diaphanous robe that had hinted at so much more than it revealed vanished without a whisper. Sheri stood in front of him clad in jeans and a soft blue shirt just the color of her eyes. It all looked so normal. She might have been any one of a million young women walking down any street in America.

Only she wasn't walking down any street. She was standing right in front of him, wearing clothes that had been nowhere in sight a moment before. And she was claiming to be something that didn't exist.

"There are no such things as genies." He said it firmly, daring her to contradict him.

Sheri settled onto the sofa, drawing her feet up under her, one finger twisting idly in the thick fall of golden hair that fell over her shoulder.

"I can understand that it must be hard for you," she told him. "You've never known one of us before."

"I don't know one of you now, either. There's got to be a logical explanation for everything." But his denial was growing weaker. He could hear it in his voice. He sat back down, needing to feel something solid.

Sheri didn't try to argue with him. She nodded slowly. "I know it is not easy to accept. Your uncle was very unusual."

"Uncle Jack knew about you?" Jack demanded. "I mean, he knew what you claimed to be?"

"He knew what I was," she corrected gently.

"And he didn't mind?" Jack chose to sidestep the question of whether she was what she claimed.

"Your uncle was a man with vast dreams. Such people believe more than others."

"Believe? You honestly expect me to believe that you're a genie? Fine. Prove it. Wiggle your nose or blink or something and do something genie-ish."

"What would you like?"

The question threw Jack off balance—a position that was beginning to feel normal. She sounded so confident, so sure of herself.

"Let's start simple. How about a cup of coffee?"

He sat back, wishing he felt more smug. For the sake of his own sanity, he needed to believe that nothing was going to happen. He needed to know that this whole charade was going to end right here and now.

Sheri held out her hand, palm up. Jack stared at it, feeling less sure than he would have liked. He was almost unsurprised when the air over her palm began to shimmer as if she held a glowing light. There was an instant of disorientation and then her palm was no longer empty.

Jack reached out and wrapped his fingers around the mug of steaming coffee. It felt solid and real. The rich scent that wafted to his nostrils was real. He stared down into the dark liquid. The entire pattern of the world had just shifted, settling into a new design. Things he believed impossible beyond a shadow of a doubt were suddenly real and undeniable. And all he could do was stare at the coffee and wonder that she'd even added a touch of cream to it.

"Are you all right?"

Sheri's anxious question brought his eyes to her face. She looked so concerned. She looked so normal. Beautiful but normal. This wasn't real. *She* wasn't real. But here he was, with a cup of coffee in his hand.

"So, how did you get into this line of work?" The flip question was the best he could come up with. Maybe if he pretended this was all some kind of cosmic joke, it would go away.

"What do you mean, 'this line of work?'"

Sheri looked so genuinely puzzled that Jack laughed. It struck him as the final touch of absurdity that *she* should be confused by *him*.

He leaned back in his chair, feeling an odd sense of freedom. It was as if, in accepting the truth of Sheri's existence, he'd lost the heavy burden of reality. In a world where genies could exist, almost anything was possible.

Sheri watched him, toying with her hair, her expression puzzled but hopeful. He could have told her that the laughter was just the final evidence of his insanity, but it didn't seem important at the moment. The laughter faded, but the feeling of having shed a heavy weight lingered.

"Where did Uncle Jack find you?" He took a swallow of the coffee that shouldn't have been there and waited for her answer. Really, this wasn't that much different from interviewing someone for a job. It was just that he'd never interviewed a figment of his imagination before.

"Hollywood."

"Oh, yes, the samovar." He looked at the squat brass urn, wondering why it hadn't occurred to him immediately that it was the perfect place to hide a genie. The thought struck him as hilarious and he grinned. "It's better than an RV."

"An RV?"

"Recreational vehicle. It's a sort of home on wheels."

She tilted her head, puzzled a moment longer, and then made the connection.

"You mean because my samovar moves?"

Her laughter came softly, like warm breezes and blue skies. Her eyes were bright with humor.

"The thought did occur to me." Jack rested his ankle on his knee, relaxing. Whatever was happening here, he might as well sit back and enjoy it. Maybe there was something in the water in northern California that fed illusions and fantasies. When he left here, this whole thing would seem like a dream. "So how did Uncle Jack come to buy the samovar?"

"He told me that he was drawn to it. That happens sometimes, you know."

"No, I didn't know. I'm afraid I'm not really conversant with the circumstances that usually surround the acquisition of a genie."

"Well, it doesn't always happen like that, but sometimes a person is drawn. Usually because they can believe."

"And Uncle Jack believed?"

"Your uncle was a man of infinite dreams. To him all things were possible."

Her words brought back memories of his childhood. When his father had been so sure Jack would follow him into the family business, Uncle Jack had been the one to encourage him to dream of being an astronaut or a carnival barker.

For his fourteen birthday, when his father had given him a small portfolio of stock to manage, Uncle Jack had given him a pair of swords, souvenirs of World War II. They'd spent hours speculating on whom they might have belonged to and what might have happened to the officers who'd worn them.

Yes, Jack had certainly been a man of infinite dreams. It wasn't hard to imagine him being attracted to the samovar. It was just the kind of exotic oddity that would catch his eye. And when Sheri popped out in a cloud of smoke and announced she was a genie, Uncle Jack had probably accepted it with hardly a blink.

He'd always envied his uncle's ability to set reality aside in favor of a more pleasant fantasy. But reality had always been an overbearing presence in his own life and he'd long ago stopped trying to fight it.

"Why didn't Uncle Jack tell me about you? If not while he was alive, then in the letter I got after he died? All he said was that he wanted me to come take a look at the house. Not a word about any exotic surprises I might find."

"I told him he should have warned you about me, but he wouldn't do it. He could be very stubborn." Sheri shook her head, remembering.

"He must have had a reason for not telling me."

"He said that you wouldn't let yourself believe. That you'd have to see to believe."

"Well, I suppose he was right about that. I guess it's not the kind of thing you tell someone in a letter. 'It's been a long time since I've seen you. Hope you're well. By the way, I've got a genie in the house these days.'" Jack laughed, swallowing the last of the coffee and setting the cup down.

"Would you like some more coffee?" Sheri leaned forward, eager to help, but Jack shook his head.

"No, thanks. One cup of magic coffee is my limit. It's probably worse than caffeine."

"The coffee isn't magic," she assured him.

"Close enough." She seemed disappointed and he almost changed his mind. But he'd had enough demonstrations of the impossible. Enough to last him a lifetime. "How long were you with Uncle Jack?"

"Almost three years."

Sheri smiled, and the expression warmed her eyes in a way that would have taken his breath away if circumstances hadn't already left him with little to spare.

"He was very good to me. He taught me so much."

"I'm sure you must have taught him a thing or two," Jack said dryly, but the subtlety escaped Sheri. She took his words at face value.

"I don't know if I taught him anything, but I think he enjoyed my company. He was a lonely man. Did you know he had once almost married a woman he loved very much?

She died, and I don't think he ever quite got over the loneliness of being without her."

"He never told me that." He wasn't sure why he should feel surprised. There were apparently a great many things the old man hadn't told him. "I wish I'd made it up to see him."

Sheri reached out to touch his hand. Comfort flowed from the light touch just as it had the day before. Of course, the day before he hadn't known she wasn't just an ordinary woman who happened to be particularly sympathetic. He shifted his hand, suddenly uneasy beneath hers. Not that he really believed she was what she claimed. But still . . .

He glanced at Sheri, catching the look of hurt that darkened her eyes before her lashes fell, concealing the expression. He felt as if he'd swatted a spaniel puppy unjustly. Whoever—or whatever—she was, she had been kind to him. More important, she'd been good to his uncle.

"I'm sorry."

"It's all right. I understand. I should have realized you would find it difficult to accept what I am."

Her words had been spoken evenly, without inflection, as if his reaction held little importance. But Jack had seen the look in her eyes and he knew he'd hurt her feelings by his withdrawal.

"Look, I didn't mean to be rude. You've been very good to me and I really appreciate all you did for Uncle Jack. It's just that . . . well, you're . . . I mean—" He broke off, at a loss. How did he explain what he was feeling when he didn't even *know* what he was feeling. He ran his fingers through his hair and stared at her.

"I understand. You don't like me," she said.

"No. No, it isn't that I don't like you," he protested. "I *do* like you."

"You do?"

Her eyes lifted to his and he found himself lost in the shining depths.

"I—yes, I do like you." Actually, he wasn't sure that was an accurate description at all. "Like" was such an anemic word. When he was with her, he felt a number of emotions, all of them confusing. There was a sweetness about her that made it impossible *not* to like her. Last night... What he'd been feeling last night was certainly something considerably more complex than simple liking.

He'd been drawn to her in a way an engaged man had no business being drawn. He'd felt the softness of her hand in his and he'd wanted to know if the rest of her could possibly be as soft. His dreams last night had held images of deep blue eyes and pale hair.

And then he'd come downstairs to find— No, he didn't want to think about what he'd seen. Better to try to block that memory if he wanted to retain any pretense of sanity. She'd tumbled his world upside down within the blink of an eye and now she wanted to know if he *liked* her.

Looking into those eyes, he found that reassuring her was more important than pinning down a precise description of his feelings at the moment. He didn't want to say anything to bring back that look of hurt.

"Of course I like you. It's just that you're the first genie I've ever met and I guess I'm having a hard time adjusting," he finished weakly.

Sheri's smile was dazzling. "You will get used to me. I'm really not all that different. You'll see."

Jack doubted he'd see any such thing. Whether she was a genie or a figment of his imagination, it was a sure bet he'd never met anyone like her.

"Would you like some breakfast?"

Breakfast was not high on Jack's list of priorities, but it seemed a safe enough thing to do. Maybe with some food in his stomach, he'd be able to make some sense of what was going on.

"Sure. Breakfast would be great."

"What would you like?"

"Whatever's out there." He caught Sheri's eye and realized that to her "whatever was out there" wasn't as limited as it might seem. "Bacon and eggs would be great."

He distinctly remembered seeing bacon and eggs in the refrigerator. However she chose to cook them, at least he wouldn't have to imagine them popping out of thin air.

"It will only take a moment."

Sheri slipped off the sofa, looking so normal, so average that Jack felt much as Alice must have felt when she toppled into the rabbit hole. At this point, if a white rabbit in a waistcoat popped out of the chimney, murmuring he was late, Jack wasn't sure he would feel any real shock at all.

Sheri left the room with a light, gliding step that seemed almost not to touch the floor. Jack pushed the thought away. God knows, she was probably quite capable of floating along. He reached for his coffee cup, taking a deep swallow before he remembered that there wasn't supposed to be any coffee left. Yet the cup was full. With a muttered oath, he set it down.

Somehow all his plans had gone awry. He'd thought he'd come up here and say a last farewell to his uncle. And he'd needed the time away, a chance to take a deep breath, figure out why his life wasn't as satisfying as it should be. A few days in the country with nothing to do but think. A simple enough concept.

Only it hadn't worked out that way. Electricity that shouldn't be on, dishes that shouldn't be clean and one delicate, exquisite person who claimed to be something that *couldn't* exist. Not only claimed it, but could prove it. No, this wasn't what he'd planned.

As he rubbed the back of his neck, his gaze settled on the samovar. The sun was creeping in through a south window and a beam of light splashed across the top of the brass urn. Jack glowered at it. It symbolized all the confusion that had entered his life. He would have loved to get up and pitch it out the window, as if he could throw the craziness with it.

"Breakfast is ready."

Sheri's voice made him jump. "Don't sneak up on me like that!" His tone held more of a bark than he'd intended, and her smile faded.

"I'm sorry."

"Oh, hell." Jack stood up, running his fingers through his hair and forcing a smile. "I'm the one who should be sorry. I didn't mean to snap at you. I guess I'm just having a bit of a hard time adjusting to this situation."

"That's all right."

Her ready forgiveness only made him feel guiltier. Did she have to be so damned nice?

The bacon was perfectly cooked, the eggs just as he preferred. He ate, refusing to think about the unconventional methods that had produced the meal. Jack leaned back in his chair, cradling a cup of coffee between his palms. Outside, the sun was shining with a brilliance that dazzled the eyes. The worn old kitchen looked so real, so normal, that it might have been a set in a movie. Which was exactly where Jack felt as though he was, smack in the middle of a Hollywood extravaganza. Any minute now the director would yell "Cut!" and life would go back to the way it had always been.

"The breakfast was delicious. Thank you."

Sheri beamed with pleasure and reached for the plates, but he stopped her.

"No, just leave them." He didn't want to see how she dealt with dirty dishes. It would spoil the fragile sanity he felt he'd achieved. "We should talk."

"All right."

She settled back in her chair, her hands clasped in her lap, her eyes on his face. She looked like a painting of an angel he'd seen when he was a child. There was the same gentle wonder in her eyes, the same fall of liquid gold hair. Only looking at the angel hadn't made him feel the way looking at Sheri made him feel.

"So, what do you plan to do now?" The question came out too loud, breaking the silence abruptly.

"Do?" Sheri was puzzled by the question. She tilted her head, a faint frown drawing her brows together. "What do you mean?"

"What do you plan to do? You know, now that Uncle Jack is gone. Where do you plan on going?"

"Wherever you go."

Her tone said that the answer was obvious.

"Wherever I go? What have I got to do with it?" Jack set his coffee down with a thud.

"Well, I'll go wherever you go."

She'd said it so calmly, as if her words weren't enough to shake the very foundations of his life.

"You'll what?" The thin-voiced question was all he could manage.

"I'll go wherever you go. Won't I?" A thread of uncertainty had crept into her voice.

"No." Jack got the word out quickly before the look in her eyes could change his mind. "Look, I'm sorry, but that's just not possible. You see, I'm a banker, and bankers don't have genies. We have Jaguars and houses in the best part of town, but we do not have genies."

"Your uncle felt that you needed me."

"Uncle Jack probably had a lot of odd thoughts. But I do *not* need a genie. It's nothing personal, you understand. It's just that my life is all set. I've got a career and I'm engaged to Eleanor. Eleanor! My God, I don't even want to think about what she'd say if I brought home a genie." Jack shuddered, imagining Eleanor's expression when he tried to explain about Sheri popping out of a samovar and pulling electricity out of thin air.

"But your uncle wanted me to stay with you," Sheri protested.

"Look, I'll tell you what. Why don't you just give me three wishes and we'll call it quits. You'll have done your duty by Uncle Jack."

"It's not about doing my duty. It's about fulfilling your uncle's wishes."

Jack pushed his chair back, standing up to pace to the back door. It looked so normal outside. The sun was shining. He could hear a jay squawking somewhere near the old barn. What was he doing in this worn old house, arguing with a woman who claimed she lived in a bottle?

He should have followed Eleanor's suggestion and sent a lawyer up here to take a look at the place. He could have sold it and never even known Sheri existed. Damn Uncle Jack! It was just like the old man to get his favorite nephew into a mess like this. The old goat was probably laughing his butt off somewhere. He'd finally managed to throw a huge monkey wrench into Jack's life. But he was damned if he was going to let Uncle Jack screw up all his careful plans.

It was one thing to admit that he'd had a few doubts himself. It was something else altogether for someone else to start pulling the strings. Especially from beyond the grave.

He turned abruptly, pinning Sheri with a look that had been known to make junior executives shudder. Sheri didn't even flinch. She just stared back at him with that wide-eyed gaze that seemed much too trusting, too vulnerable.

"Look, you owe me three wishes, right?"

"If that's what you want."

"Well, that's the way the stories all go. Is that the way it works or not?"

"Sometimes that's all that's required to fulfill the debt. But it doesn't have to work that way."

Jack moved back to the table, gripping the back of his chair and leaning toward her. "Suppose my first wish was for you to go away somewhere and stay out of my life. Would you do that?"

Sheri stared at him for a long moment, her face without expression. Then her eyes slowly lowered from his.

"Yes, I would do that."

Jack had to lean closer to hear her whispered assent.

He smiled, feeling as if he'd just concluded a particularly difficult bargaining session. He could end this entire incident right here and now. No one would ever have to know any of this. Sheri could take her samovar and steal away into the night and he could sell this place and pretend none of this had ever happened. It was perfect. He opened his mouth to tell her he wished exactly that: that she'd go away and never darken his door again. Nothing came out.

He stared at her downcast head, remembering the quiet sympathy she'd offered him; the way she'd tried so hard to make him comfortable; most of all, the way she'd cared for his uncle. If it hadn't been for her, Uncle Jack would have died alone. Genie or not, like it or not, he owed her.

"If I were to wish for you to go away, where would you go?"

She shrugged without looking at him. She'd drawn her hair forward so that it formed a pale cape over her shoulders.

"Nowhere."

"Nowhere?" Jack questioned. "Come on. There must be somewhere you'd like to go. God knows, airline tickets aren't going to be a problem. You can just twitch up a magic carpet or something, can't you?"

"There is nowhere."

She seemed to have withdrawn from him in some way he couldn't quite put his finger on.

"How about Egypt?" he pressed. "If ever there was a country built for a genie, Egypt has got to be it. Or Ireland. They understand things like this. They've already got leprechauns and pixies and things like that. I'm sure they wouldn't mind a genie. You could sort of expand their repertoire."

"No."

"No?" The simple refusal infuriated him. Here he was trying to be nice, trying to make sure she'd have a nice time when she left him. So maybe he wasn't doing the greatest job in the world, but he'd never wanted to be a travel agent for a genie.

"Why not? If you don't want to go to Egypt and you don't want to go to Ireland, where *do* you want to go?" he demanded. "There must be someplace."

"You don't understand. If I don't go with you, I shan't go anywhere. A genie who has no ties to a human is not truly alive."

Jack stared at her, appalled. "You mean you'll die?"

"Not death as you're thinking. It's more a state of non-existence. Until someone appears who can believe." She glanced up at him with a sad smile. "There are fewer people in the world today who can believe in us."

"*I* don't believe in you!"

"Yes, you do. You don't want to believe, but you do."

Jack wanted to deny her words, but he couldn't. Against every grain of common sense he possessed, he did believe. He spun away from the table, throwing his hands out from his sides as if in plea to an unseen force.

"I don't need a genie. I've got my life nicely in order. I don't *want* a genie. Damn you, Uncle Jack. Damn you." He knew it had to be his imagination that put the sound of far-off laughter in his ears.

He turned back to Sheri, wishing he could say the words that would send her out of his life, wishing his damned conscience would keep its opinions to itself. But as his father had so often said, if wishes were horses, beggars would ride.

"I hope you're going to like Los Angeles."

Chapter Five

Jack pulled the Jag into the driveway of the big house and stared at the lights blazing from the windows. The way his luck had been going lately, he shouldn't have been surprised to find that everyone was home. It simply wasn't in the cards that something could go right. He'd hoped to find the house nice and empty so he could get Sheri acclimated. Maybe get a chance to try to prepare his mother for her new houseguest. How did a man go about preparing his mother for the presence of a genie in the house?

He glanced at the genie in question as he turned off the engine. She was staring wide-eyed at the huge Spanish-style building he'd called home for the past thirty-odd years.

"It's so beautiful. How lucky you are to live here."

Lucky? Jack looked at the house again, trying to see it through her eyes. Yes, he supposed it was rather beautiful. Funny, he'd never really paid much attention to it. It was just the place his family lived.

"Well, I hope you like it. It looks like my mother and sister are both home, so you'll get to meet them right away." His voice must have reflected his uneasiness at that thought because Sheri turned to look at him. Odd, how even in the gathering darkness, her expression was easy to read. It was as if she were lit from within.

"You are worried about my meeting with your family."

It was more statement than question, but he answered her anyway. "It's not everyday that I bring home a house-guest who just happens to be something I don't even believe in."

"I know it will be difficult for you. If you'd like, I could—" She gestured at the back seat, where the samovar rested in stately solitude.

"No! No, thank you." One of the first things they'd established on the drive down the coast was that there was to be no more popping in and out of pots. Jack had always considered himself almost nerveless, but the idea of Sheri appearing and disappearing in a cloud of smoke was more than his nerves could stand. "That's all right. Mom and Tina are going to have to meet you sooner or later. It might as well be now."

Sheri shrugged and turned her eyes back to the house. "I will try not to cause you any problems, Jack. I know my arrival in your life is not welcome."

Jack's conscience gave a painful pinch. She sounded so forlorn. He reached out to touch her hand where it lay in her lap. It was the first time he'd voluntarily touched her since she'd set his world on end.

She looked at his hand and then her eyes lifted to his face. He forgot what he'd planned to say. His fingers tightened over hers. Awareness flowed into him. He should have known she was something more than human just by looking into her eyes. A blue so clear, so deep could never belong to a mortal.

She turned her hand so that their palms lay together, and the awareness intensified. Without thinking about it, Jack closed his fingers over hers. Her hand felt so small. Into him came the urge to protect her, to shield her from the blows life could so carelessly deal.

With his other hand he brushed back a lock of fine hair, feeling it twine around his fingers, another gentle link. There was such a sense of peace about her. And in him was a deep hunger for peace, a need he'd never acknowledged.

He leaned toward her, seeking... Seeking what? He couldn't have said. He only knew that she could give him what he sought. Surely it was possible to become lost in those eyes.

Behind him, the neighbor's dog barked sharply as a stray cat leaped across the lawn. Jack jerked back, blinking to clear his vision. What was he doing? He pulled his hands away from her, the silky lock of hair clinging as if to draw him back.

Sheri continued to watch him, but he avoided her eyes. He must be feverish. What had he been saying? Oh, yes. He cleared his throat, wishing he could clear his mind as easily. "I don't mean to make you feel unwelcome, Sheri."

"I know."

"It's just that—" He stopped. "Look, I—" How did he find the words to explain without hurting her that he needed this complication is his life the way he needed a hole in his head?

"Jack, you don't have to explain to me. I know that I've created a problem for you, but truly, everything will be all right. You'll see. I will not cause problems in your life. I'm going to learn how to be human. Soon I won't be different at all."

She was so sincere, so earnest. Looking at her, he couldn't imagine how anyone could see her and not realize immediately that she was not of this earth.

"That's good" was all he could manage. He reached for the door handle, then hesitated. "Now remember, my mother and Tina are *not*, under any circumstances, to be given any reason to think you're a— Well, that you're different.''

"You mean I'm not to pop in and out of a cloud of smoke or wave up a dinner or twitch a new dress while they're watching.''

She slanted him a mischievous look, and Jack couldn't help but smile. Did she have to be so damn cute? "Exactly. I want them to think you're completely normal.''

"But I am completely normal." She gave him a wide-eyed look, her mouth tucked into a solemn line.

Jack was surprised by a sudden urge to kiss that look from her face, to see if her lips could possibly be as soft as they appeared.

"Completely normal for a genie, I suppose,'' he said dryly, pushing stray and inappropriate thoughts away.

"Soon you won't be able to tell me from your sister.''

"Oh, I don't think that's too likely.'' The thoughts he had when he looked at Sheri bore no resemblance to the way he felt about Tina. Jack sighed, thinking wistfully of the joys to be found in a Tibetan monastery. Did they allow genies in monasteries? "Come on, if we don't go in soon, Mother is going to think I've died out here.''

He got out, but Sheri hesitated a moment before opening her door. Now that she was here, she was surprised by how uneasy she felt. With Jack, she felt a certain sense of rightness. They belonged, even if he didn't realize it yet. But now, meeting his family, she was suddenly full of doubts. What if they didn't like her?

"Is something wrong?''

Cool air filled the car as Jack pulled open the door. He looked so handsome, his hair falling over his forehead in a thick dark wave. She almost reached up to push it back, but knew he wouldn't welcome the gesture. With an effort she forced a smile and shook her head.

"No. I am a little nervous." Jack's face softened into a smile that Sheri thought more magical than anything she herself could produce.

"Don't worry about it. Tina is going to love you and Mother... Well, Mother likes just about everyone." He reached out and took her hand, drawing her out of the car. "Just don't do anything... odd and everything will be fine."

Sheri heard the doubt in his voice and knew Jack wasn't as sure as he'd like her to believe. Well, it was up to her to make sure that everything *was* fine.

Up close the house was even more exquisite. The smooth plaster walls gleamed pale in the twilight, reminding her of pictures she'd seen of the Spanish missions, the red tile roof a dark counterpoint. Arched windows spilled a warm glow of light onto the expanse of lawn.

The double front doors were heavily carved. A stylized sun spread across the two doors, its deeply etched face offering a greeting. Sheri reached out, feeling the warmth of the carving under her fingertips.

Jack turned his key in the lock and she felt the deep breath he drew before he opened the door and ushered her inside. The entryway was laid with thick red paving tiles, both warm and solid. To the right was an arched doorway, and she caught a glimpse of book-lined walls.

On the left, up two tiled steps, was the living room. The ceiling soared twenty-five feet above the floor. Small windows set high in the south wall broke the plastered expanse. A huge fireplace with a tiled hearth dominated the opposite wall. She could imagine that in the winter, a crackling fire would soften the almost overwhelming dimensions of the room.

She had only a moment to get an impression. Jack was leading the way up the steps. An older woman rose from a chair, setting aside the needlework she'd been doing.

"Jack! We weren't expecting you, darling." She reached out to take his hands and lifted a cheek for him to kiss.

"Mother. I decided to come home rather suddenly. There wasn't as much to do at Uncle Jack's as I'd thought there would be."

"Well, it's certainly nice to see you. You know, Eleanor was not at all pleased with you—" Her eyes went past him to Sheri, hovering in the background. "You didn't tell me you'd brought someone with you, Jack."

"Mother, this is Sheri. She took care of Uncle Jack the past few years of his life. She's also taken care of the house since he died. I thought it was the least we could do to offer her a place to stay for a while."

Sheri wondered if his mother could hear the tension in Jack's voice as clearly as she did. "Mrs. Ryan, I am very happy to meet you."

"Ms.... er... Jack, you didn't give me our guest's last name."

Sheri caught the panicked look Jack threw her.

"Jones. Sheri Jones," he answered.

"Ms. Jones, how nice to meet you." Glynis Ryan held out her hand and smiled graciously. "Of course you're welcome to stay with us as long as you'd like."

"Thank you, Mrs. Ryan. I'll try not to be any trouble." Was it her imagination, or did Jack look as if he doubted that were possible?

"Won't you sit down, Ms. Jones." Glynis gestured to the sofa, upholstered in deep red silk.

Sheri eased onto the sofa. When Jack sat next to her, tension in every line of his body, she wanted to reach out and take his hand, assure him there was no need to worry.

"Does your family live in northern California?" Glynis asked, settling back in her chair and picking up her needle and the rolled canvas she'd been embroidering.

Glynis Ryan's question was friendly, but Sheri sensed the concern under it. She was wondering just who her son had brought home.

Jack, even more than Sheri, was aware of the direction his mother's probing was likely to take. "Sheri is an orphan, Mother," he hastily explained.

"Oh, dear, how sad for you." Glynis's caution was overwhelmed by sympathy. "Were you very young?"

"She was just a child."

"Jack, really, let Ms. Jones answer for herself," Glynis said, giving her son a stern look.

"Jack's right, Mrs. Ryan. I was hardly more than an infant. I was raised by my godparents. Unfortunately they passed away a few years ago. They were acquaintances of Mr. Ryan, which is how I came to know him."

"So you're all alone in the world."

"Oh, no. At least not as long as people like you and Jack are so kind."

Glynis all but melted beneath Sheri's smile.

"Well, naturally, you must stay with us as long as you like."

"Thank you. I am grateful for your hospitality. Is that crewelwork you're doing? My godmother did crewelwork." Sheri leaned forward to view the embroidery Glynis held up. "Oh, that's lovely. I've never seen anything quite like that. It must be your own design."

Glynis preened a bit, her pride evident. "You know, my dear, you really have to do your own designing these days if you want anything truly unique. The needlework companies seem to be fatally infatuated with dancing teddy bears and kittens playing the piano. Do you embroider yourself?"

"I dabble a bit, but I'm afraid my work isn't this fine."

Jack relaxed, knowing his mother was not going to be a problem. Anyone who showed such a sincere admiration of her work would have to have a fault considerably graver than merely being something out of a fairy tale. Whether she knew it or not, Sheri was in like Flynn.

There was a clatter of footsteps in the hall and a small dark whirlwind blew into the living room. At least, that was Sheri's first impression.

"Mom have you seen my red skirt? I wanted to wear it tomorrow and I can't find it. Jack, what are you doing home? Boy, Eleanor was sure ticked off when you high-tailed it north."

Jack stood up, catching his little sister's arm in a grip that expressed his exasperation. He drew her forward as Sheri also stood.

"Yes, thank you, I'm glad to be home."

"Sorry."

The grin Tina gave him was unapologetic. "I didn't know you'd brought a guest. Are you dumping Eleanor?"

Tina didn't seem in the least regretful. Jack gave her arm a not-so-gentle shake. "You have the manners of a warthog. Sheri, this is my obnoxious sister, Tina, the bane of the family. Tina, this is Sheri Jones. She took care of Uncle Jack and now she's going to be staying with us."

"Hi." Tina held out her hand, not in the least disturbed by her brother's uncomplimentary introduction.

"Hello." Sheri took the younger woman's hand, feeling the vibrancy of Tina's personality in the touch of her fingers. "I can see the resemblance between you and your brother."

"Horrors." Tina threw Jack an impish look, her eyes dancing with mischief.

Sheri had meant there was a similar feeling of intensity in both of them, but she could hardly say as much. And the physical resemblance *was* marked. Tina's eyes held more blue than Jack's pure gray and her hair wasn't as dark, but there was no mistaking their relationship.

"Tina, your manners grow more appalling every day. Is this the kind of behavior you're learning in college?"

Glynis's tone lacked any real bite. Her eyes held pride and affection as she looked at her children.

"Sure." Tina settled herself on the arm of her mother's chair, one jeans-clad leg swinging back and forth. "I'm taking Appalling Manners 101 and I'm getting straight A's."

"I can believe it," Jack said dryly, sitting back down. "Believe it or not, Sheri, underneath this ruffian is a mathematical genius. One of these days she's going to prove that the theory of relativity is all a bunch of hokum."

"Really?" Sheri searched her mind for some knowledge of the theory of relativity, but it hadn't been among the things old Jack Ryan had considered important for her education. She had a vague idea that it had something to do with an elderly gentleman with a shock of white hair. "I'm afraid I don't know much about math," she told Tina apologetically.

"That's okay. I only know enough to fake out my professors."

"Tina, why don't you show Sheri to the blue guest room," Glynis suggested, adding to Sheri, "I'm sure you'd like a chance to get cleaned up before dinner."

"I'll take Sheri up, Mother," Jack offered. He was a little uneasy about Sheri spending time alone with his boisterous sister, at least until he was sure that disaster didn't lurk around the corner.

"Let Tina take Sheri up to her room while you bring in her luggage."

"She doesn't—" Jack broke off, coughing. He could hardly tell his mother that not only did Sheri not have any luggage, she didn't *need* any.

"I would like to change before dinner."

At Sheri's words Jack met her look and he knew he'd find more than his own luggage in the Jag. He smiled weakly.

"You don't have to be so protective, Jack," Tina admonished. "I promise not to throw Sheri down the stairs."

"Thanks." Jack hesitated a moment longer, but there was really no graceful way to insist that Sheri stay in his sight. He could hardly suggest she help him carry in the luggage. He exited, feeling as if he were leaving a disaster in the making behind him.

"Gee, Jack must really like you," Tina commented, giving Sheri a speculative look.

"I think he's just concerned." Sheri stood up, smoothing the soft linen of her skirt. She was suddenly anxious to have a few minutes alone. There were so many conflicting emotions in this room, too much to try to deal with all at once.

"Well, I think there's more to it than that," Tina persisted. "He's never worried about Eleanor."

"Tina, show our guest to her room." Glynis's voice took on a firm edge. "And don't chatter her ear off."

Glynis watched the two women leave the room, Tina's characteristic bouncy stride a contrast to Sheri's gliding step, so light she almost seemed to float. She usually enjoyed this quiet time before dinner, immersing herself in her needlework, content to know that her family was nearby. But tonight the delicate embroidery lay forgotten in her lap.

The front door opened and Jack went through the hall, carrying a pair of ivory suitcases—pigskin, if she wasn't mistaken. In fact, they looked identical to the set she'd bought Jack when he took his first trip to Europe alone, only the color was different. So Sheri must have a comfortable amount of money. Vuitton luggage was not inexpensive. If she was comfortably off, why had Jack brought her to stay here as if she'd had nowhere else to go?

Glynis stared at the fine wools in her lap without seeing the brilliant colors. Sheri Jones seemed like a perfectly nice young woman, but her instincts told her there was more to the politely spoken young woman than met the eye. Though she herself might have wished for more subtlety, Tina had expressed Glynis's own feelings quite well: Jack seemed quite protective of their guest. Too protective?

She set aside her needlework and stood up, crossing to the phone. She tried never to interfere in her children's lives. Still, this wasn't really interference: it was more in the nature of a reminder, she decided as she dialed a familiar number. The phone rang twice before being picked up.

"Eleanor, my dear, I have a wonderful surprise. I hope you don't have plans for this evening."

SHERI RAN HER FINGERS over the top of the mahogany dressing table, avoiding her reflection in the mirror. She knew what she'd see there. Confusion. It wasn't an emotion with which she'd had a lot of experience, but since meeting Jack, it was becoming very familiar.

The room she'd been given was as exquisite as the rest of the house. Decorated in royal blue and a gray the color of palest smoke, it radiated serenity. She closed her eyes, taking a slow breath, trying to draw some of that serenity inside herself.

It was no use. Her eyes came open and she sighed. There was so much to think about, so many new things to understand. Life with Uncle Jack had never presented so many potential pitfalls. He'd lived alone and he'd been accepting of who and what she was. It had been much simpler.

This business of being human appeared to be somewhat complex. There were many aspects she did not yet understand. She would have to learn quickly so that Jack wouldn't worry so much.

She frowned, staring at her reflection. Jack. In many ways he presented the greatest difficulty of all. She didn't understand her feelings for him. She felt warm when he was near. And alive. More alive than she'd ever felt before. It was not an entirely comfortable feeling.

With a sigh she turned away from the mirror. It had been so much simpler before. She wandered to the window, pulling aside the heavy drapes to look out into the darkness. Simple was not always best. She was needed here. Jack needed her. More than he realized.

She smiled softly, thinking of him. He didn't like the fact that she'd disturbed his orderly life. He didn't like it at all. But he'd still been kind to her.

Sheri allowed the curtain to fall and turned back into the room. Jack didn't know it yet, but she could help him. She would consider her own feelings later. Uncle Jack had been right. His nephew needed her help. All she had to do was prove it to him.

"MOTHER, don't you think it's a bit much to have invited Eleanor and Roger here on Sheri's first night with us?" Jack made an effort to keep his voice at a modulated level. His mother's news was the last thing he wanted to hear.

"Is there something you're not telling me about Sheri, Jack?" Glynis asked.

Jack twitched, spilling scotch onto the walnut bar top. "What do you mean?" Was that his voice? He sounded so casual. Not at all like a man on the ragged edge of insanity. He turned, leaning against the bar, the old-fashioned glass clutched a little too tightly in his fingers. "What could there be to tell about Sheri besides the fact that she took care of Uncle Jack and I think we owe her a place to stay?"

"I don't know." Glynis frowned down at the linen she held, one finger stroking the swath of royal blue stitches. "You've been acting a little . . . strange this evening. And you seem worried about her."

"Nonsense." Jack managed a light smile. "I just think she's been through a lot of changes lately and I don't want her to feel overwhelmed. That's all. I hardly know her really."

Glynis looked up at him, her eyes full of doubt. "Perhaps I worry too much—"

"Of course you do."

"But I don't want to see you make a mistake. You've done so well with the bank. Your father would be very proud of you. And Eleanor is a lovely girl. She'll be able to do a great deal for you once you're married. I'd hate to see you throw all that over on a whim. Your father and I always dreamed of seeing your life like this."

And what about what he'd dreamed? The question popped up uninvited, and Jack tightened his fingers over the heavy glass. Where had the thought come from? He was doing what he'd dreamed, wasn't he? Not those silly adolescent dreams he'd had of living in the country somewhere and raising horses. But the real, adult dreams of success.

"Don't worry, Mother. I'm not about to forget my responsibilities. You didn't have to invite Eleanor to remind me that I'm engaged. But if you're trying to remind me of the joys of being a responsible adult, Roger is an odd choice of guest. God knows, he's more likely to encourage me to run off and be a hermit in the South Pacific."

"I thought Roger might be good company for Sheri. He may be a trifle irresponsible, but he really is a charming boy. As long as she's going to be staying with us, we might as well do what we can to make sure Sheri has a good time."

"Matchmaking?" Jack's tone was light and indulgent, a masterful piece of acting. Of course Roger and Sheri would be perfect together. If ever there was a man who knew how to dream, it was Roger. Wasn't that what Sheri had said—that it took someone who could dream? It would certainly solve his problems if Sheri and Roger hit it off. So why didn't the idea have more appeal?

Before he could answer that question, Sheri and his sister came downstairs. He'd forgotten to warn Sheri that they dressed for dinner, but Tina had apparently told her. Or she'd discovered it by methods he preferred not to know about. She was wearing a soft silk dress in a color that hovered somewhere between blue and green. She'd pinned her hair up into a pale gold coronet. She wore no jewelry and no makeup, but none was needed. Jack knew he'd never seen a woman look softer, more feminine, more exquisite. Next to her, every other woman he'd known seemed hard and overdressed.

He took a step toward her, but the doorbell rang before he could say anything. It was just as well. He wasn't sure what he'd planned to say, but it was a sure bet it was better left unsaid.

Later he was able to see that the evening had gone remarkably well. At the time he was convinced that his hair would be solid gray before the evening ended. It wasn't that Sheri said or did anything that extraordinary. It was just so obvious to him that she was something more than human, something different. At any moment he expected someone to leap to his feet, point a finger at her and announce that he knew her secret.

That never happened, but he couldn't quite get the scene out of his mind. In fact, he seemed to be the only one who was at all uneasy. Sheri met Roger and Eleanor with the same easy grace with which she did everything. Her shy smile had Roger eating out of her hand before the introductions were through. Eleanor was more reserved, but, then, that was just Eleanor.

He'd almost managed to relax by the time they sat down to dinner. After all, dinner table conversation should be safe enough. But the first words out of Eleanor's mouth shattered that hope.

"You have an interesting accent, Ms. Jones. I can't quite place it." Eleanor shook out her snowy linen napkin.

Jack wanted to shake her out. "Sheri has done a lot of traveling. I understand that tends to affect a person's speech patterns. Would you like a roll, Eleanor?"

"No, thank you, Jack." Eleanor gave him a polite smile and returned her attention to Sheri, who was sitting across the table from her. "Where are you from originally?"

"Didn't you say you were born in Europe, Sheri? Have some of this salad, Eleanor. It's really quite delicious." Jack thrust the bowl at her.

"Really, Jack, you'd think Sheri couldn't speak for herself."

That was Roger, ever-helpful Roger. Jack glared at him and received a bewildered look in return.

"Yes, Jack, do let Ms. Jones speak for herself," Eleanor said.

Jack sat back, trying to resign himself to the end of life as he knew it. Sooner or later Eleanor was going to ask Sheri something she couldn't answer. Something *she should* be able to answer. Something like "What do you think of Elvis Presley?" The fact that Eleanor despised Elvis Presley and probably knew no more about him than Sheri did was irrelevant at this point. Jack reached for his wineglass, wondering if he should casually spill it on his fiancée.

"Please call me 'Sheri,' Ms. Fitzsimmons."

"And you must call me 'Eleanor,' of course." Eleanor bared her teeth in a polite smile.

"Thank you. As a matter of fact, I have spent a great deal of time in Europe. I'm afraid my accent is impossible to trace. It's a little bit of everything, I guess."

"Well, I think it's lovely," Roger said, his eyes fixed on her face.

He looked like a lovesick calf, Jack decided uncharitably, downing most of his wine.

"Thank you."

Sheri's soft smile appeared to leave the never-without-a-reply Roger speechless.

"I myself have always thought it a pity that more people don't speak English correctly," Eleanor announced as she reached for her wineglass. "It's the reason Americans have such a terrible reputation, not only with other languages but with our own."

The edge in her voice made it clear she didn't share Roger's opinion of Sheri's accent. It was so clear that for a moment no one knew quite what to say. Roger's brows rose; Jack resisted the urge to kick Eleanor under the table; Glynis looked down at her plate. Only Tina opened her mouth, her eyes flashing indignantly.

But Sheri spoke first. "You are absolutely right. I have always been ashamed that my speech is so often incorrect. But it is quite difficult to hear one's own mistakes. Perhaps while I'm staying with Jack's family you would be willing to help me, Eleanor."

"Help you?" Eleanor reiterated in a scratchy voice.

"Teach me, perhaps."

"Teach you?" She was incapable of doing more than repeating Sheri's words.

"Oh, I did not mean that you should spend any of your time on something so unimportant, but maybe you could tell me when I have said something incorrect. So that I may learn, you understand."

The silence that settled over the table was nearly visible. There could be no doubting the absolute sincerity of Sheri's request. It was written in her eyes. She wasn't trying to make Eleanor look bad. There was no ulterior motive. Her request had come straight from the heart. She hadn't seen anything nasty in Eleanor's comment. Her very innocence made Eleanor look small, and everyone at the table knew it.

From the corner of his eye, Jack could see the color rising in Eleanor's smooth cheeks. Her fingers were rigid around her fork. The silence stretched to awkward lengths. Jack cleared his throat but couldn't think of anything to say.

"Have I said something wrong?" Sheri looked to Jack, sensing the atmosphere but uncertain of the reason for it.

"Of course not." Roger reached over and took her hand, squeezing it gently. "You just caught us by surprise, that's all."

"I shouldn't have asked Eleanor to help me?"

Sheri turned those eyes on Roger and Jack was amused to see that Roger didn't handle that look any better than he did.

"Well, no. It's not exactly that. Really. It's just that—"

"What Roger is trying to say is that I hardly have a reputation as a teacher," Eleanor answered in a tight voice, but her tone was polite. "Besides, you don't need anyone to tutor you. You speak beautifully."

It was a gracious apology and Jack's respect for his fiancée inched up a notch. She'd made a mistake and she was acknowledging it.

"Well, I like Sheri's accent," Tina announced with a touch of belligerence. "I think it makes her sound very interesting and exotic."

If only you knew how exotic, Jack thought. However, the crisis was past. Conversation picked up slowly, but it did pick up. All in all, he supposed he should be grateful that that was the worst that happened. There were odd gaps in Sheri's education, but it was remarkable how much could be explained by a European upbringing.

By the end of the evening Tina was clearly a devoted fan, Roger was blatantly smitten, his mother liked her with reservations and Eleanor might not be crazy about his guest, but she'd pulled in her claws.

Jack couldn't even begin to describe his own feelings about Sheri. The last thing he'd wanted was a major complication in his life. He had enough on his plate now, what with the bank and his upcoming wedding—a wedding he couldn't seem to get up any real excitement about.

Still, there was something about Sheri, a sweetness. He couldn't put his finger on what it was exactly, but he couldn't bring himself to wish her away. God knows, he'd felt more alive in the past few days than he had in the past few years. That was something, wasn't it?

Chapter Six

"So, Jack, what's wrong?" Roger signaled for the waitress to bring a round of beer, then returned his attention to his friend.

"Why should something be wrong?" Jack leaned back as the waitress set the bottle in front of him. Harry's Pub wasn't known for its elegant presentation or even its smooth service. Nevertheless the place was always packed. The sign over the battered bar boasted the best chili size east of the Pacific. The clientele agreed.

"Something's got to be wrong."

Roger's voice drew Jack's attention away from the odd mix of hard-hat and business-suit types who made up the lunch crowd. He reached for his beer, taking a pull directly from the bottle. "Why does something have to be wrong?"

"Because this is the first time in the past five years that you've called me up and suggested lunch."

"Maybe I decided I'd been neglecting an old friendship," Jack offered.

"No, I don't think so. Something's bugging you, Jackson, and you want to tell your old pal all about it."

"How's the ranching operation going?"

Roger blinked at the abrupt question. He reached for his beer. "It's going okay. I don't get up that way very often and I leave the managing to the manager, but the reports look good. We're turning out some good quarter horses. Another year or two and we may be in the black. Why do you want to know?"

Jack shrugged, his eyes on the scarred table. "Do you ever think about the plans we made when we were in high school?"

"Which one? The one where we were going to become astronauts, or the one where we were going to become race-car drivers? Or just the general plan to become irresistible to women, means unspecified?"

"The one where we were going to move to Wyoming and raise the greatest horses in the world."

"Oh, that one. Yeah, I think about it once in a while."

"What happened to it?" Jack asked moodily.

"Life, my friend. Life happened to both of us. I suppose my little operation north of Santa Barbara isn't quite the same as what we'd planned, is it?"

"No." Jack rubbed the back of his neck, wondering what he was doing here. He should never have called Roger and suggested lunch.

"What's bothering you, Jack? If you didn't want to talk about it, you wouldn't have called me."

Jack leaned back as the waitress smacked plates heaped with chili down in front of them. Roger was both right and wrong. Something was certainly bothering him, but he didn't want to talk about it. It wasn't the kind of thing you could talk about, even with an old friend.

"I told you. I just decided I'd been neglecting an old friendship. Maybe I'll make a trip up to see what you're doing with this place. Just for old time's sake. I haven't been on a horse in nearly five years. Might be interesting to see if I can still stay on one.''

"It's Sheri, isn't it?" Roger asked, cutting into what was threatening to become a monologue.

Jack lost hold of his fork, and chili splashed over the side of the plate and onto his pale yellow silk tie. "Dammit!" He dabbed at the spot and succeeded in spreading it into a large blotch.

"You should have dressed for the place," Roger told him without sympathy.

"Some of us work for a living." Jack glared at his friend's polo shirt.

Roger lifted his hands. "Don't blame me for that. I've offered several times to introduce you to the joys of hedonism, but you're always too busy doing something worthwhile. I've explained time and again that it's not as easy as it looks. There's a certain style that takes time and practice to achieve." He dunked a French fry in a mound of chili and bit into it, chewing reflectively.

Jack glared a moment longer, and then his sense of humor won out. "We all have to make the best of our skills, Roger. You have a talent for being useless. I don't."

Roger nodded thoughtfully. "Sad but true."

Jack laughed, feeling tension slip away. "Doesn't anything ever get to you?"

"Sure. Lots of things. Just the other day, I saw someone driving a maroon car with green upholstery." He shuddered. "It was enough to ruin my lunch."

"You are utterly worthless."

"Thank you. Now do you want to tell me what the story is on Ms. Sheri Jones—an alias if I ever heard one, by the way."

Jack started to shake his head, then stopped. If he didn't tell someone, he would surely go completely mad. On the

other hand, Roger was likely to think he'd already gone
over the edge if he tried to explain what was going on. He
wasn't even too sure about his own sanity at the moment.

"Would you say I'm a relatively sane person?"

Roger raised a brow at the abrupt question. "Sure.
Much too sane, if you ask me."

"That's what I've always thought. I mean, it isn't like
I've been prone to flights of fantasy. I'm a practical, down-
to-earth kind of guy. Dependable. Maybe even a little
dull."

"Jack, you're beginning to babble, which is not a sign
of mental health." Roger dunked another fry and fixed his
friend with a demanding eye. "Spit it out. What's with the
gorgeous houseguest? Are you considering eloping with
her? Because I've got to tell you, if I had to choose between the lovely Sheri and the fair Eleanor, it wouldn't
take me long to make a choice."

It was a measure of Jack's mental disturbance that he
didn't even notice the slur to his fiancée.

"I'm not considering eloping. Not unless we go on a
magic carpet."

"Excuse me?" Roger's brows rose in question. "Did
you say 'magic carpet'?"

Jack looked up suddenly, his eyes showing the strain of
the past few days. "Look, Roger, if I don't tell someone
about this, I'm going to go completely crazy. Or maybe
I'm crazy already. But one way or another, I've got to talk
to someone."

"Sure. Sure, Jack. You know I'm always here for you."
Roger put down his fork and gave Jack his undivided attention. "What's wrong?"

"It's Sheri."

"I'd gathered as much. What about her?"

"She's . . . not what she seems."

"Okay. She seems like a nice young woman who's staying with your family. What is she really?"

"Well, she's not a nice young woman—at least, that's not all she is. And she's not staying with my family for the reasons they think she is."

Roger frowned, trying to follow the convoluted sentences. His frown deepened as a thought occurred to him. "Jack, she's not— I mean, you and she didn't— She isn't—" He gestured, unable to finish the question.

Jack stared at him, trying to figure out what he was talking about. Light dawned slowly and he gave a short laugh. "Pregnant? God, no. I wish that's all it was."

"All it was?" Roger's voice rose. "My God, Jack, what the hell is it with this girl?"

"She's different. I mean, she's not like you and me."

"I noticed that."

Jack seized on his words eagerly. "Did you really? Because sometimes I think it's obvious, and then I'm not sure."

Roger reached for his beer, taking several long swallows before setting it down with a thump. His eyes were beginning to take on a slightly wild look.

"Jack, I was referring to the fact that she's female and we're not. It was a little joke. Very little, obviously. Now if you don't just spit out what the problem is, I swear I'm going to forget that we're friends and I'm going to climb over this table and do my best to drown you in Harry's chili. *What is wrong with Sheri?*"

"She's a genie." The words seemed to fall into a pool of sudden quiet, so that Jack had the feeling everyone in the bar must have heard them. He glanced around, but no one appeared to be paying any attention to their table.

"What?"

He looked at Roger, who was looking at him as if wondering whether or not to call for the men in the white coats.

"I know." Jack nodded. "It's hard to believe, isn't it? I didn't believe it at first, but then I didn't really have any choice. There was the electricity and the food and my car. And then I saw her in the smoke and the coffee. And that doesn't even take into account the luggage that wasn't there and then it was. And yesterday. Yesterday there were Mother's rosebushes."

"Jack. Jack. You've been working hard." Roger pitched his voice to a soothing tone. "It's been years since you've taken any kind of a vacation. And then there's been the engagement and your uncle's death. It's no wonder you're feeling a little strained."

"You think I'm crazy."

"No, of course not. You're a lot saner than I'll ever be. It's just that—" Roger paused, trying to choose his words carefully. "Even you have a cracking point, and maybe you just need a little rest."

"I'm not crazy, Roger. Sheri really is a genie."

"Jack, that's ridiculous. Next you're going to tell me that she lives in a lamp."

"A samovar," Jack told him gloomily.

"A samovar?" Roger reached for his beer and found it empty. He signaled the waitress frantically. "You're serious, aren't you?"

"I can't believe I'm saying this, but yes, I'm serious. I'm not crazy. At least, I'm reasonably certain I'm not crazy, and I am sitting here telling you that the girl you met last week is an honest to God puff-of-smoke genie."

The waitress brought another round of beer and Roger reached for his, taking a deep swallow before setting it down. He pushed his plate away and leaned his arms on the table.

"This I've got to hear. Start at the beginning, Jackson, and tell me everything that happened. Between the two of us, we'll get at the real truth."

"I thought the same thing, that there was going to be a logical explanation for it. Only there wasn't. I should have noticed that something was wrong when there was food in the refrigerator."

"At home."

"No, at Uncle Jack's. And the place was clean." He proceeded to tell Roger every detail of his relationship with Sheri, from realizing there shouldn't be any electricity, to seeing her form in a cloud of smoke, to his decision to bring her back to Los Angeles.

Around them the lunch crowd finished their meals and went back to work, but neither man noticed the place emptying out. The waitress cleared away their barely touched plates and kept them supplied with beer.

Roger didn't say a word until Jack had stopped speaking. There was a long silence while he digested his friend's incredible story.

Jack leaned back in his chair, feeling a tremendous relief now that he wasn't the only one who knew the truth. Even if Roger promptly called the nut patrol to haul him off, he couldn't manage much concern. It was wonderful to have actually told the entire story, to know that somebody else knew what had happened.

"A genie. It's impossible." Roger shook his head, his eyes on the wet circles created by the bottom of his beer bottle. "But there was something kind of . . . otherworldy about her. And the way she handled Eleanor's cattiness. Only a very clever woman or a total innocent could have managed that."

"I don't think she even knew Eleanor was being catty," Jack said lazily. Now that the secret was out, he felt almost light-headed.

"I can believe that, but a genie?" Roger shook his head again. "You're asking a lot, Jackson. We've been friends for a long time, but this is a hell of a lot to ask."

"She doesn't carry a purse," Jack offered, as if it were final proof.

"What?"

"She doesn't carry a purse. Not even a wallet. Nothing. Nada. Zip. Now I ask you, have you ever known a woman who didn't carry some kind of purse?"

It might have been the beer, but this seemed to strike both men as weighty evidence that Sheri was something other than an ordinary human.

Roger nodded solemnly. "It's true. Most women carry half a house in their purses."

"Well, Sheri doesn't even own one. Of course, I suppose she could snap one up in a minute, but she doesn't even bother." Jack leaned forward, his eyes meeting Roger's. "What would a genie need with a purse? Why carry all that stuff around if you can just pop it out of the air?"

Roger nodded, but he was still hesitant. He signaled for another beer, waiting for the waitress to bring it before speaking again. "You said something about your mother's roses. What was that about?"

Jack moaned, burying his fingers in his hair. "I thought everything was going fine. I mean, she's been here a week and nobody suspects a thing. Tina thinks she's 'rad' and Mother is teaching her to needlepoint. I was just beginning to relax a little, to believe that maybe having a genie in the house wasn't such a bad thing."

"I can think of a few things a genie might come in handy for."

Jack ignored Roger's innuendo. "Day before yesterday, Mother and Sheri were talking about the rose garden, and Mother commented, in all innocence, that it was such a pity that even in L.A. roses don't bloom year-round."

"They don't?" Roger interrupted. "The florist always has them."

"Maybe they import them from Australia or something," Jack suggested impatiently. "Anyway, the point is that Mother said that *her* roses probably wouldn't bloom for another month and wasn't it a pity. She wished they'd bloom right away." He stopped, looking at Roger intently.

Roger looked back, aware that he'd somehow missed an important point.

"Don't you see?" Jack asked.

"See what? Your mother loves roses. So what?"

"She said she *wished* they'd bloom right away. She *wished*."

"She wished they'd bloom— Oh, I get it." Roger signaled for two more beers to celebrate this understanding. "So what happened? Did they burst into bloom right before her eyes?"

"No. It wasn't quite that bad." Jack leaned back to allow the waitress to set the fresh round on the table. "But yesterday morning she woke the whole household to come out and look at what had happened. The whole damned rose garden was in bloom. It looked like the middle of June."

"And what did your mother say to this?"

"Well, at first she said it was a miracle. Then Sheri managed to convince her it must have been the Zoo Doo she'd used last fall. She claimed she'd seen it happen once in a garden in France."

" 'Zoo Doo'?"

"You know, manure from the zoo. They gather it up and package it and sell it."

Roger stared at Jack, his mouth beginning to twitch. "You mean to tell me that your mother believes this miraculous occurrence was caused by elephant—" He broke off and leaned back in his chair, his shoulders shaking with laughter.

Jack's mouth curved in a barely suppressed grin, and then he began to chuckle. It did seem ludicrous, but no more absurd than the real truth of the matter. His eyes met Roger's and the chuckle became a laugh. It had been too long since he'd really laughed at something. Years too long.

Their laughter faded, leaving a lingering sense of ease. Jack took a swallow of beer, trying to remember the seriousness of the situation. But after several brews, it was difficult to feel the full weight of it.

"It's not funny, you know," he finally said into the silence. "What am I going to do with her?"

"Have her predict the stock market, become one of the richest men in the world, create a line of ever-blooming roses and corner the garden market?" Roger volunteered.

"Eleanor keeps suggesting I find her an apartment or a job or both."

"Ignore her."

"I can't ignore her. I'm going to marry her."

"All the more reason to ignore her now. You won't be able to after the wedding."

"What have you got against Eleanor? You've been sniping at her ever since I told you we were getting married."

"I don't have anything against her, Jackson. I just don't think the two of you are suited. She brings out the worst in you and you bring out the worst in her."

"Don't be ridiculous. She'll be a perfect banker's wife." Jack downed the last of his beer, wishing the thought of Eleanor as his mate gave him more pleasure.

"Exactly. But will she be the perfect wife for Jack Ryan? That's the million-dollar question." Roger signaled for another round, ignoring Jack's vague protest that he ought to be getting back to the office. "You can't go back to the office. You're drunk."

This seemed so logical that Jack didn't even try to argue. "Weren't you and Eleanor seeing each other for a while?"

Roger laughed, and if Jack's senses hadn't been more than a little dulled, he might have heard the note of bitterness there.

"That's ancient history. Ellie and I dated centuries ago, Jackson, my boy. Centuries ago. That was before I left this fair land for climes considerably less salubrious."

Jack didn't have to ask what Roger was talking about. He remembered what Roger had been like when he'd gotten back from Vietnam. He'd never been inclined toward what he called "earnest endeavors," but he'd come back seemingly determined to enjoy every moment he was given. As if he believed that at any moment his life might be snatched away.

"That was a rough time," Jack offered awkwardly, knowing the memories still haunted his friend.

"Yeah." The silence stretched until Roger broke it with a short laugh. "But we're not here to discuss old times. We're here to decide what you should do with your inheritance. You know, it's just like old Jack to leave you a genie. None of my family ever does anything half as interesting."

"Well, I could do with a little less interesting and a little easier to deal with. All I want is to get my life back to normal. How am I supposed to do that with Sheri in it?"

" 'Normal'? Who's to say what's normal?" Roger asked, waxing philosophical. "In a more perfect world, we'd all have genies and *that* would be normal. Besides, you need something to liven your life up a little. Can you really tell me you wish you could go back to what it was before you met Sheri?"

JACK WAS STILL PONDERING the question several hours later as he made his way up the front walk. The bricks were showing a distressing tendency to shift beneath his feet and he had to concentrate on where he was stepping. He'd never before realized what a swell place to while away an afternoon Harry's Pub was.

In the back of his mind was the thought that he'd probably missed several meetings that afternoon, but it didn't really disturb him. He'd had important things to discuss with Roger. There'd been decisions to be decided, choices to be chosen. Off the top of his head, he wasn't sure whether he and Roger accomplished anything, but that didn't bother him, either.

He opened the front door and tiptoed into the hallway. At least, he tried to tiptoe, but someone had placed a palm in the middle of the entryway. Fighting his way free of the plant's vicious embrace, Jack glowered at it.

"Jack?" He turned at the sound of Sheri's soft voice, executing some rapid footwork to avoid tipping back into the killer plant.

She was standing on the stairs. Sun spilled in through the arched window on the landing, haloing her hair so that it

seemed to be pure white gold. It came to him suddenly that
he knew the answer to Roger's question. He did *not* want
his life to go back to being just as it was before Sheri had
floated into it.

He gave her a smile of singular sweetness. Sheri reached
up, tugging on her hair, aware of the increased rate of her
pulse.

"Hello."

"Hello." She came down a few more steps. "Are you all
right, Jack? Your office called and said you hadn't come
back from lunch."

"That's right."

He didn't seem interested in pursuing the topic, Sheri
thought. He stared at her, an expression in his eyes she
couldn't quite read.

"You don't look like a genie," Jack said abruptly.

"I don't?"

"No. You look exactly like an angel I saw in a picture
book when I was a child."

Sheri felt a small shiver run up her spine as he continued to stare at her. There was something in his eyes—a
look she'd never seen before—a need, a promise. Something that brought a feeling she didn't recognize, didn't
quite understand. She cleared her throat and took another step toward him.

"We were worried."

The words broke the inexplicable tension. Jack blinked,
looking around the hallway as if expecting to see someone
lurking in the corners.

" 'We'? We who?"

"Your mother and I. And Eleanor came by an hour or
so ago."

"Ah, the fair Eleanor. Did you know that she hates
being called 'Ellie'? Roger calls her 'Ellie.' "

Sheri crossed the last few feet between them and put her hand on Jack's arm. He looked at her, his eyes crossing slightly as he attempted to focus on her face.

"So what have you been doing with your day? Turning water into wine, feeding the fish on a loaf of bread? Or was that feeding the bread with a loaf of masses?"

"You're intoxicated!"

Jack grinned down into her wide eyes. "So I am. It's rather nice, don't you think?"

"I don't know. Perhaps you should go upstairs. I don't think your mother should see you like this."

"Quite right. Mother never has had any sense of humor about this sort of thing. She threatened to ground me for the rest of my life the first time I came home with a few too many under my belt."

Sheri pulled him toward the stairs. He was amenable enough to direction, though he showed a tendency to waver a bit.

"I told Roger all about you," he said solemnly. "He thought I was crazy, but then I told him you didn't carry a purse."

"A purse?" Sheri frowned, unable to make the connection that was obviously clear to Jack and Roger.

"That's right. Roger thinks it's great you're a genie." He frowned. "Don't go giving him tips on the races."

"I'll try to avoid that," she assured him, guiding him up the stairs.

"Do genies drink?" He turned to look at her, and caught his foot on a stair.

Sheri braced her arm across his back, exerting all her strength to keep him from tumbling backward.

The small crisis successfully resolved, Jack paused, devoting his full attention to her. "Well, do you?"

"Generally not." She tugged on his arm, getting him started up the stairs again. "Alcohol does not really agree with us."

They reached the top of the stairs, and she breathed a small sigh of relief. His room was just down the hall.

"That's too bad," he announced suddenly.

"What is too bad?"

"That you can't drink."

"I did not say I *could* not drink." She steered him toward his door. "I said that it's generally not a good idea. It can have a deleterious effect on my metabolism."

The door opened and Jack allowed her to push him gently through. "A del-e-te-ri-ous effect," he said, prounouncing each syllable separately, and then he grinned at her. "I like that. Next time someone asks me if drinking makes me sick as a dog, I'll tell them it has a dele—" His tongue stumbled over the word and he waved one hand expansively. "You know—that effect."

"Your mother will be home soon. I'm not sure you want her to see you in this condition."

Jack flopped down into a soft chair, tilting his head back to look at her. "Why don't you wave your wand and make me sober again? On second thought, I'm very dull when I'm sober. I'm much more interesting this way, don't you think?"

"I think you're always interesting." A lock of thick dark hair had fallen over his forehead and she had the urge to reach out and brush it back, to lay her palm against his brow and draw out the pain she could sense inside him.

"Always interesting, huh?" Jack leaned back in the chair and stared up at the ceiling. "Do they teach you that in genie school? That humans are to be told they're always interesting?"

He didn't wait for an answer. He reached up and caught her around the waist. Sheri gasped as he pulled her off balance and she tumbled onto his lap. Jack laughed, a low, masculine sound that sent a strange warm shiver through her. She shook her hair back out of her face, looking at him hesitantly.

His eyes were slightly glazed from alcohol, but there was something more there, a slumberous look she'd never seen before.

Jack reached up to stroke her hair. "Your hair is so soft," he murmured, almost to himself. "I've never touched anything so soft."

Sheri watched him uncertainly. She felt an odd tightness in her chest that made breathing an effort. His eyes swept up to meet hers, full of such pain that Sheri almost cried out.

"Did I ever tell you I wanted to raise horses?"

She shook her head.

"I did. Roger and I were going to have the biggest horse ranch in the country." Jack leaned his head back against the chair, his hand still tangled in her hair. "We were just kids with big dreams. Dreams. I used to be able to dream."

"You still can." Sheri brushed his hair back from his forehead.

"Can I?" He looked at her from under heavy lids. His mouth twisted suddenly in a wry smile. "I guess I must be able to. I dreamed you, didn't I?" His lashes drifted down.

"I am not a dream," she whispered.

But a deep breath was all the reply she received. The afternoon's drinking had caught up with him.

Sheri slid off his lap and settled him in a more comfortable position. Jack stirred as her fingers rested on his forehead, his brows puckering. She brushed the frown away, feeling him slip into a deeper sleep beneath her touch.

She backed away, her eyes on him. There was so much she didn't understand, so many things she hadn't been prepared for.

Jack needed her. She knew that, even if he didn't. And she should have been happy that it was so. To be truly needed was important. But there was something more. She wanted to be with Jack, wanted him to need her. But she wanted something more—something she couldn't define, didn't understand.

She reached out, almost touching him, then drew back, suddenly sure it would be a mistake. Shaking her head, she backed out of the room, easing the door shut behind her. The window at the end of the hallway beckoned and she drifted toward it.

It looked out on the rose garden, ablaze with bloom. She frowned. That had been a mistake. She should have realized it was the wrong thing to do. But she'd only been trying to make Glynis happy. She'd sounded so wistful when she'd spoken of her roses and it had seemed a small enough thing to do. Still, Sheri knew she'd have to be more careful.

Life had been so simple with old Jack. He'd asked nothing more of her than companionship, wanted nothing but a few small comforts and a smile. There'd been no need to worry about the truth of her origins coming out since he'd never had visitors. Her small magics had amused him.

But they didn't amuse Jack. He worried about them. He worried about her. She leaned against the cool glass, tracing her finger over its surface. Her expression grew dreamy. She liked the thought of Jack worrying about her, liked the idea that he cared enough to worry.

But it wouldn't do to like it too much. Jack was engaged to be married. She frowned, her finger tracing the same design over again. He and Eleanor did not seem well suited, but that was not for her to judge. She knew so little of his world. But she could learn.

She turned away from the view of the rose garden. Tina kept a stack of magazines in the library. That would be as good a place as any to start.

Behind her on the windowpane, the tracing of a heart seemed to glow for a few minutes, as if catching the light of the fading sun.

Chapter Seven

Learning to be human was not a simple thing, as Sheri soon found out. The magazines were full of articles on how to improve oneself: how to lose weight, how to gain weight, how to find a husband, the joys of single life, planning a wedding, surviving a divorce. She'd hoped to find a clear-cut pathway to being normal, and instead found a bewildering array of choices.

Apparently a human woman was expected to be a high-powered career woman and a perfect mother whose children ate nutritionally complete meals at all times, attended only the best schools and participated in extracurricular activities. At the same time she should have the body of a twenty-year-old model, an unlined face, be a gourmet cook, a dietetic expert and have a home that was not only immaculate but exquisite—somehow combining both comfort and decor into one perfect whole.

Her relationship with a "significant other" was important, though not the sole focus of her life. A relationship was to be split right down the middle, fifty-fifty, and the magazines abounded with information on how to make sure your mate carried his fair share of the load.

Somewhere, in between jobs, classes, social engagements and self-improvement seminars, she should find time for herself.

Just reading about it all was enough to make Sheri's head spin. If this was what being human was all about, it was an exhausting affair altogether.

Still, in sorting it out, the one thing that seemed to be a constant thread was that a woman needed a job. Some articles allowed, rather grudgingly, that if you had small children, perhaps raising them could be considered fulfilling. But if you were single, there was no question that you needed a job.

Since everyone had one, how difficult could a job be to find?

"Ms. JONES, I thought you said you had experience using a keyboard." Mr. Lewis ran his fingers through the few strands of hair remaining on his head, his eyes taking on a harried look.

"I . . . well, yes, I did. But it wasn't a keyboard of quite this type." Sheri stared at the rows of numbered and lettered buttons, wondering how she could explain to him that she'd been talking about a piano keyboard.

"Keyboards don't differ that much, Ms. Jones. Can you explain to me how you managed, in the space of less than two hours, to cause a total system crash?" Despite his best efforts, Mr. Lewis's voice was starting to rise.

"I—" Sheri stopped, raising her eyes to his, her expression helpless. "No."

The simple word seemed to leave him without words. When he'd hired her for the job, he'd been dazzled more by her fine-boned beauty than her qualifications. After all, she was only to answer the phone, type a few letters and act as a general receptionist to the small real estate office. The pleasure of watching her around the office—perhaps even more than just watching—would more than make up for any minor training he might have to provide.

She'd been honest about her lack of job experience. Looking into those big blue eyes, Gerald Lewis had seen the future in glorious Technicolor. He'd provide her with the necessary skills, she'd provide him with... Well, who could say just how grateful she might be.

Only now, staring at the lines of gibberish wending their way across the lit screen of the computer, he faced the possibility that the cost of hiring with his libido might be far higher than he'd ever dreamed.

"I am sorry, Mr. Lewis. I just pushed a few of the buttons. I did not mean to break it."

"Break it? Break it? I don't even know what it is you've done." He stared at the screen in despair.

"I suppose this means you do not want me to come back tomorrow morning?" Sheri questioned hesitantly.

The look he gave her spoke volumes.

Sheri was disappointed that her first venture into the working world had turned out badly, but not discouraged. According to the magazine articles, it was important to find a position requiring skills that meshed with your own. Apparently real estate was not her field.

She soon found that any job that required mastery of a computer was a mistake. Genies and computers simply didn't mix. She didn't understand them and they clearly disliked her. Her third attempt to master one ended with her prospective employer begging her not to return.

Wandering through the rose garden, she nipped a faded flower here and there and considered her options. If a job was necessary, then a job she had to have. She could ask Jack. He'd almost certainly find her a position. She scowled at a bee buzzing nearby, her jaw set stubbornly.

She didn't want to ask Jack. This was something she wanted to do herself. She needed to prove—to Jack and herself—that she could live in his world, that she didn't have to be at best a helpless decoration, at worst a burden.

Still, it was difficult to know where to try next. With a sigh she set the problem aside. Given time, the Fates would provide. She just needed to have patience.

"YOU'RE GOING TO love this place, Sheri. They have the greatest seafood." Tina jerked the wheel, sending the little Mercedes skidding around a corner.

Sheri closed her eyes and tried to remember the names of all the presidents in order. Uncle Jack had sworn by it as a method of keeping calm. He'd obviously never ridden with his niece.

When Tina had suggested that she and Sheri go out shopping and have lunch, Sheri had jumped at the chance. Her job hunting had been discouraging, Jack had been spending long hours at the office and she was finding time lying a bit heavily on her hands.

Tina's offer of lunch was heaven-sent. Not only would but she get to see something beyond the walls of Jack's home, she could observe Tina and learn from the other woman's behavior. Besides, she liked Jack's little sister.

But she didn't need a lot of experience in this new life to know that one thing she did *not* want to learn from Tina was how to drive. The other woman was completely fearless and appeared to have a boundless faith in the ability of other drivers to anticipate her every move and compensate before disaster occurred. The fact that it had worked so far didn't reassure Sheri.

Tina spun the wheel again, and the car bounced over a shallow dip in the road as it hurtled into a parking structure. Sheri breathed a sigh of relief when they were safely parked between a gray Honda and a bright red Corvette. Tina threw herself out of the car with the enthusiasm she showed for everything she did. It was hard to reconcile her quick movements and impatience to get at each new experience with the kind of patience and discipline required by higher mathematics, but Tina seemed to balance the two.

Over the past few weeks, Sheri had learned that Tina was one person she could relax with. Tina never questioned any odd gaps in her knowledge, never probed for information she couldn't give. If Sheri didn't know something, Tina was more than happy to fill her in. She was quite capable of carrying ninety percent of the conversation by herself, and required little more than an occasional comment from her companion.

Now and then Sheri caught a shrewd look in Tina's eye that gave the lie to the scatterbrained image she projected. But she never questioned. Sheri was content with that.

The restaurant was in a slightly scruffy area of Pasadena. Tina referred to it rather sarcastically as a "revitalization target." Sheri followed her gaze out the window to across the street, where a bright neon sign advertised Chi Chi's vintage clothing. Next to it was a run-down storefront whose sign proclaimed adult movies for rent. She'd already learned that adult movies did not mean documentaries and educational specials.

"You don't approve of revitalization?"

"Oh, it's not that exactly." Tina picked up a breadstick and crunched into it, a frown puckering her forehead. "It's just that any time they revitalize an area, a lot of people are displaced. Sometimes it's people who've lived in the area for years. Look what's happening in Venice."

"Italy?" Sheri searched for anything she'd heard about the famous city, but the only thing that came to mind was that it was ever so slowly sinking.

"No. Venice, California. You know, on the beach."

"Sorry. I wasn't thinking." Sheri reached for a breadstick, hoping this lapse wasn't too severe. Tina seemed to take it in stride, however.

"A few years ago Venice was a pit. It was run-down and property values were really low. Only then property values in all the surrounding communities climbed so high that people started looking at Venice as an alternative to Santa Monica. A bunch of artists moved into the area. After all, what does an artist have that's worth stealing?"

Sheri considered pointing out that an artist might think his or her work was worth something, but she sensed it wasn't relevant.

"Anyway, before too long, Venice started to be seen as this artsy community. Property values started to climb and all sorts of pseudo-artistic types began to move into the area. The streets were cleaned up and clever little shops opened up all along the boulevard. Which brought the tourists in, which brought more money, which made the property values go higher."

Sheri frowned. "Is that bad? It seems to me that it would be a good thing that the streets were safer and nice shops were opened."

"That's just what it seems like on the surface. But that's not all there is to it." Tina waved a breadstick for emphasis, her face alight with emotion. "There's another side to the story. As property prices increased, landlords suddenly realized they could sell buildings they'd neglected for years and make huge profits. If they kept the buildings, they raised the rent to outrageous levels because all these artsy types were willing to pay to live in Venice."

"I still don't see what's so awful."

"Well, what about the people who used to live in those buildings? The people who used to run businesses where those clever little shops are now? Some of those people were there for decades, renting their apartments or shops and going on with their lives. Now suddenly they're forced out because Venice is 'revitalized.' It's not right."

Sheri crushed a tiny crumb with the tip of her finger, feeling Tina's passion. "And yet it's progress of a sort," she pointed out. "You said that this Venice was not a nice place to go before the changes started. It's inevitable that something would change that. Cities are like people—they don't stay the same for long. If this hadn't happened, perhaps things would have gotten even worse."

"Maybe." Tina stared moodily across the street. "But I can't help but wonder how many people ended up homeless because some nitwit wanted to try his hand at becoming the next Picasso."

"It's rare that a change doesn't displace someone or something. Even good changes aren't good for everyone. All you can do is try to lessen the impact on those whose lives must change whether they wish it or not."

"I suppose," Tina allowed, then eyed Sheri shrewdly. "You're awfully philosophical for someone so young. You're not much older than I am, but you're so rational. Don't you ever get passionate about things?"

"Many things." Sheri glanced up, and smiled in relief when she saw the waiter approaching with their plates. "Especially about food. It looks wonderful."

The subject was safely dropped, but Sheri doubted it had been forgotten. Tina didn't forget much. The conversation moved in lighter channels over the meal, and by the time they left the restaurant, the tentative bonds of friendship had been drawn a little tighter.

"There's a shop across the street where they have the greatest Italian shoes." Tina caught Sheri's look and shrugged sheepishly. "Well, if you can't beat 'em, you might as well enjoy 'em."

The two women laughed and headed for the crosswalk. They were waiting for the light to change, when a gruff voice spoke from behind them.

"Excuse me. I'm sorry to bother you."

They turned to see a man of about forty standing nearby. His clothes were ragged and dirty, but showed signs of having been cared for once. His hair was as neatly combed as fingers could manage. His face was lean and worn. But it was his eyes that caught Sheri. Never had she seen eyes so old, as if the man had seen centuries of hard living. There was almost pride there. Pride and strength. Beaten down and almost destroyed, but still struggling to survive.

"I'm sorry to bother you," he said again. "But I was wondering if you could spare any change."

Tina was already reaching for her purse, but Sheri took a step closer to the man, drawn by his need.

"Are you lost?"

He appeared surprised that she was addressing him, then he laughed without humor. "Lost? In a manner of speaking, I suppose. I haven't been able to find a job for over a year now."

"How awful."

He drew himself up, pride in every line of his body. "I don't ask for your pity. We're managing all right. Most of the time."

"Here. This is all I have." Tina held out a handful of bills and grasped Sheri's arm with her free hand, trying to draw her back.

The man looked at the money, and Sheri could see how much he hated needing it. She took the money from Tina's hand and thrust it into his.

"Please. She can afford it." Tina murmured a slightly alarmed protest, but Sheri ignored her. "You said 'we.' Are you married? Do you have children?"

He shoved the bills into his pocket and half turned to walk away. But something in Sheri's eyes persuaded him to stay. "I have a wife and daughter."

"How old is your daughter?"

"Sarah is ten."

"Do you have a place to stay?"

"We've been living in the car for the past couple of months, but it isn't going to last much longer."

"That's terrible! Don't you think that's terrible?" Sheri turned to Tina for support.

Tina mumbled something, clearly at a loss about how to deal with the situation.

"You can't continue to live like that," Sheri said. She turned back to her new acquaintance, her expression determined. "What's your name?"

"Melvin. Look, I didn't mean to start any trouble."

"You haven't started any trouble at all, Melvin. We just can't allow this to continue. It's terrible to think that you and your family are living in your car. We'll have to do something about it, won't we, Tina?"

Tina stared at her helplessly. It wasn't that she didn't feel compassion for the man's situation. She felt tremendous compassion for him and his family. That's why she'd given him all the money she had with her. But never in a million years would it have occurred to her to engage him in conversation.

She had a sinking feeling that Sheri planned on a lot more than talking to him.

JACK STARED at the abstract print on the wall across from his desk. Squiggles of blue and red darted across a vaguely gray background. He wondered why he'd never noticed how much he disliked that print. He'd have to ask his secretary to find something that wasn't reminiscent of a depressed four-year-old's scribbling.

Of course, if he didn't manage to focus on the report in front of him, he would be telling his secretary she was going to have a new boss. He'd been working on the Carter deal for almost a year. Now that he had it virtually in the palm of his hand, it didn't seem all that important. It didn't even seem interesting. He rubbed a hand across his forehead, trying to remember what a coup this was. Where was his concentration these days?

He focused on the stack of papers again. Two lines into the report, his attention wandered once more, this time to the framed portrait of Eleanor that sat on one corner of his desk.

She really was a lovely woman. Not beautiful, and certainly nothing as frivolous as pretty. There was an elegance about her that he'd once found soothing. Why was it that lately it seemed more grating than anything else? When they went out together, he kept wondering what she'd look like with her hair mussed about her face, maybe her cheeks flushed.

He supposed that if he suggested it, she would have no objections to sleeping with him. But he had no desire to suggest it. He told himself that he was just observing a little propriety, something that was too seldom done these days. Yet he had a sneaking suspicion that it was lack of interest, not propriety, that kept him out of his fiancée's bed.

When he considered making love with a woman, it wasn't Eleanor's face he saw. It was Sheri's. No matter how firm he was in putting her from his mind, she always slipped under his guard, catching him at odd moments.

There was no reason for it. It wasn't as if he'd even kissed her. *But oh, how he wanted to.* He hadn't been so drunk that he hadn't noticed how right she'd felt on his lap. And he didn't have to concentrate to remember the soft scent of her—not quite a perfume, but a gentle scent that lingered in the memory.

With a muttered curse, he pushed his chair back from his desk and strode over to the window. Looking out over the Glendale financial district didn't do a thing to help him concentrate. Sometimes, if he tried really hard, he could almost believe his own story—that Sheri had been his uncle's nurse and nothing more. He could almost believe it.

It wasn't even the fact that she could twitch coffee cups out of the air and came with her own home away from home in the form of a samovar. Since the incident with his mother's roses, she'd been careful not to do anything out of the ordinary. She might have been just a normal houseguest, not too obtrusive and fairly easy to get along with.

In fact, he'd seen very little of her these past two weeks or more. Which was just the way he wanted it, he told himself. She was keeping out of trouble and that's all he asked.

So why couldn't he get her out of his mind?

The discreet buzz of the intercom interrupted his thoughts. He spun back to the desk and jabbed the button irritably. "What is it, Ms. Sanders?"

"It's your mother on line two, Mr. Ryan. She sounds very upset."

He jabbed line two and snatched up the phone.

"Mother?"

"Jack, you've got to come home immediately. It's just awful. I don't know what to do with these people. They're in the hall and they won't go away. They might go away, but she won't let them. She keeps insisting we've got to do something, but it's not my responsibility, Jack. Really it's not."

"Calm down, Mother. She who? What people?"

"Sheri. And she brought them home. Eleanor is here and she agrees with me. Only, Tina and Roger are siding with Sheri, and I don't know what to do. It's not that I'm not a compassionate woman, Jack. You know I'm a compassionate woman."

"You're a very compassionate woman, Mother," Jack told her soothingly. "Now tell me what's going on."

"I told you. They're in the hall and she won't let them leave. It's not right, Jack. It's not proper. You've got to come home and do something."

"I'll be there in twenty minutes." Jack set down the phone in the midst of more protests from his mother that she really was compassionate. He didn't have the faintest idea what was going on at home, but it was obvious Sheri was right in the middle of it. That was enough to fill him with foreboding.

It was closer to fifteen minutes than twenty when he pulled the Jag into the driveway. The house looked much the same as it always had. From his mother's garbled explanation, he'd half expected to find people camped on the doorstep. Thrusting open the front door, he stepped into a scene he could guarantee the old house had never witnessed before.

The hallway was filled with people. On one side stood Sheri and Tina and Roger. Tina was arguing passionately that this kind of thing was everyone's responsibility. Sheri was silent, but her stance said she agreed with every word his sister uttered. Roger's eyes held more than a tinge of slightly malicious amusement, but his position bespoke his support.

On the other side of the hall stood Eleanor, looking a great deal like the paintings Jack had seen of Liberty on crusade. Her jaw was set, her dark eyes full of fury, and the flush on her cheeks made it clear the argument had been going on for some time. His mother stood next to her, her eyes full of confusion; she was clearly undecided about the proper stand.

In the middle was a ragtag trio of total strangers. Obviously a family: a man of about forty, a woman a few years younger, though hard living had etched premature lines in her face, and a little girl, who was holding her mother's hand so tightly her knuckles were turning white.

"Good grief!" The exclamation escaped his lips before he could think to back out the door, leaving this obviously volatile situation to resolve itself without him.

There was a moment of silence as everyone turned to look at him and then they all converged at once.

"Jack, thank heavens you're here. I don't know what to do with these people."

"Jack, you've got to tell Mother and Eleanor we can't turn our backs on these people. We have to do something."

"Jack, perhaps you can add a voice of reason to this whole mess. I've been trying to explain how impossible this situation is, but your sister and your 'guest' don't seem to understand."

"Jack, I'm sorry. I did not mean to cause trouble, but they haven't enough money for food and they have been living in their car and I just could not leave them there."

"Jackson, welcome to the circus. If you had any sense, you'd have stayed at the office."

Jack realized that his back was pressed to the door, much like an animal at bay. He straightened up, raising his voice to be heard above the cacophony.

"Hold it! Hold it! I can't hear a thing when you're all talking at once." Silence descended and he drew a deep breath, trying to look as though he was in control of the situation. "Okay, now somebody explain to me exactly what's going on."

"We were—"

"They brought—"

"I couldn't—"

"I can't believe—"

"QUIET!"

The bellowed command had the desired effect. They all stared at him, waiting. He thrust his fingers through his hair, his gaze settling on the strangers, who looked as bewildered as he felt. He gave them a distracted smile before looking at the assembly in front of him.

"Roger, you seem to know what's going on. Do you think you could explain it to me?"

"Sure. It's really very simple."

Jack braced himself, recognizing the look in Roger's eyes. Roger was enjoying this entirely too much. Which meant that simple or not, things were not going to be easy.

"Tina and Sheri went out for lunch, and when they came out of the restaurant, this gentleman—" he gestured lazily to the strange man "—approached them and requested a small amount of money, apparently to buy food for his family." This time his gesture encompassed the woman and child. "Tina gave him some money, but Sheri engaged the man in conversation. When she discovered he'd been without work for over a year and he and his family were attempting to make their car into a home, she felt he needed more than money."

"And she brought them home?" Jack questioned weakly, beginning to understand his mother's hysteria over the phone.

"Yes, indeed. She brought them home. I personally think it was an act of great humanitarian spirit that puts the rest of us to shame," Roger answered, his eyes sparkling with amusement. It wasn't that he didn't sympathize with the man's plight, but he could see the humor in the current circumstances.

Jack was not really up to seeing the humor at the moment.

"Jack, Sheri's absolutely right. Melvin and Louise need more than just a handout. And there's Sarah to consider. Do you want to think of her growing up on the streets?"

"Tina, be quiet." He raised his hand when Eleanor started to speak. "Pardon me for being rude, but if you'd all just shut up for a minute, it would make it a lot easier to think."

He met the stranger's eyes again, and he saw pride beneath the confusion. Yes, he could just imagine Sheri taking one look at the man and deciding she had to help him.

"Sheri, could I talk to you for a moment? If you'll all excuse us?" He drew her into the library, shutting the door on the odd little gathering in the hallway.

"I'm sorry I have caused trouble, Jack. I know I promised I would fit in. But I could not leave that man on the street. He was so full of hurt and pride. He hated asking us for money, but his family had no food."

"Sheri, I know it's a terrible tragedy, but I'm not sure that bringing him into my mother's house is the right thing to do."

"I did not know what else to do, and I knew you would know how to help them. You can help them, can't you?"

When she looked up at him with those eyes, he was ready to promise her the world. He dragged his gaze away, trying to order his thoughts.

"Look, there are agencies who handle this sort of thing. It's too big a problem for individuals to deal with." He broke off as Sheri set her hand on his arm.

"They've been to the agencies, Jack. They would not be able to stay together. They're a family. All they want is a chance to stay together. That's not so much, is it?"

"No, of course not, but—" He stopped, running his hand through his hair again. How did he explain this to her? How did he make her understand that this wasn't the way things were done? She made it seem so reasonable, as though she'd done the obvious thing.

"Sheri, I—" He stopped again, caught by the shimmer of tears in her eyes.

"Jack, I am sorry I have caused trouble again, but I could not leave them there."

He reached up, catching a tear on the end of his finger. "No, of course you couldn't." And he knew it to be the truth. She could no more have left Melvin and family on the streets than she could have stopped breathing. "It's all right. Don't cry anymore. It's all right."

Somehow, she was in his arms, her head pressed against his chest, her tears dampening the front of his shirt. He bent his head over hers, inhaling the sweet fragrance of her hair.

Jack felt an ache in his chest, as if her pain were his. He wanted to comfort her, to take the hurt away. Her gentle soul could never understand the harsh realities of the world. Yet he realized he wouldn't want it any other way. He tightened his arms around her and pressed his cheek to the top of her head, his expression tender. "It's going to be all right."

"I don't see how you can say that, Jack."

He jerked his head up. Eleanor stood just inside the door, her eyes cool as she took in the sight of her fiancé with another woman in his arms. "This whole situation is ridiculous."

Jack dropped his arms from Sheri. She turned to look at Eleanor, apparently unaware of the possible implications of the scene the other woman had just witnessed. Eleanor stepped farther into the room, shutting the door behind her. The furious color faded from her cheeks, and she was as coolly in control as ever.

"Really, Jack. Maybe you should explain the realities to your little guest. This kind of thing may be acceptable in some places, but this is hardly the place. One just doesn't bring people of that sort into one's home. And especially not into the home of one's hostess. Glynis was practically in tears when I got here."

Sheri flushed. "I'm sorry if I upset Glynis, but I couldn't leave Melvin on the street."

"So you brought him here where he can do God knows what sort of damage? I hate to point out the obvious, but you know absolutely nothing about these people."

"I know they are good people," Sheri insisted stubbornly.

Eleanor gave a short laugh, expressing total incredulity. "On the basis of a five-minute conversation on a street corner, you're willing to risk not only your life, but the lives of Jack's entire family? The man could be a killer for all you know. My God, that's a bit arrogant, don't you think?"

Sheri paled, her fingers furiously twisting her hair.

"That's enough, Eleanor."

Jack's abrupt tone only fueled Eleanor's anger. "Enough? Jack, you can't possibly condone this. What about your family? Have you thought of what could have happened to Tina when this woman so blithely invited these people home?''

"Nothing happened to Tina," Jack said wearily. "And I don't think any good can come of overdramatizing the situation."

"Pardon me. I thought I was simply showing a normal concern for the welfare of the people I thought you cared about."

Eleanor's tone could have created instant icicles in the tropics. She turned and left the room before Jack could say anything more.

"I'm sorry, Jack. I did not mean to cause trouble."

Sheri's eyes, wide and troubled, settled on his face.

"Stop apologizing. You did what you thought was right, which is more than most of us manage these days." He rubbed the back of his neck, feeling the tension settle in a knot at the base of his skull.

"Still, I have made Eleanor very angry."

"She'll get over it." He was vaguely appalled to realize how little he cared whether she did.

He pushed the thought aside to concentrate on the problem at hand. "You must have had some idea of what to do with Melvin and Louise when you brought them here."

Sheri brightened somewhat. "Well, I did think that perhaps you could hire them."

"Hire them?" He tried to picture Melvin or Louise on the payroll at the bank. Did Sheri see them as the executive types?

"Your mother told me the cook is going back to Europe next week. Louise is a good cook. Sarah told me so."

Jack thought of pointing out that what a ten-year-old considered good cooking might not be quite what his

mother had in mind. Goodbye *osso bucco*, hello maca-
roni and cheese.

"And what about Melvin?"

"Well, he likes plants. He told me so when I asked. And
your mother told me how hard it is to find a good gardener—someone who really cares about their work."

She was looking at him so eagerly, as if she'd just solved
a major problem for him. He pictured his mother's immaculately manicured two acres and then tried to picture
her face if he suggested that she hire the scruffy individual
he'd seen in the hallway.

He sighed. Roger had been right. He should have run the
minute he heard his mother was on the phone. Saint
Thomas was nice this time of year.

"Why don't you ask Melvin and Louise if they'd like to
come in here, and I'll talk to them. Maybe they have some
idea of how they'd like their future settled."

Sheri flashed a dazzling smile. "I knew you would understand. I knew you could help them."

The light in Sheri's eyes told Jack she believed he could
do anything. "I haven't helped them yet," he said hastily.
She caught his hand in hers and he felt the same jolt of
awareness he did every time they touched. It was like
coming into contact with something so intensely alive that
there was an almost electric shock. He pulled his hand
gently away. There was nothing he wanted more than to
take her in his arms and try to absorb some of that vibrancy into himself. But the very intensity of his desire
made him pull back.

"Ask them to come in here. And see if you can calm
Mother down a bit. I think this has been a bit of a shock."

If finding Melvin and Louise in her foyer had been a
shock to Glynis Ryan, it was nothing compared to having
her only son suggest that the couple be hired.

"Jack, we don't know anything about them." She stared at her elder child as if trying to decide where she'd gone wrong with him.

"They're good people, Mother."

"They're living in a car."

"They wouldn't be living in a car if we hired them. The guest house hasn't been used in years."

"Really, Jack. This is ridiculous."

Eleanor's tone left no room for doubt about her opinion of her fiancé's suggestion.

"You can't possibly be serious about this. You're willing to risk your mother's safety and Tina's just because your little 'friend' brought home this riffraff? I can't believe you've thought this out clearly."

"If you manage to speak a little louder, Ellie, maybe the poor souls will get an even clearer idea of what you think of them."

Eleanor flushed at the lazy sarcasm in Roger's tone, but she didn't back down.

"I don't think they're terribly concerned about my opinion. Tina is probably encouraging them to help themselves to everything in the kitchen, including the silver."

"The silver isn't in the kitchen," Sheri told her soothingly.

Eleanor turned on her, her eyes bright with rage. "Don't get smart-alecky with me! This situation is entirely your doing, and if I had anything to say about it, you'd be leaving along with your filthy friends."

"But you don't have anything to say about it."

Jack's quiet words reverberated in the silence that followed Eleanor's harsh words. His eyes met hers, flashing cool gray to furious brown. Two spots of color appeared high on her cheekbones. There could be no doubting that Jack was letting her know she'd overstepped her bounds.

"You're right, of course," she said tightly. The rigid set of her back left no doubt as to her feelings. "I apologize."

She didn't look at Sheri and her tone was flat, but Sheri didn't seem to notice a lack of sincerity.

"It's all right." Sheri's smile held no enmity. "I know you are concerned. Truly, Melvin and Louise would never do any harm."

Roger pried himself loose from the wall and moved over to Eleanor. "The truth is, Ellie, my pet, this really isn't any of our business. What say we go explore the rose garden?"

Eleanor hesitated only a moment before rising and shaking out the folds of her full silk skirt. She looked at Jack. "I hope you give some consideration to my feelings in this matter. After all, after the wedding it *will* be my concern."

"Of course, Eleanor," Jack said, his tone saying he was apologizing for his earlier harshness. He watched Roger and Eleanor leave the room before turning back to his mother.

"You know I wouldn't suggest this if I thought there was any possibility at all that they weren't completely trustworthy. Melvin has a letter of recommendation from his former employer." He didn't mention that Melvin's former employer had been a garbage company.

"I don't know, Jack." Glynis pleated the folds of her shawl uneasily. "This all seems so peculiar."

Sheri leaned forward, taking the older woman's hand between hers. "I am sure Melvin and Louise would be a wonderful addition to your home, Mrs. Ryan. You know how much you need a gardener, and Louise would be a fine cook. Hiring them would solve many of your concerns."

"Do you really think so?" Glynis clutched at Sheri's fingers.

"I'm sure of it."

"Well, it still seems very odd, but I suppose if you're both so sure, we could give them a try. Heaven knows, Tina will make my life a misery if I don't agree. But on a temporary basis only, mind you."

Sheri looked at Jack, her smile dazzling, her eyes sparkling with pleasure. Seeing only her face, aglow with gratitude, Jack promptly forgot all his doubts.

Chapter Eight

"So, are you going out to celebrate?"

Bob's question shook Jack out of the fog he'd been drifting into.

"Celebrate? Celebrate what?" He looked at the company's youngest vice president, wondering what the man was talking about.

"The Carter deal," Bob said, surprised. "You've been working on this long enough. I'd think you'd want to do a little celebrating now that you've tied the knot."

"Tied the knot," Jack repeated, the Carter contract forgotten. "You're married, aren't you?"

Bob blinked, wondering what he'd missed. "Yes," he admitted cautiously.

"I'm engaged, you know."

"I know."

Jack toyed with a pen, his eyes on the aimless movement. "How long have you worked here?"

"Five years."

"Five years. That's a long time. Do you like it here?"

"Yes." Bob tugged at his tie, wondering if he was about to get the ax.

"Did you ever want to do something else?"

"Something else?" Bob questioned cautiously. Was this some kind of a test?

"Some other career. You know, scuba diving or raising horses or something."

Bob relaxed. Either Jack was kidding, or he was just making idle conversation. No one would ask that question seriously.

"Sure. When I was a kid, I wanted to be an astronaut." He grinned, but Jack's responding smile didn't reflect much amusement.

"Why didn't you?"

Bob shifted uneasily in his seat. Maybe Jack had been working too hard. He shrugged. "Well, you know. That's kid stuff. Everybody has silly dreams when they're a kid. When you grow up, you want other things."

"I guess you do." Jack toyed with the pen a moment longer before dropping it and straightening in his chair. "Thanks, Bob. You've done a great job on this project."

Jack watched the other man leave, then leaned back, his eyes focused on nothing in particular. Bob now thought he was crazy and he couldn't blame the guy. He rubbed his fingers over the niggling ache that lurked between his eyes. He couldn't seem to get up any real enthusiasm for the business of Smith, Smith and Ryan these days. Sometimes he wondered if he'd *ever* had any enthusiasm.

In those first months after his father had died and he'd thrown himself into the business, he'd busted his butt to keep the bank going. He'd enjoyed the challenge. But sometime in the past ten years, the challenge had gone out of it—out of the business, out of his life.

Maybe Sheri was right. Maybe he didn't dream enough these days.

But there had to be something more to life than dreams, he argued with himself.

If you didn't have dreams, what was life really worth?

Plenty. He'd accomplished a lot in his life. He knew men twice his age who hadn't done half as much.

But was he any happier than they were?

He slammed a desk drawer shut and shot to his feet. The only problem with him was that he'd been spending too much time in this damned office. The fact that he was having arguments with himself was a strong indication that he needed a break.

His secretary looked up, startled, as he strode through the outer office.

"I'll be out the rest of the afternoon, Ms. Sanders. I don't have any vital appointments, do I?"

Since he was already at the outer door, it was clear it would have to be a very vital appointment, indeed, for him to be interested.

"No, sir."

"Good. If anyone calls, tell them I've gone fishing. Better yet, why don't you wrap up whatever you're doing and go home yourself."

He shut the door on her surprised expression. Climbing into the Jag, he felt pleasantly truant, a sensation he hadn't experienced in a very long time. The late-spring weather was particularly mild, even for Southern California. The temperature hovered in the seventies, just warm enough for shirt sleeves. He rolled the window down as he pulled out of the underground parking lot and into the sunshine.

With no particular destination in mind, he turned toward home. That was the trouble with keeping one's nose to the grindstone. When you lifted it, you didn't quite know what to do with it.

By the time he marched into the wide hallway, Jack was feeling vaguely disgruntled. Now that he'd fled the burden of responsibility, he wanted something to do, someone to share it with. He stopped just inside the door, frowning. He shouldn't have come home. You didn't go home when you played hooky. It had been a long time since his grade school days, but he distinctly remembered that you did *not* go home when you ditched school.

Guilt niggled at the back of his mind. He really did have a lot to get done. It was all very well for Roger to talk about running away and Sheri to make obscure comments about the importance of dreaming, but neither one had people depending on them.

He wandered into the library, still arguing with himself. There was a small fire burning in the grate, an odd circumstance when the weather was so warm. He moved closer, stepping off the rich Oriental carpet onto the oak floor. At the first click of his heel on the floor, the fire winked out as if it had never been, leaving no embers or ash to mark the immaculate marble hearth.

"Sheri."

Two slender legs disappeared from where they draped over the arm of a wing chair and Sheri peered over the side, her anxious expression fading when she saw that he was alone.

"Hello, Jack."

"Hello. You know, you can't just go around popping fires in and out of existence. People notice things like that."

"I'm sorry. It looked so pretty, even though it's warm out. I could not resist."

"Don't worry about it." He waved away her apology as he sat on a thickly padded footstool, stretching his long legs out in front of him.

She was curled up in the big chair, her feet tucked under her. She was wearing a soft cotton skirt of a yellow so pale it was hardly a color at all and a plain shirt in a shade that hovered somewhere between blue and green.

"What do you do with yourself all day?" he asked abruptly, suddenly aware he'd never taken the time to wonder how she occupied herself when he wasn't with her.

"I've been reading a lot. You have so many wonderful books." She gestured at the floor-to-ceiling shelves that lined the room. "Have you read all of these?"

Jack glanced at the volumes that filled the shelves, leather-bound first editions packed next to the latest paperback best-sellers.

"No. You know, when I was twelve, I swore I was going to read every one of these books, shelf by shelf." He reached out to take the book she held, staring at the spine without seeing it.

"Why didn't you?"

"I got bogged down in *Plutarch's Lives*." He laughed, handing the first edition of *Little Women* back to her. "The most god-awful dull book you can possibly imagine. By the time I gave up on it, I'd sort of lost my taste for literary endeavors. So what else do you do besides read?"

Sheri tilted her head, studying him, sensing that he wanted to be distracted. "Your mother is teaching me to needlepoint. I'm halfway through a pillow." She wrinkled her nose. "I'm not very good at it, I'm afraid. I think your mother's fingers twitch with the urge to redo everything I've done. But she's very tactful about it. You know, she's really quite a good teacher. I think she should open a shop where she could use some of those skills."

"Oh, I've been trying to get Mother to open a shop or take up teaching for years, but she won't do anything about it."

He picked up a delicate Meissen figure of a woman, studying it absently. "Where is Mother, anyway?"

"She's arguing with Melvin, I think."

"What are they arguing about this time?"

In the weeks since Melvin and Louise had entered the Ryans' employ, Glynis's arguments with Melvin had become legendary. She was determined that he do things her way and he was equally determined that he do them his. Whether it was roses or plumbing, they were bound to have differing opinions.

"He doesn't believe it was the fertilizer that made the roses bloom earlier," Sheri said, watching Jack, trying to sense his mood.

"Oh, he doesn't, does he?" Jack's eyes met hers, an amused glint in them. "What is Melvin's theory for the miraculous occurrence?"

"He thinks it was a convergence of Mercury with Mars. Or was it Venus with Saturn?" She wrinkled her brow, secretly pleased when she drew a laugh from him.

"Mother is sticking by the Zoo Doo theory, I take it."

"Oh, yes. She showed him the bag of manure and Melvin said it would take more than zebra—" she hesitated, seeking a more delicate word "—droppings to make roses burst into bloom like that."

"Good for Melvin. I'm glad to see he's sticking by his guns. Of course, if he gets her too frustrated, she may fire him."

"I don't think so. I think she rather likes arguing with him. Besides, Louise is a wonderful cook, and if your mother fired Melvin, she'd have to fire Louise. And she's teaching little Sarah to needlepoint. She wouldn't want to give that up. Sarah is a much better pupil than I am."

"I would think there wouldn't be much you couldn't do if you set your mind to it," Jack said.

Sheri shrugged. "I guess I haven't spent much time working with my hands."

He laughed softly. "I suppose it's a lot easier to twitch things up when you need them."

She laughed but shook her head. "You overestimate the amount of . . . twitching I do."

"Do I?"

There was something in his eyes that put an odd little flutter in her breathing. She touched her fingers to the base of her throat, feeling the quickness of her pulse. It was odd the way her heart beat sped whenever Jack looked at her this way. There was a warmth in his eyes, a feeling she couldn't quite put a name to. Just as she couldn't quite put a name to her own feelings.

He looked away and the moment was gone, leaving her to wonder if she'd only imagined it. Silence lay between them, not uncomfortable but holding something best left unexplored.

Jack stood up abruptly, making Sheri jump. She tilted her head back to look up at him, sensing something in his mood she'd never seen before.

"Let's go somewhere." He reached down and caught hold of her hand, drawing her to her feet.

It was one of the rare occasions when he initiated physical contact between them. Sheri wondered if he felt the same tingling awareness that she did, that feeling of being connected to something vibrantly alive.

"Go where?"

"I don't know." He frowned down at her, thinking.

"We could go on a picnic," she suggested tentatively.

"A picnic." Jack considered the idea and then nodded slowly. "I haven't been on a picnic in years." He grinned, looking suddenly years younger. "I take it you can supply the food?"

Sheri grinned back, picking up his lighthearted mood. "I can only do my humble best."

"I'm sure that will be good enough." He tightened his fingers around hers. "Let's get out of here before someone catches us and suggests we do something worthwhile."

"So, what do you think of L.A.?" Jack leaned on one elbow, feeling wonderfully content. The sun was beating down, warming him in a way central heating could never match. His suit jacket lay in the back of the Jag, his tie stuffed in one pocket. His collar was loosened; his sleeves were rolled halfway to his elbows.

The rest of the world was hard at work, and here he was, slothing the afternoon away on top of a grassy hilltop, surrounded by tall pines. But not a twinge of guilt accompanied the thought. At the moment, work, responsibility and the rest of the world seemed very far away. He was determined to keep it that way, at least for a little while.

He was pleasantly full of fried chicken and potato salad, not to mention the half-dozen other dishes that Sheri had felt appropriate for a picnic. On the blanket between them, the remains of the meal invited nibbling.

He had to admit there were definite advantages to not having to worry about spending hours in the kitchen to prepare a meal like the one they'd just eaten. It certainly made spur-of-the-moment alfresco dining a lot easier.

Sheri sat on the edge of the blanket, nibbling on a grape, her skirt spread out around her like the petals of a pale flower. Her hair was pulled back from her face, and it spilled over her shoulders, all shining pale gold in the warm sunlight.

Jack thought lazily that he'd never seen anyone quite so exquisite.

"It's a strange place," she said thoughtfully.

Jack had to drag his mind back to the conversation and make an effort to remember what he'd asked her. Oh, yes, her opinion of Los Angeles.

"I think that's an understatement," he commented dryly, reaching for a grape.

"There are so many people. And they all go about their business. They hardly ever seem to know there are other people around them."

"Most big cities are like that."

"It seems rather lonely."

"Lonely?" He nodded, staring across the grassy park to the small lake that nestled in the midst of some pines. "I suppose it is lonely in a way. But you can't be friends with everyone."

"No, of course not. But it seems as if people have so few friends."

Jack thought of himself. How many friends could he lay claim to? Roger, of course. And one or two people he worked with. But he rarely saw them outside of work. When it came right down to it, he could count his friends on the fingers of one hand and have a finger or two left over. It was not a cheering thought.

"Are you lonely, Sheri?"

She looked at him, surprised by the question. "Lonely? No. There are many things to think about, to do. I don't feel lonely."

"Just what do you do all day? You can't spend all your time reading and needlepointing." Jack felt a twinge of shame when he realized how little thought he'd given to how she was occupying her time. "Do you get bored?"

"Bored?" Sheri laughed. "Never. You don't realize how interesting it is for me, being in your world. It's very different. I've never known anything like it."

"Before Uncle Jack, who were you with? I mean, did you have another—" He stopped, wondering if he was treading on delicate ground. "That is, if this world is so different, I just wondered— Never mind." He waved one hand as if he could erase the words. "It's none of my business."

"No, it's all right," Sheri told him quietly. She smoothed a hand over her skirt, her expression pensive. "You know that a genie who has no human connections is not truly alive. We exist, but we do not live. Before your uncle..." She trailed off, shaking her head, the sadness deepening. "It had been a very long time, longer than you can perhaps imagine. That, for us, is true loneliness. Such times drain the soul, leaving us weak, our powers thin.

"Before that..." She shrugged. "I remember little. Some compensation. It would be too cruel if we had to forever remember all that was lost."

It occurred to Jack that he'd accepted her existence by pretending she was an ordinary woman, at least as much as it was possible to pretend that. Only now was he acknowledging that there were many unanswered questions.

"Sheri, do you mind if I ask you something?"

"From you I have no secrets."

"Are you immortal?"

"Not truly immortal. Our life spans are... different from yours, but all things have an end." She squeezed a crust of bread in her hand, watching as the bread crumbled. "When I read your books, immortality seems an end devoutly to be wished. But everything has a price."

"And what's the price of immortality?" he asked.

"To see those around you grow old and die. To be always left alone."

She'd uttered the stark words quietly, but there was pain in her eyes.

"I'd never quite thought of it that way."

They fell silent and Jack felt as if a cloud had passed over the sun, dimming the pleasure of the day.

Sheri spoke first, her tone deliberately light. "It's not all bad. There are advantages." She made a quick gesture with her hand and the remains of the picnic vanished, leaving the thick grass empty.

After a startled moment, Jack laughed. "I suppose there are a few advantages." He leaned back, hands behind his head, and stared up at the sky. "So what else do you do with your days?"

Her answer was so long in coming that he turned his head to look at her, his curiosity aroused by the hesitancy in her expression. "You look guilty. What are you doing?"

"I am looking for a career." She made the announcement with a mixture of pride and defiance.

"You're what?"

"I am looking for a career," she repeated a little less certainly.

"As what?" Jack sat up, staring at her.

"I do not know." She frowned. "I thought it would be simple, but it has turned out to be much more difficult than expected."

"I— Have you been on any interviews?" Jack was having a difficult time picturing her on a job hunt.

"Oh, yes. I was even hired twice."

"Twice? How long have you been looking?"

"Two weeks."

"And you've been hired twice?" Jack thrust his fingers through his hair. "Why are you still looking?"

"Those careers did not work out."

"They didn't? What happened?" he questioned weakly.

"Computers and genies do not go together," she informed him succinctly.

Jack shuddered, trying to imagine the damage she could have done to a system. "Why?"

"Perhaps it's because computers have no soul."

"No, no. I mean, why are you looking for a job?"

Her eyes dropped. "I have been trying to become as human as possible so as not to cause you so much trouble."

"And you thought that having a career would make you more human?"

"It seemed to be something I should have. Unless one had children. If one has children, it is suitable to stay home and see to their care."

The innocent words had a stunning impact on Jack. He could see Sheri, her slender figure full with the weight of a child. He shook his head, forcing the image away.

"I have done something wrong?" Sheri's anxious question dragged his attention back to the moment.

"No, no. You haven't done anything wrong. If you want a job, you should certainly have one. I could find you something if you'd like." He closed his mind to the possibilities for disaster that lurked in the concept of Sheri working at the bank.

"Thank you, but this is something I wish to do myself. You will be surprised at how human I can become."

Jack bit back the urge to tell her he didn't want to see her change too much. He lay back, staring unseeingly at a thick white cloud overhead. He hadn't realized he'd come to cherish Sheri for her uniqueness.

A flutter of movement caught his attention and he turned his head, rising up on one elbow as a mourning dove settled on the ground near Sheri, cooing softly as if in inquiry. Sheri laughed and held out her hand. The dove hesitated a moment, eyeing the inviting crust of bread. Jack wondered if it was his imagination that made it seem as if those beady little eyes looked at him suspiciously before the dove sauntered forward and took the crust from Sheri's fingers. She was soon joined by a second dove and then a third.

Watching Sheri feed the small creatures, Jack wondered how it was possible to see her and not know that there was something unique about her, something that set her apart from everyone else. It wasn't just the fact that the birds ate from her fingers with such trust. There was something in her eyes, in her smile, in the tilt of her chin. She was different—special.

"Sheri." The birds started, taking flight as he sat up. Sheri turned her head, meeting his eyes in a look so open, so honest, it brought an ache to his chest. What did it feel like to have nothing to conceal? No secrets—even from yourself.

"Jack?"

Her tone was questioning, but he didn't have a reply. Perhaps he'd just needed to reassure himself that she was real, that her beauty wasn't a figment of his imagination.

The rustle of footsteps nearby and the sound of a child's crying provided a distraction. Sheri scrambled to her feet. Jack followed more slowly, not sure whether to regret the interruption or welcome it. Whatever he might have said was probably better left unspoken.

Stepping around a sprawling oleander shrub, he found Sheri kneeling on the grass in front of a little boy who couldn't have been more than three or four. Tears had left tracks down his grubby cheeks and sobs still made the small frame quiver, but his attention was irresistibly caught by the woman in front of him. Jack knew just how he felt.

"Look at this. See the pretty leaf?" Sheri was saying to the youngster.

As Jack moved up to join her, she closed her hands over a wide sycamore leaf, crumpling it. The little boy was no more interested in the results than Jack. Sheri opened her fingers and a baby bunny sat trembling in her palm.

Jack glanced over his shoulder, hoping there was no one over the age of four close enough to witness what she was doing.

"See the bunny?"

The little boy reached out to touch the creature, his tearstained face reflecting his awe.

"This is Larry and his parents are lost."

She didn't change her tone from the same soft cadence she'd used with the child, and it took Jack a moment to realize she was talking to him.

"Do you think you could find them for him?"

Jack pulled his gaze from the bunny that shouldn't have been there and nodded. "Sure. I'll see what I can do. Try not to conjure up a pony or anything that's too big to be explained. Okay?"

As he strode off, he heard Larry say "Pony?" in a hopeful tone. He winced, hoping Sheri would use some restraint in her efforts to distract the child.

Larry's parents were not difficult to locate. Nearing the lake, he heard them calling their missing offspring in frantic tones. Jack felt vaguely heroic at telling them their son was safe. Since Larry's mother was at least ten and half months pregnant, only Larry's father accompanied Jack back up the hill. As they approached, Jack muttered a prayer that they weren't going to find a camel or an elephant in addition to little Larry.

Perhaps Sheri had heard them coming, because there was nothing untoward lurking behind the oleander. The minute the boy spotted his father, he was reminded of his lost condition and a wail of anguish shattered the quiet.

His father snatched him up, scolding him about wandering away. Since he was also clutching him so tight that the child was having a hard time getting enough breath to sob, Jack didn't think it likely that the reprimand was going to have much effect. With a heartfelt thanks, Larry and his dad disappeared down the hill.

Jack turned to look at Sheri, surprising a wistful expression in her eyes.

"He is a beautiful child, don't you think?"

Jack considered the dirt-smeared countenance, filthy jeans, torn T-shirt and shock of tangled hair. "He was certainly...healthy."

The answer seemed to satisfy her. "Do you ever think about having children, Jack?"

"Sometimes," he admitted slowly. "But I'm not sure I'd make the best of fathers."

"You would be a wonderful father." Her eyes met his, full of belief.

"Would I?" He reached out, hardly aware of his actions as he fingers caught a lock of her hair. It felt like the finest of silks in his hand—warm, alive, full of promise.

"I think any child would be lucky to have you for a father."

"Do you?" His finger slipped deeper into the fall of her hair, as if irresistibly drawn.

"Yes."

There was a breathless quality to the word that drew his eyes to hers. As always, he felt lost in the clear blue, sinking deeper to find the green that lurked beneath the surface.

The sunlit park faded away until only the two of them existed—alone, isolated, in a private world that couldn't be touched by reality.

His fingers slipped through the silk of her hair to cup the back of her neck. Sheri's palms touched his chest, light as thistledown, yet the touch went straight to his soul.

His eyes held hers as he lowered his head until their lips were barely a breath apart. He hesitated and her lashes fluttered downward, forming dark shadows on her pale skin.

If he kissed her, he'd surely be lost. Yet kissing her was as necessary as breathing.

His lips touched hers and a feeling of homecoming flowed through him. How had he lived without this? Without her?

He slid his hands around her back and drew her closer. Sheri rose up on her toes, her hands slipping upward to his shoulders. Her body fit against his as if made to be there. Her taste, the warm scent of her, the feel of her in his arms . . . it was all so right, so inevitable.

A breeze whispered by. Sheri's skirt drifted forward, wrapping itself around Jack's legs as if in silken embrace. Desire swept over him like a slow tide. His hands tightened around her back as need replaced wonder.

He heard Sheri make a soft sound as her lips parted for his tongue, fanning the deep hunger that gripped him. She tasted of everything and nothing. Femininity, passion, warmth, strength and softness—all lay in the sweetness of her kiss. It was like nothing he'd ever experienced before. It was magical.

Magical. The word stayed in his mind. *Magical.* His hands loosened slowly. *Magical.* Sheri's fingers drifted down to rest against his shirt front. *Magical.* He broke the kiss slowly, reluctance in every movement. *Magical.*

Their eyes met and Sheri saw the question in his, read the thought in his expression. Her fingers touched his mouth, feather light.

"No, Jack. What is between us is not of magic." A smile flickered over her mouth. "It's more of dreams. But not magic. Never magic."

Jack stared at her, his arms still around her, reluctant to give up the contact. More than anything, he wanted to keep her in his arms and shut out the world with a kiss.

But he had responsibilities, commitments. He was engaged, for God's sake. The world existed. But for just a little while longer, he could pretend it didn't.

He grinned suddenly. "Do you like movies?"

THE KNOCKING on the door was not gentle. Roger dragged his eyes from the television set. He wasn't sure if he'd been watching a sitcom or a soap opera. It was getting harder and harder to tell the difference. The knocking came again as he reached for the remote control and shut the set off.

"Hold your horses," he muttered as the knocking came a third time before he was more than halfway to the door. He jerked it open, his eyes widening when he saw who was on the other side.

"Is Jack here?"

Eleanor's tone was not one of friendly inquiry. In fact, she looked furious. And beautiful. Her dark hair was swept up in a simple chignon that set off the strength of her features. A simple black sheath of watered silk molded to her figure. But not even the most carefully applied makeup could conceal the rage in her eyes.

"Well, are you trying to think up a lie?" she demanded when Roger stared at her in silence.

"No."

"No, what? Oh, you're impossible."

She pushed him out of the way with one disdainful hand and stepped into his apartment. Roger's mouth twisted with amusement as he shut the door and turned to lean against it, watching as she swept the living room with her eyes.

"Jack isn't here, Ellie."

She spun around, her eyes flashing frustrated rage. "Don't call me 'Ellie.' And how do I know he isn't here? You'd probably lie for him."

"Undoubtedly," he agreed without apology. "But it's hardly Jack's style to hide in a closet when his fiancée comes looking for him." He pushed himself away from the door and crossed to the built-in bar. "Why don't you have a drink? You look like you need one."

"I don't want a drink," she snapped, too angry even to try for good manners. "If Jack isn't here, where is he?"

"Well, at a guess, I'd say he's not where he's supposed to be." Roger turned away from the bar and held out a glass. Eleanor took it absently, clenching the cool glass. "Did he stand you up, Ellie?"

"I waited for almost two hours at that damned restaurant."

Roger's brows rose. If she was cussing, she must be pretty far gone.

"How rude of him," he commented mildly. "Have a sip of scotch. It's good for the nerves."

"I told you I didn't want a drink."

But she took a swallow, anyway. It didn't seem to help her mood.

Roger poured himself a gin and tonic, then leaned one hip against the edge of the bar, watching as Eleanor paced restlessly across the room to stand at the window. He didn't think she was admiring the panoramic view of the Los Angeles basin.

"He's out with her. I know he is."

He didn't have to ask whom she was talking about. He took a swallow of his drink and wandered over to join her at the window.

"What makes you think Jack is out with Sheri?"

"I just know it. Nothing's been right since he brought her here. Nursing his uncle, indeed." She spit the words out, making them sound like a curse. "More likely she was hoping to bilk the old man out of his money."

Roger considered what he knew of Sheri. "I don't think so. She seems like a nice enough girl."

The remark was like throwing gasoline on a fire.

"Nice! She's not nice. She's manipulating Jack, using him. Look how she talked him into hiring those awful people."

"They seem to be doing quite well."

"Hah!" Eleanor tossed back the glass of scotch and thrust it out for a refill. "They're probably cohorts of hers. God knows what they're stealing."

Roger picked up the scotch bottle, weighing it in one hand, weighing obscure concepts like ethics and morality in the other. With a faint shrug for obscure concepts, he filled the glass with straight scotch.

"It's possible they're just what they seem, you know."

"None of this is what it seems." She took a swallow. "That woman isn't what she seems. I know she isn't."

Roger stared at his drink. She didn't know just how right she was, and he wasn't going to be the one to try to explain it to her.

"Jack seems to like her." He carefully tipped a little more fuel on the fire.

"Jack is like most men. You all think with your zippers. Just because a woman is pretty and looks helpless, you think she's an angel of goodness and light. Hah!" She tossed back another gulp. "That's the trouble with men.

They don't have any sense. It's so easy to fool them just by batting your eyes at them. They're gullible."

"Do you think Jack's gullible?" he questioned idly.

"I thought he had more sense than the average man. He *did* have more sense until that woman wound her fingers around him. *She's* the one to blame for this."

"You don't appear to have a very high opinion of Jack's ability to think for himself."

"I—" She stopped, frowning down into her almost-empty glass. "Naturally, my opinion of Jack is high on every score."

"Except when it comes to thinking for himself. Do you think the same of me, Ellie?"

Her eyes came up to meet his and he saw the memories there—reluctantly recalled and fought against, but still there.

"The trouble with you is that you're determined to go your own way. You don't care what the rest of the world thinks, do you?"

"Not much," he admitted. He set his glass down and took a step closer to her. "I care what you think, Ellie."

"No, you don't." She backed away a step, but bumped into the window. She watched him, her eyes wide, showing a vulnerability few had seen.

"I do care, Ellie. I've always cared."

"No." She stopped and swallowed hard. "If you'd cared, you wouldn't have gone away."

"But I came back." He stopped inches away, so close he could see the way the pulse fluttered at the base of her throat.

"Roger, no..."

She tried to turn away, but his hand wound into her hair, holding her where she was. He stepped closer, pinning her to the cool glass. Her hands came up, pressing against his chest in silent protest. A protest he ignored.

"It's been a long time, Ellie. Do you still remember what we were like together?"

"No." But her eyes told him that she lied. "Let me go."

"We weren't much more than kids, but I've never forgotten it. I've compared every other woman with you."

"And there've been so many," she spat at him, her eyes burning. Roger's mouth curved in a smile of pure male satisfaction and Eleanor realized just how much she'd revealed. Color mounted her cheeks and she stood rigid in his hold. "Let me go."

"Jealous, Ellie?"

"Never!"

"I'm glad." He stroked the soft skin behind her ear with his thumb. "I like the idea of you being jealous."

"You always were a conceited ape." She twisted in his hold, but he only crowded her closer against the window.

"And you always were a stubborn little idiot."

"Coming from you, I'll take that as a compliment."

"We used to fight like this. Remember?"

"No." But the word was uttered breathlessly. Her eyes met his and she pushed frantically at the solid wall of his chest. "Roger, no. Please."

It wasn't a gentle kiss. His mouth plundered hers, expressing fifteen years of frustration. Years of broken dreams, shattered hopes. For a split second she fought him. And then she melted against him, her lips opening to his.

He dragged his mouth from hers, his breathing ragged. "You tell me if Jack has ever made you feel this way. Tell me if you've ever felt with him a tenth of what I make you feel." His voice was raspy, all the lazy humor gone.

She didn't answer him with words. Instead her arms came up to circle his neck, her eyes pleaded with him.

With a groan, Roger bent, his arms sweeping her feet out from under her as he lifted her against his chest. His mouth found hers again, and tried to slake a thirst that burned deep inside both of them. But the thirst wouldn't be quenched.

"BREAK THE ENGAGEMENT, Ellie." She jumped at the sound of Roger's voice. Her eyes flew toward the bed, where he lay propped against the pillows, the sheet draped across his waist.

"I can't."

The refusal was barely audible. Roger could see her fingers trembling as she reached for her dress. "You don't love him."

"I'm very fond of Jack." She tugged the dress into place, reaching behind her back to struggle with the zipper.

"You can be very fond of a puppy. It's not enough to base a marriage on."

"Jack and I understand each other."

"And you and I don't?"

"I thought Jack was your best friend." She snatched up her shoes, clutching them to her chest.

"He is my best friend. If it wasn't for Jack, I'd probably be in a psych ward somewhere. When I came back, he's a lot of what held me together. There wasn't anyone else."

Eleanor sucked in a breath, feeling the impact of Roger's words like a blow. Her eyes were wide and vulnerable on his, but he didn't soften his look. He wanted her to remember just how grim that time had been for all of them.

"Jack is like a brother to me. And this marriage would be as disastrous for him as it would be for you."

Her eyes dropped from his and she shook her head. Roger swung off the bed, catching her halfway to the door, his hands firm on her shoulders.

"Let me go, Roger." She didn't look at him.

"No. Ellie, don't be a fool. You can't go on with the marriage, not after tonight."

"All the arrangements have been made."

"Arrangements can be canceled. Ellie, look at me." He shook her gently until her eyes lifted to meet his. "Tell me that you melt in Jack's arms the way you melted in mine."

"Don't."

Her voice held a wealth of despair, but he didn't back down. "Tell me you cry his name the way you cried mine tonight."

"Please. Don't."

"Tell me he makes you feel what I feel. Tell me that, Ellie, and I'll let you go."

Tears filled her eyes, spilling down her cheeks. Her mouth quivered with pain. "Roger, please don't. I beg you."

"Tell me."

"Jack and I haven't . . . we don't sleep together." The admission was soft, broken.

"I knew it." Roger's eyes blazed with triumph and he tightened his hands on her shoulders, pulling her closer to his bare form.

"No." She turned her head away, her hands pressing against his chest. "I'm going to marry Jack." She backed out of reach.

"You can't marry him," Roger protested incredulously.

"I can and I will. The arrangements are made. Jack will make a good husband. He's steady and dependable."

"So is my car, but I'm not walking it down the aisle."

"He's your best friend."

"He's not going to be any happier in this marriage than you are."

"The arrangements are made." She repeated the phrase like an incantation.

"Damn the arrangements! Ellie, we're talking about your life. Jack's life. My life," he added more softly.

"Stop it." She pressed her hand against her mouth, her eyes tortured. "Just stop it. You don't understand."

"Explain it to me."

"It's not just Jack and I. People have expectations. My family." She caught her breath as fury blazed in his eyes.

"Is that what this is about? Your damn family! You wouldn't fight them fifteen years ago and now you're letting them push you into a marriage that's going to make you miserable. When are you going to grow up and stop worrying about what your family thinks?"

"Please." The word broke on a sob. "Please, Roger. If you care about me at all, just let me go."

He stared at her, his hands clenched. The dimly lit bedroom was taut with emotion. For several long moments neither of them spoke. Eleanor watched him, her eyes swimming with tears. Slowly, moving like a very old man, Roger stepped out of her way, clearing a path to the door.

She moved to rush by him, but his hand caught her forearm, holding her still for one last moment. Eleanor was rigid in his clasp, her eyes fixed on the door as if salvation lay beyond it. He was so close his breath stirred the hair at her temple.

"I'd feel guilty about what happened here if I thought Jack gave a damn. But he doesn't love you any more than you love him. You think about that while you're walking down the aisle.''

He released her and she bolted out the door as if all the hounds of Hell were on her heels. Roger didn't move as he listened to the sound of her stumbling progress across the living room, then the opening and closing of the front door.

Chapter Nine

The restaurant was small, dark and crowded. It made Jack think of opium dens and dungeons, neither one of which put him in a particularly good mood. It also happened to be one of Eleanor's favorite places to lunch.

Ordinarily he would have tried to talk her into eating somewhere that the lights held bulbs of more than two watts. But considering the fact that he'd completely forgotten their date the night before, it had seemed that the least he could do was graciously agree to her choice of restaurant.

Eleanor was already seated at a table in the most dimly lit corner in the place. As Jack approached, she looked up, her expression shadowed and impossible to read. Jack bent to kiss the cheek she presented and then seated himself across the table.

"I'm sorry I'm late. I had a hard time finding a parking place." He reached for the menu in the vain hope that they'd added something edible since the last time he'd been there.

"That's quite all right. After last night, I suppose I should just be grateful that you showed up at all."

Jack shut the menu with a snap, feeling guilty and annoyed. "I've already apologized for that, Eleanor."

There was a moment of tense silence and then she sighed, the stiffness going out of her shoulders. "You're right. I'm sorry, Jack. I guess I'm just a little snappish today."

The unexpected apology threw him off balance and added to the guilt he was already feeling. "I couldn't really blame you if you held it over my head." He gave her a half smile. "I really am sorry I forgot our date. Things have been difficult at the office."

"It's okay. I know you're not all that fond of the opera, anyway."

"Well, I have to admit it doesn't break my heart to have missed it, but I am sorry to have been so rude."

"It doesn't matter." She waved one hand, dismissing the incident.

The waiter appeared just then and the subject was dropped as the orders were given. When he was gone, silence settled between them.

Jack reached for a breadstick, one of the few things in the place he didn't consider undercooked and overpriced. Eleanor was studying her fork as if she'd never seen one before and Jack took the opportunity to study her.

She was a lovely woman. Her features were strong but not unfeminine. Her hair was thick and dark, the style softer today than the one she usually wore. There was none of Sheri's gentle sweetness—

The breadstick shattered between his fingers. He was *not* going to make comparisons between Sheri and Eleanor. Eleanor was his fiancée. He was going to marry her. And Sheri was— Just what the hell was Sheri?

"Jack."

He looked at Eleanor, grateful for the interruption. She didn't say anything for a moment, as if debating her words.

"I think you should ask Sheri to move out."

The words were flat, lacking any real emotion. Jack wondered if it was his imagination that put an underlying passion in them. He drew a deep breath. Maybe he should have expected this, but he hadn't.

"Why?" It wasn't quite the brilliant reply he'd have liked, but he was groping for time.

She looked away, uncharacteristically indecisive. "I think she's had a detrimental effect on our relationship." She lifted a hand, stopping him when he would have spoken. "Please let me finish, Jack."

Jack sat back, wishing he were almost anywhere but in this dingy restaurant. How was he supposed to explain to Eleanor that no matter how reasonable her arguments, he couldn't ask Sheri to leave. He didn't even fully understand why himself.

"I am not a jealous woman, Jack. I think you'd agree with that. Even if I were inclined toward jealousy, our relationship is not one where it would be an appropriate emotion. After all, I realize that what we share is more in the nature of a strong friendship than a grand passion.

"When we decided to marry, we both knew it wasn't a love match in the generally accepted sense of the term. I want the stability you offer. You need a wife who understands your world and your business. I am not unhappy with that bargain. I don't think you are, either." She paused, as if waiting for him to confirm this.

Jack stared at her, trying to think of an appropriate reply. He was grateful for the interruption provided by the arrival of their waiter, bearing plates of artistically arranged, semiraw vegetation. He tried to look terribly excited by the prospect of the meal, hoping Eleanor would forget what they'd been discussing, but Eleanor's memory was considerably better than that.

"I think your friend Sheri is creating an undue strain on our relationship," she reiterated.

Jack set down his fork and looked across the table at the woman he planned to marry. The reasons for that marriage were becoming more blurred in his mind lately. But then, everything in his life had grown a little fuzzy around the edges since the advent of Sheri.

Sheri. There was the crux of the whole problem. The center, it seemed, of most of his problems these days. Certainly she was central to Eleanor's problem.

"Eleanor, Sheri nursed my uncle for almost three years before he died. She did that without any expectations of recompense. I can hardly throw her out now."

"I didn't expect you simply to throw her out." Eleanor stabbed a sliver of carrot with more force than was necessary. Her smile was strained. "But I'm sure it wouldn't be that difficult to find her a job and a place to live."

"I don't see any reason to rush her into making any decisions."

She set down her fork and clasped her hands in front of her, her expression intent. "This is important to me, Jack. Important to our future together. I'll help you find her a job. I'll help her find a place to live."

Jack looked away. The request wasn't unreasonable. God knows, most women would have made it long ago. If this had been an ordinary situation, if Sheri had been an ordinary houseguest, if anything about this whole damn thing had been ordinary— But it wasn't and she wasn't.

He ran his fingers through his hair, feeling a headache nagging between his eyes. Around them, the other diners seemed unaware of the tension at their table. He envied them their oblivion.

"I'm sorry, Eleanor," he said finally, his tone flat. "After what Sheri did for my uncle—for the family, really— I simply can't urge her to move."

"I see."

The silence stretched interminably, until Jack felt forced to break it, offering her reassurances he wasn't sure he had faith in himself.

"There's nothing to be concerned about. I consider her a friend, but nothing more than that—" He broke off, remembering that kiss yesterday. There'd been nothing of friendship in that kiss. "I just wouldn't feel right about asking her to leave," he finished weakly.

"Then of course you mustn't do so," she said without inflection. She glanced at her watch. "Heavens, look at the time. I really must be going."

Jack automatically rose as she stood. "Eleanor, perhaps we should discuss this further."

"Are you going to change your mind?" Their eyes met and Jack shook his head. "Then I really don't see any reason to discuss it further."

Her tone was quite pleasant, as if they'd just disagreed on whether or not to serve lobster at the wedding supper. She leaned down to him and Jack kissed her. It was a light kiss, perfectly suited to their surroundings. It was disturbing to realize that even if they'd been alone, he wouldn't have had any particular urge to turn the kiss into something more.

After Eleanor left, he sat down again, picking at the meal he hadn't wanted in the first place. There were too many things changing too damned fast to suit him. For years his life had gone along on an even keel. He'd had things planned, organized, settled.

In the space of a few weeks, all his planning, organizing and settling had begun to totter like a badly stacked tower of children's blocks. He rubbed at the ache in his fore-head and stood up, throwing a handful of bills on the table.

He'd been spending too much time thinking lately, that's all it was. This constant analysis of the state of his life wasn't healthy. Maybe he'd call Roger and see if he could arrange a game of racquetball. Some nice cutthroat physical competition was just what he needed right now.

SHERI WAS CURLED UP on the sofa, laboriously threading Persian wool through the appropriate holes in the needle-point canvas. It didn't seem to matter that she had put the stitches in the right place, which Glynis Ryan swore was all that was necessary. They might be in the right place, but they managed to look unhappy there. In fact, the peony she was supposed to be needlepointing didn't look happy at all.

When the doorbell rang, she put the canvas down, grateful for an interruption. From the direction of the kitchen, she could hear Louise drilling Sarah on her multiplication tables. She smiled, thinking of how Sarah had blossomed in the weeks since her family had moved into the guest house.

Her smile widened when she opened the door to find Roger standing on the step. She liked Roger.

"Hi. Twitched up anything interesting lately?" He wandered into the hallway.

"I've been trying very hard to restrain myself from 'twitching.' It bothers Jack." Sheri shut the door and followed him into the living room, watching as he slouched down into a chair. She returned to her position on the sofa, but didn't reach for the abandoned needlepoint.

"Jack doesn't know how to have fun," Roger complained. "Now if I'd been lucky enough to have an uncle leave me someone as interesting as you, I'd know how to take advantage of it.''

"What would you ask for?'' It was a pleasant change to be able to talk naturally with someone without worrying about her words revealing what she was.

"Oh, I don't know. Stock market tips, maybe.''

"Jack says you have absolutely no interest in the stock market.''

"True, but it might be amusing to know where everyone else is going wrong.''

"A lot of things seem to amuse you,'' she commented.

"Most things,'' Roger agreed easily. "If you just have the proper perspective, there isn't much in life that isn't amusing in one way or another.''

"Is there anything you take seriously?''

"Sure, food and drink. Two very serious subjects.''

Sheri laughed at the exaggerated solemn expression he conjured up.

"Speaking of which,'' he continued, "I don't suppose you'd like to get me a drink.''

"Of course.'' She uncurled her legs and stood up, moving to the bar. "What would you like?''

"No, no, no. I didn't mean for you to get up.'' Roger stood and joined her at the bar. "Now you're making me feel guilty. I just thought you could pop it up for me.''

"I thought we'd just discussed the fact that I've given up that sort of behavior.'' She watched as he poured himself a very short scotch with a lot of water.

"Jack spoils all my fun,'' he whined pathetically, drawing a laugh from Sheri. "So, what have you been up to lately?''

"I'm looking for a career.'' Roger's brows rose, Sheri noticed, but he didn't seem to find the idea as remarkable as Jack had.

"Really? How's it going?"

"Not well. I seem to have a great deal of difficulty with computers. I do not think they like me."

"Then they have no taste."

"Thank you, but perhaps they are right. I do not seem to be very good for them, either."

"What you need is a job where you work with people."

"I would like that."

"How about charity work? Have you thought of that?"

"Charity work?" She frowned. "Can that be a career?"

"I don't see why not. Look at what a good job you did with Melvin and Louise. There are a lot of people out there just like them. Maybe you could help them."

She considered that, a smile slowly brightening her face. "That would be very nice. How would I go about finding some of this work?"

Roger looked uneasy and stared down into his glass for a moment before meeting her eyes. "I could put you in touch with some people," he muttered.

"You could?"

"I...ah...do a little work for an organization. Nothing major, you understand. Just a little now and then...." He trailed off as if he'd just confessed a crime.

"I promise to keep your secret," Sheri told him.

Roger laughed at his own foolishness and held out his hand. Sheri took it and they shook, sealing the bargain.

To Jack, who was just entering the room, the scene appeared cozy and intimate. Sheri and Roger were standing in front of the bar, Sheri's face tilted up to his, laughter warming her expression. They seemed like old and close friends, and Jack discovered he didn't like the idea at all. He cleared his throat. They turned to look at him, displaying none of the guilt he half thought they should.

"Jack, you are home early. How nice." Sheri's smile held nothing but pleasure at seeing him.

"Jackson, your wish is my command. I await the pleasure of trouncing you on yon court of racquet, just as you requested." Roger waved his hand in a vaguely medieval salute.

"That wasn't exactly what I had in mind," Jack said dryly, coming farther into the room.

"But that's going to be the end result. You're out of practice."

"Maybe, but I can still run your butt off." Jack wondered if it was his imagination that put wariness in his friend's eyes. And if it wasn't his imagination, what was causing that look? "Have you been here long?"

"Just long enough to fail at convincing Sheri to demonstrate her unusual talents for me."

"Since I presume Mother and Tina are home, not to mention Melvin and family, I'm glad she had the good sense to turn you down," Jack commented, pouring himself a drink of mineral water.

"Your mother is upstairs," Sheri said, "but I'm afraid she and Tina had an argument and Tina left. She said she'd be spending the night with a friend."

Jack sighed, rubbing the back of his neck. "I suppose they fought about Tina going for her master's?"

Sheri nodded. "Don't worry. I'm sure they will work it out." She reached out to smooth the collar of his shirt.

Roger's sharp eyes noted the casual intimacy of the gesture, but there was nothing more than mild curiosity in his tone when he said, "Your mother isn't a fan of higher education?"

Jack shook his head, a frown drawing his dark brows together. "It isn't that. She's just worried that Tina's education is going to get in the way of her personal life. She's got this idea that no man is going to want to marry a math professor."

"Ah, the ever elusive 'suitable marriage,' She should be satisfied that one of you has made such an excellent choice."

There was a note in Roger's voice that Jack couldn't quite define. "Eleanor, you mean?"

"Unless you're engaged to two women, I must mean Eleanor."

"After the way lunch went today, I don't even know if I'm engaged to one woman."

Roger tightened his fingers around his glass, a subtle shift in his expression revealing his interest, but it was left to Sheri to ask the obvious question.

"Did you and Eleanor quarrel?"

Jack shook his head, obviously regretting having said anything. "Not really. A minor disagreement. I'm going to go change. I'll be down in five, Roger. You might as well have another drink. Alcohol can be a cushion to the pain of defeat."

Roger lifted his glass in acknowledgment as Jack left the room. Sheri watched Roger for a moment, tilting her head as if to get a better angle.

"You don't like the fact that Jack and Eleanor are going to be married, do you?"

Roger's eyes met hers. His look was guarded, but not so guarded that she couldn't see the pain he felt.

"I don't think they're suited," he admitted cautiously. "Do you?"

"I don't know. There are many things I don't yet un-derstand." She frowned, feeling her way carefully. "It does seem as though they don't make each other very happy. And I do think that if you're going to marry someone, they should make you happy—and you them."

"Eleanor appeals to the stuffy side of Jack, the side that thinks duty is the most important thing in the world."

"Isn't duty important?"

"Sure. But it's not a god. And it shouldn't be the be-all and end-all of your life. Ever since Jack's father died, he's been trying to do everything his father would have done. What about what Jack wants to do?"

"You don't think Eleanor will encourage him to follow his own dreams?"

"Ellie is worse than Jack when it comes to doing what's 'right.'" His tone held an odd mixture of bitterness and affection. "No, she'll encourage Jack to keep on doing just what he's doing because it's safe and predictable. Ellie's big on predictablity."

"And you aren't predictable?" she questioned softly.

"Not at all." His eyes met hers, a wry acknowledgment in their depths. "You know, for someone who's spent her life in a samovar, you're pretty shrewd."

"I watch people. They're so interesting."

"This coming from a woman of your 'interesting' talents?" Roger's brows rose in comical question.

Sheri grinned and reached for his empty glass. "What talents?" The glass shimmered in her hand for an instant and then was gone.

Roger stared at her hand and then lifted his eyes to hers. For once there wasn't a trace of cynical amusement to be found in his expression. It was one thing to hear Jack's descriptions, to see the evidence of Sheri's uniqueness in an out-of-season rose; it was something else altogether to see the impossible happen right before his eyes.

"Good God."

"That's almost exactly what Jack said," Sheri commented mildly, her eyes sparkling with mischievous amusement.

Roger shook his head, some of the bemusement fading, to be replaced by a look of genuine humor. " 'There are more things in heaven and earth, Horatio,' " he quoted softly.

"Hamlet. Act 1, Scene 5," Sheri said demurely.

Roger laughed out loud. "Jack is a fool if he can't see what's under his nose."

Sheri cocked her head, puzzled, but before she could ask him what he meant, Jack walked in. Faded jeans molded to his thighs in a way Levi Strauss had never envisioned. A blue chambray shirt with the sleeves rolled up and a pair of slightly scruffy running shoes completed his transformation from executive to sportsman.

Sheri smoothed her hair, her pulse oddly accelerated. She'd never seen Jack look quite so...so masculine. The shirt emphasized the width of his shoulders, the open throat exposing a hint of dark hair. Another quote came to mind: "Yon Cassius has a lean and hungry look."

There was something lean and hungry about Jack tonight, a restlessness she could feel as if it were a fourth presence in the room. Out of practice or not, she didn't think Roger should count on winning tonight.

"Sheri?"

Jack's voice penetrated her preoccupation and she jumped, realizing it wasn't the first time he'd called to her.

"What?"

"You looked like you were a million miles away," Jack commented, his eyes curious.

"I'm sorry. I was thinking." She hoped the soft lighting would serve to conceal the flush that had crept up her cheeks. She was aware of Roger watching her with an expression she didn't quite understand.

"I just asked if you would tell Mother not to expect me for dinner. We'll probably get something at the club."

"Alfalfa sandwiches and watercress juice," Roger grumbled under his breath.

"It'll be a nice change for your stomach," Jack told him without sympathy. "After a steady diet of burgers and fries, I suspect it will welcome a change."

"A hasty change in the diet can be hazardous to one's health."

Jack ignored him, his eyes on Sheri. "I guess I'll see you later."

"Yes."

The silence stretched for several slow heartbeats while they continued to look at each other. Sheri could only guess at Jack's thoughts. Her own were hardly more clear. This breathless feeling was new to her, still unexpected. It was left to Roger to break the moment.

"Sometimes I'm amazed by the stupidity of the human race." The apparently irrelevant remark was addressed to no one in particular. He clapped Jack on the shoulder. "Come on, I've been waiting all afternoon for a chance to grind you to dust on the court."

"Fat chance," Jack mumbled, turning to follow him out the door.

Sheri curled up on the sofa and picked up her needlepoint as she listened to the sound of the car backing out the driveway. It wasn't the well-bred purr of the Jaguar, which meant they must have taken Roger's ancient M.G. She smiled, remembering Jack's bitter complaints about the car having been built for someone without legs.

Her smile faded as she tugged the yarn through the canvas. She and Jack had spent a wonderful day yesterday. She hoped he didn't regret it. She'd felt almost normal. As though she really belonged here.

There was nothing she wanted more than for Jack to see her as normal. To have him look at her without wondering what new disaster lurked around the corner. To have him forget that she wasn't human. To live in his world as if she belonged.

She smoothed her fingers over the slightly lumpy surface of the canvas. Jack had asked her if she was ever lonely. She'd lied, not knowing how to express the deep loneliness of being different from those around her, so different that she could at best find only a shaky meeting ground. Oh, she could pretend to fit in, but deep inside, she was always on the outside looking in.

There had been moments when she'd felt truly a part of his life. She didn't need to close her eyes to remember the way his arms had felt around her. They'd felt strong and warm and right. Just as the kiss had felt. In Jack's arms she'd felt as if she belonged.

She sighed. If there was one place she didn't—couldn't—belong, it was in Jack's arms. Jack was engaged to Eleanor. She might not yet understand everything that went on in Jack's world, but she knew that engaged men were not supposed to kiss other women.

Yet it had felt wonderfully right. And it was a memory she would hold to her always—that moment of belonging.

Chapter Ten

"Now *that* is a gorgeous dress."

Sheri turned from the mirror as Tina plopped down on the bed. "Do you really think so? It's very plain."

"It's perfect. It'll make all the other women look fussy and overdressed."

Sheri frowned, turning back to her reflection. The dress was a pale gold crêpe de chine. It was, as she'd said, very plain. A high, rolled collar, long straight sleeves and simple bodice topped a wide waistband over yards and yards of fabric gathered into an extravagantly full skirt that fell to midcalf. There was nothing flashy about the dress, but it managed to catch the eye, anyway.

"I don't want to make anyone else uncomfortable," she said uncertainly, touching her collar.

"You're much too nice, Sheri." Tina sighed when she saw that the words didn't reassure the other woman. "You look perfectly appropriate."

"Are you sure?"

"I'm positive. And if you happen to make the other women just a teeny-weeny bit jealous, where's the harm in that?"

Sheri laughed, turning away from the mirror to study Tina. "You look very nice yourself."

Tina tugged at the narrow skirt of her simple black dress and grimaced. "I want Mother to notice that I'm in mourning."

"In mourning?" Sheri sat on the bed next to Tina. "Who are you mourning?"

"Not who," Tina corrected. "What. I'm mourning my career aspirations."

"Is this what you quarreled about night before last?"

"It's what we always quarrel about. I don't know why she's so stubborn about it. It's not as though I don't have the money to go for my master's."

"Then why don't you do it?"

"Because Mother has control of the trust fund. I don't get control of it until I'm thirty." She scowled. "Thirty. My grandfather didn't think women could handle money, so he tied mine up until I turn thirty. He didn't do that to Jack."

"It doesn't seem very fair," Sheri agreed cautiously. "Why doesn't your mother want you get one of these master's?"

"She thinks I'm going to forget all about my personal life in my pursuit of a degree. She also thinks that most men are going to be threatened by a woman with a master's in math."

"You don't agree?"

"Of course not. No man worth having is going to let something like that stand in his way. Besides—" she hesitated, her eyes flickering to Sheri and then away "—I've already met a wonderful man who doesn't care what kind of a degree I have."

"Have you told your mother that?"

Tina studied her fingernails. "No. She wouldn't approve of him."

"Why not?"

"Well, he's older than I am—almost ten years—and he's not exactly the conventional type. He has a degree in marine biology and he's working with dolphins, trying to break their language down so that we can understand what they're saying."

Once she started talking, the words seemed to tumble from her. "He's tall and he has the most incredible blue eyes you've ever seen and blond hair and I don't think he's ever been in a tux in his life. It's not that he thinks there's anything wrong with money. It's just that it's not very important to him. He lives in this tiny little apartment right next to the water and he drives the oldest, most beat-up VW I've ever seen in my life. But he doesn't care, because that's not important to him, either."

She stopped, drawing in a quick breath, as if surprised to realize how much she'd said. "And he wants me to get my degree if that will make me happy," she finished defiantly.

"He sounds very special. Why do you think your mother wouldn't approve of him?"

Tina frowned, flicking a bit of lint off her skirt. "Because he's not rich and he doesn't have any plans to get rich. And because he isn't part of 'society' and he doesn't have any interest in being part of it. Because he's different."

Sheri shook her head. "I think you're doing your mother an injustice. All she really wants is to see you happy. Maybe she'd prefer it if you married someone who shared her world, but that's only because that's what she understands and it's what she believes would make you happiest. It seems to me that you should talk to her about this man, reassure her that you're not so buried in your education that you're letting your personal life fall by the wayside."

Tina's frown deepened. "I don't know."

"What do you have to lose? She's already said she won't fund your education. What more can she do?"

"I guess. I hadn't thought of it that way." Tina brightened a little, her natural optimism coming through. "Maybe you're right. Maybe if she met Mark, she'd see how wonderful he is."

"From your description, I don't see how she could help it." Tina caught the gentle teasing in Sheri's tone and flushed, but she laughed, too.

"You know, I'm really glad Jack brought you home. I think you're good for all of us."

Sheri returned her quick hug, keeping her doubts to herself. She'd feel better if she could be sure that Jack shared his sister's opinion.

JACK STRAIGHTENED his tie for the tenth time, aware of a deep feeling of foreboding. This was not where he wanted to be. Ordinarily he enjoyed his mother's parties. Good food and good conversation were not to be sneered at. But tonight was different. Tonight Sheri was going to be there.

He thrust his fingers through his hair. He wondered what Sheri was going to think of her introduction to a larger swath of society. God alone knew what they were going to think of her.

"Don't be an idiot," he muttered under his breath. He moved over to the heavy mirror that dominated one corner of the living room. Meeting his own gaze, he realized that he looked as panicked as he felt. His hair was standing on end and his eyes held a slightly wild look reminiscent of a man facing a firing squad. He drew in a deep breath, smoothing his hair back into its usual neat style.

"There's nothing to worry about," he told his reflection. "There's no reason for anyone to suspect a thing.

She's just a houseguest. It isn't as if she has 'genie' tattooed on her forehead. She's just a perfectly normal young woman.''

"Begging your pardon, but if you're talking about Sheri, you're one hundred percent wrong."

Jack jumped at the sound of Melvin's voice and turned away from the mirror. He'd been so busy concentrating on his one-sided conversation he hadn't heard the other man come in. With the small portion of his mind that was still functioning in a normal fashion, Jack noted that Melvin had been pressed into a tux for the occasion. With his habitual lugubrious expression and his lanky frame draped in black and white, he looked like something out of an Alfred Hitchcock movie. The thought did nothing to calm Jack's nerves.

"Wrong about what?" he asked. Just how much had Melvin heard? And what exactly had he said?

"Wrong about Sheri being perfectly normal."

"I am?" His voice threatened to break into a squeak and he cleared his throat, repeating the question in a deeper tone. "I am?"

"Anyone can see that she's not normal at all."

"Really?" Was that his voice? He sounded so casual. Just what the hell did Melvin know and how was he going to deal with whatever it was?

"Yes, sir. You just have to look at her to see that she's different," Melvin said earnestly.

"Different?" That was a masterpiece of understatement if ever he'd heard one. "In what way?"

"She's sweet and kind and there's not an ounce of malice in her."

"And you think you can see all that just by looking at her?" Jack felt limp with relief. The way his life had been going lately, he'd fully expected Melvin to have guessed the worst.

"I do. It's all right there in her eyes. When she looks at you, you know there's nothing but goodness in her." He might have continued, but Sarah appeared in the doorway just then, her frantic signals indicating some domestic crisis in the works. Melvin bowed in Jack's direction, his long face completely solemn again as he exited the room.

Jack tugged at his tie again, wishing his mother had held off on this little gathering. Just until he'd gotten used to the idea of having a genie in the house—say, another ten or fifteen years.

He heard them coming down the stairs, Tina chattering away at a mile a minute, Sheri making an occasional reply in her soft voice. Turning toward the doorway, he realized he felt like a teenage boy about to go on his first date. He was long past his teenage years and this was definitely *not* a date, but he couldn't shake the nervous tension that gripped him.

The feeling didn't ease when he saw her. Her hair swirled over her shoulders, a pale golden cape that almost exactly matched the color of her dress. He couldn't have said just what the dress looked like, but he knew it made her look like a princess in a fairy tale. Her eyes were wide pools of blue in the delicacy of her face.

He stepped forward, hardly aware that Tina was standing next to Sheri. There was something about Sheri—a look of wisdom mixed with such innocence. The unawakened expression in her eyes drew him so, made him wish he could be the one to awaken her.

He stopped in front of her, never taking his eyes from hers, losing himself in their clear blue depths. For a moment they weren't standing in his mother's living room.

They were somewhere far away, alone, the world a distant presence.

"Sheri." Just her name seemed to say everything he was feeling, all the thoughts he couldn't express. He started to reach out, needing to touch her to assure himself of her reality. But then Tina cleared her throat and shattered the fragile fantasy.

Jack dropped his hand and shook himself, dragging his eyes from the melting depths of Sheri's gaze to meet the shrewdness of his little sister's.

"Gee, Jack, for a moment there, I wondered if I was invisible."

"Don't be silly." His laugh was a little strained, but it *was* a laugh. "You both look stunning." His eyes flickered over Sheri and then away again. "Can I get either of you something to drink?"

The moment was gone, but not so easily forgotten. In that one instant Jack knew he could have walked away from everything just for the chance to be with Sheri, to hold her in his arms. The question was, why?

But this wasn't the time to try to answer it, for within a few minutes the guests began to arrive. Jack allowed himself to be drawn into his duties as host, grateful for the distraction.

Sheri did her best to fade into the background, retreating to a quiet corner and watching the colorful swirl of guests. Her eyes drifted to Jack more often than not. He looked so handsome in the dark dinner jacket.

There'd been a moment when she and Tina had first come downstairs—just a moment—when it had seemed Jack was about to say something important. What would he have said if Tina hadn't been there?

There was a stir in the doorway, and she smiled when she saw Roger come in, wearing a slouchy silk jacket and jeans. Utterly inappropriate but so suitable for Roger that he fit right in. He saw her and waved a greeting. As he reached for a glass of wine, his eyes fell on Eleanor. For an instant Sheri could see pain wash over his face, but just as quickly the expression was gone, leaving his habitual cynical look.

She reached up to toy with her hair, her expression thoughtful. There was something between Roger and Eleanor, something a great deal deeper than the surface animosity they both displayed. Why did they pretend to dislike each other, when it was obvious they cared very deeply?

Her eyes shifted to Melvin, who was moving silently about the room, refreshing drinks and making sure the trays of canapés were always full. His eyes caught hers and he returned her smile with a slow wink, making her laugh softly. She might not entirely understand this world of Jack's, but she'd been right in thinking that Melvin and Louise belonged in it. Even Glynis admitted, somewhat reluctantly, that the couple had been an excellent addition to the household.

"Sheri, I have someone who wants to meet you."

She turned at the sound of Roger's voice, meeting the amusement in his eyes before her gaze shifted to his companion.

She'd seen the young man come in with an older couple she assumed were his parents. He was perhaps nineteen years old and at that awkward stage when he wasn't quite an adult but well past childhood.

"Sheri, this is Alan Brinkman. His parents are old friends of the family."

Seeing the look in Alan's eyes, Sheri knew the source of Roger's amusement. She didn't need to have spent a lot of time around young men to recognize an instant infatuation when she saw it.

"Hello, Alan." The look she threw Roger carried equal amounts pleading and threat.

Roger simply grinned and wandered off.

"I saw you the minute I came in," Alan told her fervently.

"Did you really?"

"Yes. You are the most beautiful woman in the room. I've been told I have an eye for beautiful women."

The attempt at sophistication would have been laughable if it hadn't been clear that he was painfully serious. With a sigh, Sheri resigned herself to the inevitable.

JACK WAS DOING HIS BEST to play the part of the attentive host. It wasn't easy when at least half his attention was on Sheri. He wanted to talk to her, hear her impressions of the guests. He wanted to make sure she was having a good time. He wanted to feel the peace that was such a palpable part of her presence.

He saw Roger introducing young Alan Brinkman to her and relaxed slightly. She'd be safe enough with Alan. The boy wasn't likely to ask any questions she couldn't answer. From the awestruck, worshipful look on his face, it would be a miracle if he managed to get out a coherent word.

"Jack, Mr. Toffler was just telling me the most interesting story about his trip to Greece." Eleanor slipped her hand through his arm, drawing his attention away from Sheri. "Perhaps we should consider going there on our honeymoon."

Jack knew Eleanor had no intention of setting foot in Greece, but Harold Toffler was an important client at the bank and it never hurt to make important clients feel as if their opinions were of vital interest. It was exactly this kind of social skill that made Eleanor such an asset to his career. It was unfortunate that *he* couldn't seem to get up more interest in his career these days. Jack shoved the thought away, smiling at the older man and commenting that Greece was certainly a lovely country.

Twenty minutes later Jack knew far more than he'd ever wanted to learn about the country. Mr. Toffler was just launching into a column by column description of the Parthenon, when Jack's eye fell on Sheri.

There was something odd about the way she was standing. Something slightly off balance. He shook his head as Eleanor drew his attention back to the conversation. It was probably just his imagination. But five minutes later, his eyes drifted in her direction again.

Alan was still with her, talking earnestly in her ear, but Jack didn't think she was listening. Her attention seemed to have wandered. And there was definitely something wrong with the way she was standing. She looked taller somehow. Almost as if she wasn't touching the ground.

"Holy—" He covered the exclamation with a cough.

"I beg your pardon. What did you say, Jack?"

"I said that it sounds wholly interesting, Mr. Toffler. But I'm afraid I'll have to ask you to excuse me. I'm neglecting the rest of the guests."

As departures went, it could have been worse. Toffler seemed willing to buy it, but Jack was vividly aware of Eleanor's eyes following him. She wasn't going to be happy that he'd abandoned her and an important client to go to Sheri. But he couldn't worry about that now. Right now he had more important things to worry about. Much more important.

He skidded to a halt at Sheri's side, pinning a bright smile on his face. He set his hand on her shoulder, pushing downward until he felt her feet hit the floor.

"Alan, good to see you."

"Jack." Alan did not look at all happy to see his host.

"I noticed you and Sheri over here talking and I couldn't help but wonder what you were talking about so earnestly." He kept the jovial smile in place, along with the heavy hand on Sheri's shoulder.

"We were just talking," Alan said, a touch of sullenness revealing his youth.

"Alan was suggesting that I might like to leave the party with him," Sheri announced brightly. She looked at Jack, her eyes showing a slight tendency to wander.

"He was, was he?" Jack took the glass from her hand. "Did Alan get you a drink?"

"Yes, a juice. Wasn't that nice of him?"

"Very nice." Jack took a swallow, tasting the vodka under the sickly sweet fruit juice. Alan squirmed under the anger in Jack's eyes. But Jack didn't have to worry about punishment. Sheri delivered that all unknowingly.

"Alan says that in the locker room, his nickname is 'Stud.' Why do you suppose that is, Jack?" She looked at him, her eyes wide with puzzlement.

Out of the corner of his eye, Jack could see the color climb in Alan's face until the boy looked as though he were going to have a stroke. Despite his irritation, Jack had a moment of genuine pity. Still, maybe this would teach the puppy a lesson. With a garbled farewell Alan beat a hasty retreat. Sheri didn't seem to notice his departure.

"What's a locker room, Jack?" She reached up to straighten his tie.

"It's a room full of lockers," he told her absently. The door was on the opposite side of the room, making a casual exit difficult. Eleanor was shooting dagger-sharp looks in his direction, but he couldn't worry about that now.

"Why did they call Alan that, Jack?"

He looked into her unfocused, totally innocent eyes that searched for an explanation. "Because he has a laugh like a horse," he finally offered in desperation.

She frowned. "That doesn't seem like a nice thing to call him."

"I'm sure he doesn't mind at all. Sheri, just what exactly happens when you drink?"

"When I drink? I'm not thirsty anymore." This seemed to strike her as amusing and she giggled softly.

Jack tightened his hand on her shoulder. "Sheri, what happens when you drink alcohol?"

"Alcohol? I told you. It has a deleterious effect on my powers." She drew the words out slowly, savoring them.

"Yes, I know. But what exactly happens?"

"I don't know. I've never drunk anything. Drank? Drinked?"

She giggled again, but this time the giggle ended in a sneeze. Over her head, Jack watched as a delicate Limoges vase lifted off the mantel, hovered in midair for a second and then crashed to the hearth. The sound of shattered porcelain brought a few startled cries, then complete silence as everyone turned to look at the shards of glass.

"Boy, these tremors are getting worse all the time." Jack knew his voice was too loud, a little too hearty.

"Tremor? I didn't feel a thing," said one of the guests, her face reflecting bewilderment.

There was a murmur of agreement as everyone checked with his neighbor to see if he'd felt the quake. One or two people muttered that maybe they *had* felt something.

Jack's smiled widened to a maniacal width. "It wasn't very strong. And quick. It was very quick."

"I'm surprised it would knock a vase off like that," Mr. Toffler commented.

Jack considered immediately canceling the man's account.

"It does seem remarkable," Eleanor commented, her sharp eyes still on her fiancé.

"You know, I noticed earlier that that vase was sitting right on the edge of the mantel."

That was Roger, reminding Jack of all the reasons they'd been friends since grade school.

Roger moved forward to give Glynis an apologetic smile. "I'm sorry, Glynis. I should have said something. I feel as if this is my fault."

Glynis rushed to assure him it was nothing of the kind. Melvin appeared with a whisk broom and removed the debris. Losing interest, the guests resumed their conversations. Catching the panic-stricken look in Jack's eye, Roger made his way over.

"Hello, Sheri. Jack."

"Hello, Roger. Did you know that Alan's friends all call him 'Stud' just because he laughs like a horse? I don't think that's very nice of them, do you?"

Roger met Jack's eyes over Sheri's head. He bit his lip, trying to maintain a sober expression. "I'm sure they don't mean any harm by it, Sheri. What's going on, Jack? You look like you expect a police raid."

"That would be easier to deal with," Jack muttered, keeping a firm grip in Sheri. "That little twit slipped Sheri a glass that was at least fifty percent vodka."

"Alan? I didn't think he had it in him." He caught Jack's eye and erased the half-admiring smile. "I take it genies don't drink?"

"It has a deleterious effect on our powers," Sheri informed him solemnly, then sneezed again.

In the blink of an eye, an immaculate arrangement of gladiolus became a tousled basket of daffodils. Jack held his breath, but no one appeared to have seen the transformation.

"Look, I've got to get her out of here," he told Roger.

"That seems like a wise move. Why are you leaning on her?"

"Because she was floating a few minutes ago."

"I was not. I have my feet planted firmly on the ground. But I could float if you wanted me to," Sheri offered in a helpful spirit.

"No! No, that's all right. We're going to leave now. Can you walk?"

"Of course I can walk. I can fly, too."

Roger snorted with muffled laughter, drawing a rather fierce look from Jack, who wasn't up to seeing the humor of the moment.

They'd taken only a few steps, when Sheri sneezed yet again. Roger lunged to catch a cut-glass plate of crudités as it lifted from the table and executed a figure eight in midair. Several people turned to look at him. He looked back, wondering how to explain the fact that he was clutching a plate of carrot sticks to his chest.

"I...ah... was just noticing that the tray was a little low. Thought I might take it out to the kitchen." The explanation was weak, but it was better than the truth.

Melvin appeared at Roger's side, giving him a sideways glance that questioned his sanity. "I'll take care of that, Mr. Bendon."

Roger handed him the plate and edged away from the table. Jack had Sheri almost halfway across the room, but they'd run into a snag in the form of an elderly neighbor. Roger was almost to them, when Sheri sneezed once more.

Over Roger's shoulder, Jack watched almost resignedly as a tray of smoked salmon began to move, arranging itself into the shape of a fish, complete with two olives for eyes. For several long moments he almost dared to hope no one would notice this phenomenon. That hope was dashed by a shrill cry as the fish rose on its tail and began to walk the length of the table.

Everyone turned to look. There was the sound of breaking glass as fingers, slackened with shock, lost their grip on wineglasses. The fish stepped over a fork and Jack closed his eyes, shuddering. His entire life flashed beneath his lids, but it was the future he saw that bothered him.

"That's amazing!"

"Incredible! How are they doing that?"

"Must be a puppet."

Several people stepped forward to investigate, but before they reached the table, Sheri sneezed again and the lights went out.

The repeated shocks to their nerves had left the guests without a reaction to this latest assault. Jack waited numbly. Anything from Attila the Hun and his hordes to a troupe of singing dogs was to be expected at this point.

"Look! On the ceiling."

Jack recognized his sister's voice. He looked up, wondering what new disaster lurked above them.

Pinpoints of colored light hung in midair. They swung back and forth, slowly at first, then more rapidly. With each swing they showered colored light over the room, like droplets of sparkling rain. Where the drops landed they clung, still glowing. There was a general exclamation of wonder as hair and clothes developed bright patterns of warm light.

In the illumination cast by the shining dots, Roger made his way to where Jack was easing Sheri from the room. He took her other arm as they edged through the awestruck guests.

They were almost to the door, when Sheri drew a quick breath, preparatory to another sneeze. Jack's hand came up and clamped her mouth as they swept her out the door, no longer concerned with the fact that her feet weren't touching the floor.

From across the room, Eleanor couldn't see Jack's hand over Sheri's mouth. All she saw was Jack and Roger leaving the room with Sheri, their attention focused completely on her. She turned away, oblivious of the exquisite dancing lights.

IT WAS NEARLY midnight. The last of the guests had left an hour earlier, still talking about the dancing fish and the spectacular light display. Jack had explained them away by the use of mirrors and a friend who worked for George Lucas. Lucky for him, no one had insisted on names and details.

He'd gotten through the rest of the party running on adrenaline, hardly conscious of what people said to him or what he said in response. He and Roger had tucked Sheri safely in her room, where her sneezing couldn't cause any new disasters. By the time they'd closed the door on her, she'd been sound asleep.

He'd made excuses to his family for Sheri's absence. Now the headache he'd claimed for her nagged at his temples. Still, it could have been worse. Nothing had happened that couldn't be more or less explained away. At a safe distance he could even see the humor in the evening.

Jack grinned, shutting the door to his room behind him. The fish had really been a classic. All it had needed was a top hat and tails and he could picture it doing a little soft shoe in the dill sauce. He took a deep swallow of black coffee. The caffeine would probably keep him awake all night, but right now he needed its restorative effects more than he needed sleep. Many more evenings like this and he was going to grow old before his time.

He rubbed the back of his neck as he crossed to the window to pull the drapes. He paused, looking out into the moonlit garden. The roses were covered in blooms, the wonder of his mother's garden club. In the glow of the full moon, the blossoms of pale yellow and white caught the milky light.

A flutter of color near the far end of the garden caught his eye, and his hand tightened on the drapes. He shouldn't go out there. It was midnight, the witching hour. If Sheri was in the garden at midnight, she wasn't looking for company.

He took the stairs two at a time, turning toward the rear of the house when he reached the darkened entryway. He barely noticed the chill in the air as he stepped out the back door. Sheri fingered a rose washed white in the moonlight. Her golden gown glowed and her pale hair seemed the color of moonlight itself—neither silver nor gold but an amalgam of the two.

She turned at his approach, her face in shadow. "Hello." Her voice was subdued.

"A little late for a walk in the garden, don't you think?" Though there was no one to hear, he'd automatically lowered his voice in response to the stillness.

"I like the way it looks at night." She caressed a showy blossom. "All the color is washed away. It's so clear and simple."

As life should be and so rarely was, Jack thought.

"You looked very beautiful tonight."

She turned to face him, her eyes wide. "How can you say that? I caused so much trouble."

"Well, it could have been worse."

"I don't see how." She refused to be comforted.

"Well, nothing that awful really happened. The vase can be replaced. The fish had a certain air about him that I rather liked. Everyone thought the light show was spectacular. I've already had five people ask me for the name of the firm that did the special effects," he lied. When he saw some of the tension go out of her shoulders he laughed.

"You aren't furious with me?" She tilted her head questioningly and Jack had to suppress an urge to take her in his arms and kiss her thoroughly.

"For what? It wasn't your fault Alan spiked your drink."

"But I should have realized. I promised I wasn't going to cause any trouble. I wanted to make your life easier. Better. Not cause difficulties."

Jack caught her hands in his, drawing her forward so that the moonlight illuminated her face. "You didn't cause any real problems. You just livened things up a bit. Don't beat yourself over the head about this."

"But I—"

"No." He placed a finger across her lips. "Not another word about it. Do I have to make that an order?" he asked with mock sternness.

Her hands slowly relaxed in his and he saw a smile flicker over her face. "Your wish is my command."

"That's much better. For a minute there, I thought I was going to have to get tough with you."

"You have only to ask," she said softly.

He had to drag his eyes away from the softness of her. He released her hands, realizing how much he wanted to pull her closer, instead. If he had any sense at all, he'd go in. That would be the safe thing to do. The sane thing.

"So, do you always come out to the rose garden at midnight?"

"It's a nice place to think." Sheri half turned from him, looking out over the quiet garden. "If you listen carefully, you can almost hear the roses whispering to one another."

"What are they saying?" Jack watched her profile.

"Oh, silly things. They wonder why we're out here instead of safe in our beds where we belong. They discuss the weather. They gossip about their neighbors."

The moonlight made the curve of her cheek like porcelain, the drift of her lashes a silken shadow. Sheri seemed unaware of his regard. She cupped a rose in her palms, bending down to inhale the night-gentled scent.

"I love roses. They're so full of beauty and mystery."

"Like a beautiful woman," Jack murmured, his eyes never leaving her face.

"Don't you think all beauty has an element of mystery?" she asked, her fingertips caressing the full bloom. "We're never quite sure just why something is beautiful, what it is that takes it out of the ordinary."

"Sheri, do genies ever fall in love?" She was quiet for so long he had time to ponder the foolishness of his question.

"Sometimes," she said, her voice so low it was nearly a whisper. She tugged uneasily at a rose leaf. "But we have to be very careful. Love isn't the same for us as it is for humans."

"Why not?"

"Love is something we are, not just something we feel. Many of our powers are lost when we fall in love. We don't have as much to lose in these times. We had more power when the world had more dreams." She sighed, her expression troubled. "If something happens to that love..."

She trailed off and Jack could see the frown that creased her forehead. "What happens, Sheri?" He caught her hand, stilling its restless movement. "What happens?"

"We die."

The simple reply caught at his breath.

"A human dies of a broken heart only on the inside," she continued. "For us it's more than that."

Jack reached out to cup her cheek, feeling the softness of her skin against his palm, the warmth of her in his very soul.

"You are so very beautiful."

She didn't move as he bent to her. Her lips were soft under his, parting to welcome him, her body pliant in his arms.

Moonlight spilled over them, the stillness of the garden surrounded them, and for one magical instant Jack was sure he, too, could hear the roses whispering secrets to one another.

Chapter Eleven

The party affected the Ryan household in unexpected ways. Tension seemed to creep through the house, catching everyone in its grip. Sheri could sense the change in atmosphere, but couldn't quite grasp the reason for it. It wasn't in anything anyone said. It was in the way they avoided one another.

Tina and her mother were still at odds over the future of Tina's education. The two women were polite, but the distance between them was obvious. Jack threw himself into his work with a new fervor, leaving early in the morning and coming home late at night.

Sheri was left to her own devices and she filled her time exploring the area around Jack's home, enjoying the warmth of spring.

On this particular day she was in a mood to like the whole world. Roger had kept his promise, introducing her to Marty and Lisa, a young couple who ran a shelter for the homeless. They'd been more than grateful for her offer of help, taking Roger's word for it that she would be an asset to their small endeavor. In fact, it was clear that anything Roger said was okay with them.

When Roger and Marty left the room, Lisa took the opportunity to pump Sheri for information, showing her disappointment when it became clear that Sheri and Roger were nothing more than friends.

"He's such a good man, you know." Lisa smoothed her hand over the bulge of her stomach.

"I do not think Roger would want you to spread that around," Sheri told her with a smile.

"No, he doesn't like people thinking he does good things," Lisa agreed. "He finances all of this, you know." Her wave encompassed the shelter. "Marty and I could never have managed this without Roger. It was a dream of ours to help the homeless, but Roger made it happen."

"He is very kind."

"Yes, but lonely, don't you think?" Lisa sighed, her hands resting on her stomach as if she took comfort from the life she carried.

"I think perhaps Roger has not yet found what he seeks. But he will."

"I certainly hope so."

"When is your baby due?" Lisa's pregnancy fascinated Sheri.

"Another two weeks." Lisa smiled, her thin features suddenly pretty. "It seems like centuries. Besides, he's been trying to kick his way out today."

"Could I— Would it be very rude of me—" She broke off, wondering if she was breaking a taboo she didn't know about. Her eyes met Lisa's, wide and uncertain.

Lisa's smiled softened. "Have you ever felt a baby move?" Sheri shook her head. "Here. Give me your hand." She took Sheri's palm, pressing it to her stomach.

Sheri closed her eyes, dizzy with the strength of the life force she felt beneath her fingers. "A boy," she murmured, only half-aware of speaking out loud.

"Yes. How did you know?"

Sheri opened her eyes to meet Lisa's puzzled gaze. "I'm...lucky with guesses." She drew her hand away. "He seems very strong."

"But he didn't kick just then."

"I . . . it is just a feeling I got," Sheri said weakly.

"I hope you're right. We lost a baby before this."

She stroked her stomach, her expression full of such protective yearning that Sheri looked away. What would it be like to carry another life inside you? Sheri wondered. *That* was surely true magic.

She was still thinking about Lisa and Marty and her new job, which she was to start in two weeks, later that afternoon. The shelter was small, but its purpose was to get people off the street for good, not to merely offer them a place to stay temporarily.

She liked the idea of working with people, helping them. This was something she could do and do well. Her smile widened as she thought about her attempt to thank Roger. He'd brushed the words away, as embarrassed as if he'd been caught doing something shameful. Such an odd man.

She shook her head, aware she'd been paying no attention to her surroundings. On a beautiful day like this, it was a crime to miss even a moment. This was a day to savor. Which is how she came to meet Mrs. O'Leary.

Mrs. O'Leary lived on the block behind Jack's. The houses were smaller there, the properties not as large. Mrs. O'Leary's home could best be described as midwestern farmhouse, with a wide front porch and neat blue shutters against the white paint.

Sheri had walked by it several times before she actually saw its owner. She liked the house. It seemed to smile at her. And the yard was a lavish tangle of plants. She liked that, too.

Today she slowed as she approached the house, just as she always did. She paused by the waist-high picket fence, admiring the tangle of hollyhocks, calendulas and pansies that filled one corner of the yard.

"Well, don't just stand there, my girl. Come here and give me a hand with this."

The voice came from behind a sprawling shrub rose. Peering toward the sound, Sheri could just make out a tiny figure wearing what seemed to be chartreuse coveralls.

"Hurry up," the voice commanded.

Sheri let herself through the gate, hurrying up the old brick pathway until she came to the huge rose.

"Here, hold this while I get the saw. Darn thing keeps whacking me in the face. Watch the thorns. Trouble is, I didn't discipline it like I should have when it was small. Now it's got the idea that it can do what it wants. Plants are like children. They need a firm hand."

Sheri held the long cane out of the way while the old woman grasped a saw and proceeded to remove the cane at ground level.

"There now. That's better. Most of the time, he's well behaved, but this past year or so, he's been getting a mite above himself. Thinks because I'm getting old I'm getting soft. Do you like plants?"

Faded blue eyes, still fierce with life, glared up at Sheri from under the brim of a bright green baseball cap. The cap just matched the coveralls.

"Yes. I like plants very much."

"Thought so. I'm Cassie O'Leary. Mrs. O'Leary," she added firmly. "I've seen you walking by the yard. Had a feeling you liked plants."

"I am Sheri." Sheri reached out a hand to help the old woman to her feet, half expecting it to be brushed aside.

But Mrs. O'Leary took it in a strong grip, pulling herself up to her full height, which was several inches less than Sheri's.

"Sheri. Not a bad name. Here. Hold these while I help these sweet peas find the trellis. Stupid creatures. They just wave in the air as if the trellis wasn't right under their nose. Still, nothing smells quite like a sweet pea... I've seen you at all times of the day. Don't you work?"

"I do now. In two weeks I'll be working three days a week in a shelter for the homeless." Sheri set the pruning shears down and reached out, her slim fingers guiding the delicate green tendrils to their holds on the net trellis.

"The homeless, huh? I've seen articles about them. Tragedy, that's what it is." She knelt in front of the sweet peas, deftly nipping spent blossoms from the mat of pansies at the foot of the trellis. "The trouble is that we've lost sight of the family. Used to be that you took care of your own, but people don't think like that anymore. This place could use someone young about. Liven things up some. You may come here when you have time."

Sheri bit back a smile, wondering if it was a command or a request. "Thank you. I'd like that."

Mrs. O'Leary's eyes met hers. "I'm a pushy old woman, I should warn you."

"I would never have thought that," Sheri said demurely.

A surprised bark of laughter met the comment. "I like you. At my age, you've got to make up your mind quickly. You never know how much time you've got."

Sheri laughed and the old woman gave her an approving look. "You've got a sense of humor, too. We'll work well together."

And so they did. Sheri found Mrs. O'Leary's companionship as welcome as the old woman seemed to find hers.

Jack was home so rarely. The big house was empty without him. She needed something to distract herself from the gap his absence left in her life. When she wasn't puttering in Mrs. O'Leary's tangled gardens, she walked.

This seemed a reasonably harmless way to spend time. And so it was, until a day when she didn't come home alone.

"BUT, SHERI, you don't know where he's been. And surely he belongs to someone."

Glynis eyed the "he" in question uneasily. "He" was a medium-size dog. He looked somewhat gray, though it was possible that beneath the layer of dirt he was another color entirely.

"I don't think so." Sheri reached down to stroke the animal, who sat quietly beside her. "He was very hungry. Louise fed him a few scraps of meat."

"Well, I certainly wouldn't want to see any animal go hungry, you know that. But he simply can't stay in the house. I'm allergic to dogs." Glynis confirmed this by sneezing violently.

Sheri turned to Roger, who was lounging nearby. He met her pleading look and lifted his hands in self-defense. "Sorry. My building has strict rules about pets. They aren't allowed even if they have a pedigree, and that thing certainly does not have a pedigree."

There the problem rested when Eleanor came into the room. She hesitated when she saw Roger, but it was too late to back out gracefully. With a vague smile in his direction, she approached Glynis's chair, bending to touch cheeks with the older woman.

"I thought I'd give you time to recover from the party before visiting. Good God, *what* is that?" She'd seen the dog, and her expression reflected her opinion of his presence in the immaculate living room.

"It's a dog, Ellie," Roger offered helpfully.

The look she shot him would have withered a lesser man where he stood. It had no visible effect on Roger.

"Sheri brought him home, but I've explained to her that he can't stay. Melvin and Louise were one thing. I mean, they're people after all. I'm not allergic to them. But I am allergic to dogs." Glynis sneezed again.

"I'm very sorry, Mrs. Ryan, but I couldn't leave him on the street." Sheri looked at her, distress in her eyes. "He was so frightened and hungry. I thought maybe I could find a home for him."

"Well, that's very kind of you, Sheri. But I'm afraid he simply can't stay in here. Please ask Louise to vacuum thoroughly after he's gone." Glynis retreated from the room, muffling a string of sneezes with a handkerchief.

"I can't imagine what kind of a home you'd find for a scruffy-looking bundle of fur like that," Eleanor said disdainfully.

The dog had been watching her since she'd entered the room and he chose this inopportune moment to leave Sheri's side and approach Eleanor.

"Don't you come near me. You're probably crawling with fleas." At her harsh tone, he cowered on the floor, whimpering as if expecting a blow.

"He just wants to be friends," Sheri said reproachfully.

"I have no desire to be friends with a dog." But Eleanor's tone had softened considerably. "Do get up. I'm not going to hurt you." When the animal continued to cower at her feet, she bent and patted him gingerly. "There. Now go away."

But all he'd needed was that one touch to be convinced he'd found a friend for life. He rolled over onto his back, his entire body wiggling with delight. Despite herself, Eleanor smiled and scratched his stomach.

"Looks like you've made a conquest, Ellie," Roger commented lazily. "Maybe you'd like to take him home."

"Certainly not." But her fingers found a particularly sensitive spot just behind the dog's ear.

"You know, Eleanor, he really is a very nice dog. Well mannered, too. He'd make a wonderful companion."

"I don't need a companion." Eleanor was kneeling on the floor, rubbing the dog's back. He yelped suddenly and then cowered on the floor once more. She touched the sensitive spot again, gently brushing aside dusty fur to reveal a welt. She looked up, her eyes flashing. "Somebody has struck him."

"People aren't very friendly toward strays." Roger's voice was soft. "You've got room at your place. You could take care of him, just until you find him a home."

Eleanor stroked the scruffy dog, her fingers gentle. Her expression was soft and compassionate, a far cry from her usual haughty look.

"Well, I suppose I could let him stay with me for a little while," she said hesitantly. The dog turned to lick her wrist, looking up at her with worshipful eyes.

"He loves you already," Sheri told her. "Animals can sense when someone has a kind heart."

"A kind heart," Eleanor repeated, standing up. "I suppose so." She reached for her purse. "I guess I'd better get him home. I'll have to get food and things." She looked at the dog doubtfully, as if she wasn't quite sure how he'd come to be her responsibility.

"Did you come over for something specific? I could take care of him for you if you want to talk to Mrs. Ryan," Sheri offered.

Eleanor paused, looking at her, an odd expression in her eyes. She shook her head. "No, that's all right. Actually, I came to talk to you, but it can wait. It was nothing important." She snapped her fingers at the dog, who leaped to his feet and ran to the door, clearly eager to be on his way. Eleanor smiled. "He seems to be a bit of an ingrate," she told Sheri, her tone friendly.

"That's all right."

"Well, I guess I'll be going, then. Tell Glynis goodbye for me, won't you?"

"Of course."

Eleanor's eyes flickered over Roger, her smile fading. She strode toward the door, only to gasp when her toe hit an invisible high spot in the rug. She stumbled and would have fallen if Roger hadn't lunged and caught her under the arms, pulling her against his chest.

For an instant they stood pressed together, their eyes locked. An instant only, then Eleanor pulled away, mumbling a thank-you before she rushed from the room. Roger watched her go, not turning back to Sheri until the front door had closed behind Eleanor and her new companion.

"It's a very dangerous thing to meddle in other people's lives," Roger remarked.

"Meddle?" Sheri widened her eyes innocently.

"The rug. She didn't trip without a little help."

Sheri shrugged. "Maybe it's the lingering effects of that drink I had at the party."

"That was a long time ago. I don't think it's still affecting your talents. Don't interfere in things you don't understand."

He seemed more weary than angry, and this gave Sheri the courage to pursue the subject.

"You and Eleanor care for each other, don't you?"

Roger was silent so long she thought he was going to ignore the question. When he spoke, his tone was flat. "Once, a long time ago, we cared a great deal. But that was a very long time ago. She's engaged to Jack now and I've learned to accept that."

"Have you? When you look at her, your eyes haven't accepted it."

Roger's face tightened. "Look, no matter what you think you see in my eyes, it doesn't matter. She and Jack are going to be married. That's the end of the story."

"There are so many things I don't understand."

"Join the club," Roger told her bitterly.

"You and Eleanor love each other, yet she's going to marry Jack. But they don't love each other." She frowned, puzzled.

"What makes you think they don't love each other?" Roger asked in a tone of mixed hope and pain.

"They aren't happy when they're together."

"Who told you love was supposed to make you happy? It's been my experience that love does a lot of things, but making you happy isn't one of them." He reached for his jacket.

"But it's obvious they aren't in love," Sheri protested. She'd caused Roger pain in some way she didn't quite understand.

Roger shrugged into his jacket before looking at her. "Is it obvious because of your own feelings for Jack? Don't let love fool you into seeing what you want to see. It's a painful experience.''

Sheri watched him go, too stunned to speak. What he was implying wasn't possible. She cared for Jack. Of course she cared for him. She wanted to see him happy. That was the only reason she was concerned about his engagement. She just wanted him to be happy. But it wasn't because *she* loved him, at least not in the way Roger was suggesting. She wasn't *in* love with Jack.

Was she?

She reached up to smooth her hair, aware that her fingers were trembling. The luxurious room faded away and she was standing on a grassy hill, Jack's arms around her; then she was in a rose garden at midnight, Jack's hands gentle on her skin.

Shivering, she wrapped her arms around her waist, trying desperately to refute Roger's words. In love with Jack? It just wasn't possible. It would be foolish. But, then, when had love ever been wise?

But if she loved Jack, how could she be sure of her motives in trying to force Eleanor and Roger together? It seemed clear that they loved each other. It was in their eyes, in the tension between them. Was Roger right? Was it clear because that's what she wanted to see? Had her motives been selfish all along?

Sheri heard Glynis's footsteps in the hallway. Without a second's thought, the air around her shimmered and she was gone. She sought the sanctuary of the rose garden instinctively, slipping into reality in the shadow of an arbor that arched over one end of the pathway. The afternoon sun spilled over the garden, bringing out a wondrous richness of perfumes.

For once Sheri didn't notice the beauty around her. Her eyes were turned inward, trying to comprehend the impossible. She couldn't be in love with Jack. Yet how could she not love him? The question slipped in, and she closed her eyes against the truth it held.

How could she not love him? She should have asked that question weeks ago. When she thought of the kindness in his eyes, the way he could laugh at himself, the way his lightest touch seemed to go right to her soul, it seemed almost inevitable that she should fall in love with him.

She'd been such a fool. She closed her eyes, shutting out the bright sunshine around her. The price for loving him was high, but she'd have paid it in an instant if she thought there was any chance of him returning that feeling. But he didn't, couldn't. Even if he wasn't in love with Eleanor, he planned to marry her. And even without that barrier, there was still the reality of what she was.

Jack had accepted the disruptions she'd brought to his life, but only because he saw them as temporary. In the end he expected his life to continue along the path he'd set for it. That path didn't include her.

JACK SHRUGGED out of his suit jacket and threw it on the passenger seat as he slid into the Jag. Leaving work these days felt more and more like escaping from a prison. In the office above, he'd left half the company celebrating the successful conclusion of the Carter deal. He should be there. After all, it had been his project, his baby from the start. He should be at the celebration.

Only he didn't feel much like celebrating. Somewhere along the way, the Carter deal had become just another duty to be discharged. He'd lost the enthusiasm, the excitement.

He turned the key in the ignition, frowning at the windshield. There had been a time when he'd enjoyed his work. He was almost sure of that. At least he'd enjoyed the challenge it presented. But that seemed like a very long time ago now.

He flipped on the Jag's lights as he backed out of the parking place. The problem was, he'd been thinking too much lately. And what he kept thinking about was that long-ago dream of raising horses. Stupid. He'd grown out of that years ago. It was a kid's dream. But he kept thinking about it. About how much he'd like to ride again, how much he'd like to teach Sheri to ride.

Sheri and her talk about dreams. That was what had started this line of thinking. Sheri. Everything in his life seemed to circle back to her in one way or another. No matter how hard he tried to put her out of his mind, she lingered there.

He turned on the radio as he hit the on ramp for the Ventura Freeway. The soothing strains of Mozart washed over him and he scowled, flipping the radio off. Mozart made him think of Eleanor. And Eleanor made him think of his upcoming marriage, which was beginning to loom on his horizon like an iceberg before the *Titanic*. He'd been so clear on his reasons for marrying Eleanor, so sure that it was the right thing to do, that they could make each other happy.

"She died and he never quite got over the loneliness of being without her." Sheri's voice echoed in his mind, telling him about the woman his uncle had almost married. Jack scowled at a Toyota in the next lane. There was Sheri again, poking in where she didn't belong. But her words lingered. He tried to imagine how he'd feel if something happened to Eleanor. He'd miss her. Of course he'd miss her. But spend years of his life grieving for her? No, he couldn't honestly say he would.

"But every marriage can't be based on a grand passion," he muttered aloud. There was no answer except the abiding uncertainty in his mind.

By the time he got home, he was feeling restless and just a little put upon. After all, he'd been quite content with the arrangement of his life until a few weeks ago. Maybe he was going through a midlife crisis. It was a decade or so early, but that didn't make it impossible.

The house was dark and quiet, and Jack assumed that everyone was in bed. But when he shut the front door, there was a glow of light coming from the library. He stepped into the room, already sure of what he'd find. The room was dark except for the dancing glow of the fire on the hearth. Sheri was visible only as a pair of slender legs draped over the arm of a heavy leather chair.

He cleared his throat and the legs disappeared to be replaced by a head of tousled hair and wide blue eyes. She smiled when she saw him, though he thought a touch of wariness lingered in her expression.

"No, don't put it out," Jack told her when the fire flickered on the verge of disappearing. "It's nice. Even if it is almost summer."

"You look tired." The lilting softness of her voice soothed his ragged nerves. He sank into a chair near hers, barely noticing when a footstool appeared in just the right place. Putting his feet up, he sighed. "I guess I am a little tired."

"I'll leave you alone." She stood, but Jack leaned forward, catching her arm.

"No." He realized how abrupt the word sounded and softened it with a smile. "If you're not too tired, I'd like the company."

She hesitated. Odd, Jack thought, how he could feel her uncertainty where his hand touched her arm. He wanted her to stay. She'd turned his life upside down, put a permanent crimp in his picture of the world as he'd always thought he knew it, but there was a certain peace in her company. And he wanted that right now, needed it.

"All right." She sank back into the chair, tucking her feet under her legs so that the swirl of her gray skirt covered her legs.

Silence settled over the room, a pleasant, undemanding quiet. Jack let it seep into him. Staring into the fireplace, he was reminded of those few short days at his uncle's house. That was the last time his life had seemed simple and under control.

"Do you ever think of Uncle Jack's?" he asked, his voice low.

"Sometimes. It was so peaceful there."

"I've thought about selling the place, but I can't bring myself to do it."

"It is a special place for me, too."

Jack turned his head to look at her. She was staring into the fire, her expression pensive.

"Are you ever sorry you came here?" He wasn't sure where the question had come from, but the answer was suddenly important.

She was silent for a moment. When she turned her head to look at him, there was something in her eyes he couldn't define, a deep sadness.

"No. No, I could not be sorry that I came with you."

Jack had the feeling there was some meaning in her words that he couldn't quite catch.

"You know, I wish we could be at the cabin right now. It must be beautiful."

He'd spoken impulsively, out of desire to find a simpler time more than anything else. Scarcely had the words left him than he felt a tingling that started at his fingertips, then swept over his body. There was a moment of warm darkness, a darkness so intense that it was impossible to imagine light ever piercing it. A quick wrenching feeling, like stepping off a stair that wasn't there, and then he was sitting in a thick leather chair that was not in his library.

He clutched at the arms of the chair, staring around him at the living room of his uncle's home. Everything was just as he remembered it, with the exception of the golden samovar, which no longer sat in the corner. Sheri sat in the chair across from him, her feet curled under her, just as they'd been a moment before. Only a moment ago she and Jack had been six hundred miles away.

"Your wish is my command," she said.

"I guess I'm going to have to be careful of what I wish for." Jack wasn't surprised to hear the shaky note in his voice. He had to make a conscious effort to unlock his fingers from their grip on the chair arms. He was aware of a tingling sensation again, a feeling of being vibrantly alive unlike anything he'd ever felt before.

He grinned suddenly, leaning back. Maybe Roger was right. Maybe he didn't appreciate the advantages of having a genie. He laughed.

"This gives new meaning to the words 'Beam me up, Scotty.'" He laughed once more, feeling totally carefree. His life, his fiancée and all his problems were hundreds of miles away.

"That is from *Star Trek*. I have been watching it in reruns." Sheri was pleased that she recognized the reference.

Jack laughed again. "I wouldn't think they could teach you much. Was that my first wish?"

"I have told you that it does not work that way."

"Are you sure?" He lifted his feet, watching without concern as a footstool shifted into position. "In all the fairy tales I read when I was a kid, you got three wishes."

"Those were stories. This is real life." She stared at him, puzzled, when he threw back his head and laughed deep and long.

"If I'm going to believe in you, I can hardly refuse to believe in fairy tales," he explained.

"I suppose not." Sheri laughed, too, seeing the humor in her words.

"Okay, for my second wish I'd like a cognac. The very best cognac, if you please." Jack waved his hand in a kingly gesture, but it was still a shock to see the snifter at his elbow. He lifted it, finding it warmed to the perfect temperature.

"Thank you." He lifted the snifter, inhaling the heady fragrance. "Do you suppose anyone will worry that we're not where we're supposed to be?"

"Your mother and Tina went to Santa Barbara to visit someone."

"Aunt Lydia, probably. Mother and Tina went together? I thought they were still at odds with each other."

"I believe Tina wanted to talk with your mother. She wants to try to reassure her that continuing her education does not mean she's not thinking about a personal life."

"Well, I wish her luck on that one. God knows, I've talked until I'm blue in the face. About the only thing that would reassure Mother is if Tina turned up married."

"I don't believe she is going quite that far, but she does have a man she cares very much about. I think she's going to tell your mother about him."

"Tina has a boyfriend?" Jack frowned into his cognac, not entirely sure he liked the idea of his little sister with a man.

"A man who works with dolphins," Sheri told him.

"Great. Now we'll be inviting Flipper to tea. Translation of 'works with dolphins'—he's a beach bum."

"That is one of the reasons Tina has not told you about him," Sheri informed him reprovingly. "She said you would not approve because he wasn't on the same social level. I told her you were not that narrow-minded."

There was a momentary silence.

"Ouch," Jack said. He looked at her, his eyes rueful. "For such a nice little thing, you certainly do pack a wicked punch. But you're right." He lifted one hand, palm out. "I promise to keep an open mind about Tina's friend. How's that?"

"Tina will appreciate it."

"You've been avoiding me," Jack said abruptly.

"Have I?" Sheri reached up and tugged on a soft curl.

"Yes, you have." He swirled the brandy in the bottom of the snifter. "For the past two or three days. When I appear, you disappear. You're not mad at me, are you?"

"No, of course not."

Her eyes appeared haunted, Jack thought, the tilt of her smile a little fragile.

"I guess I just thought that maybe you could use a little distance from me."

Jack leaned forward, catching the hand that twisted in her hair, feeling her fingers quiver in his. Their eyes met and he forgot what he'd planned to say. Where their fingers touched, electricity sparked. He drew a deep breath and released her hand. "When I need distance, I'll let you know, okay?"

"Okay." Her smile was brighter, but there was still something in her eyes—vulnerability. He took a sip of cognac and stared at the fire.

Around them the old house was quiet. Outside, the night lay quieter still. Somewhere far off came the hoot of an owl. Los Angeles seemed a million miles away. Part of another world.

"Did I ever tell you that I wanted to raise horses?" The question came from out of nowhere. He hadn't planned to say anything at all, and certainly not that. But now that it was out he couldn't call it back.

"It sounds wonderful. I think you'd be very good at that."

"Oh, it was just silly kid stuff." Jack swirled the cognac, watching the patterns of light in the amber liquid. "Roger and I were going to move to Wyoming. Or was it Montana? And we were going to have the greatest horse ranch the West had ever seen. Stupid, really."

"Why is it stupid?" Sheri questioned.

Jack shrugged. "Oh, I don't know. We didn't really know that much about raising horses. You know, all kids go through a cowboy stage. I guess we were just a little older than most when the urge hit."

"What happened?"

"Life. I guess life happened. God, that sounds pompous and philosophical, doesn't it?" He pushed the footstool out of the way, setting his feet on the floor and leaning forward to stare into the fire. "Roger went to 'Nam. By the time he came back, I was halfway through college. We talked about it. Roger even bought a place up above Santa Barbara. Not the million acres we'd dreamed of, but a start. I was going to join him after I got out of school—it meant so much to my father that I have my degree."

He stopped, but Sheri didn't prompt him. After a long moment he went on, feeling the need to finish now that he'd started. "Then my father died. The bank was in trouble and I had a majority interest. There wasn't anyone else, so I tackled it. I worked blind at first—I didn't know what the hell I was doing. But I made a few lucky choices. The job was only going to be temporary, but there never seemed to be a good time to step out. After a while I stopped thinking about leaving.''

He shrugged again, suddenly uneasy. He had the feeling he'd said a great deal more than he'd intended.

"It's not too late, you know." Sheri's quiet words broke the stillness. "You could still have your dream."

"You mean the horses? I told you, that was just kid stuff." He finished off the last of the cognac without tasting it.

"Was it?"

"I don't know." He stared into the empty snifter broodingly. "If you'd asked me that three months ago, I could have said yes. But something's happened since I met you." His mouth twisted. "I guess I'd forgotten all about dreams and magic before I met you."

"Are you sorry?"

The question brought Jack's gaze to her. Her face was shadowed, her expression impossible to read.

"No. No, I'm not."

He reached out, catching her hand in his, drawing her toward him. She slipped from her chair with the grace of a drifting leaf and knelt in front of him. Jack cupped her cheek with his hand and let himself be lost in her eyes.

"I want only your happiness."

How was it possible for her to be utterly perfect? The firelight cast shadows in her hair, turning it into a cloud of red gold. Her eyes were soft pools of blue, danger and sanctuary in one glance. And her mouth— How could he possibly describe her mouth? His thumb brushed across the sweet bow, feeling her lips soften beneath his touch.

"You've turned my life upside down. You've made me believe in the impossible. And you've almost made me believe in dreams again. Almost."

"Jack—"

He pressed his fingertips to her mouth, stopping her words. "Don't say anything. For now let's pretend that this is a dream. There's no one in the world but the two of us. This is all there is, only the here and now. A dream, Sheri. A sweet, sweet dream."

For a moment they stared at each other. He couldn't define what he saw in her eyes, he couldn't guess what she saw in his. But he knew that nothing had ever felt quite so right as this moment. He cupped her neck, tilting her head back, and saw her eyes widen, and knew she was half frightened, half eager.

"Jack, no." Her breathless protest didn't match the need in her eyes.

"Sheri, yes." The words ghosted against her lips an instant before his mouth touched hers. She opened to him like a flower drinking in rain. Her mouth was soft and inviting. His tongue slid between her lips, the taste of cognac mingling with a sweetness that could belong only to Sheri.

Jack felt all rational thought slip away and he let it go gladly. The past, the future—neither mattered.

He stood up, drawing her to her feet, his arms catching her close so that nothing could have slipped between them, not even a shadow. All that mattered was the here and now, the feel of her in his arms, the taste of her on his tongue and the desperate need that burned deep inside him. A need only she could satisfy.

He dragged his mouth from hers, but only to explore the length of her delicate throat. He heard her sigh, a soft sound of pleasure, another brand on the fire. He'd wanted her forever, needed her always. The pulse that beat at the base of her throat fluttered beneath his touch. Jack's mouth claimed it for his own.

She arched over his arm, trusting him with her helplessness, offering him whatever he chose to take. But in the taking there was giving.

His hand slid downward, cupping the gentle weight of her breast in his palm. His mouth closed over hers again, swallowing the quiet moan.

He lifted her in his arms, her weight as insignificant as a fairy's wing. Her lashes fluttered upward, her eyes meeting his in the golden firelight. Jack waited. She seemed to be searching for something in his eyes. Whatever it was, she must have found it, for she relaxed against him, her head coming to rest on his shoulder; she gave herself into his keeping with a trust so complete it made him ache.

The house was still as he carried Sheri up the stairs, the only sound his footfall on the steps. He shouldered open the bedroom door, unsurprised when the lamp beside the bed came on.

Stopping beside the bed, he let Sheri slide down his body until her feet touched the floor. Her hands rested on his chest, one palm over the rapid beat of his heart.

Her blouse opened at his touch, seeming to melt away. The skirt dropped to the floor with a whisper of sound and she stood before him, wrapped in nothing more than the silken fall of her hair. Jack stared at her, her beauty leaving him without words. She was all pale gold. He reached out, needing the sense of touch to prove her reality.

She caught his hands, a half smile tilting her mouth as she placed them at his side, a silent command. Jack obeyed with an effort that became greater with each passing moment. His shirt fell open beneath her touch and

Jack's breath caught at the feel of her fingers against his chest.

Sheri looked up at him, her eyes reflecting wonder as she explored the muscles she'd bared. There was such innocent sensuality in the look that Jack groaned. He buried his hands in the rich length of her hair, letting it spill over his forearms. Her mouth yielded to the hungry pressure of his, her body pliant in his arms.

Jack released her only long enough to tug the rest of his clothes off, impatient with anything that kept him from her. He lifted her onto the bed, following her down, fitting the length of his body to hers.

The bed cradled them, a gentle cocoon against the world outside. There was no tomorrow, no yesterday. Nothing that mattered beyond this place, this moment.

Jack's hands shook as he explored her slender body. He'd never wanted—needed—like this. There was a soul-deep need that only Sheri could fulfill. Her soft touch, her murmurs of pleasure fed that need, yet stoked it until it threatened to consume him.

He lifted himself above her, bracing his weight on his hands. Her legs came up to cradle him, but he hesitated a moment. Her hair was spread across the pillows, framing her delicate features, her deep, shining blue eyes. In that moment, he knew that he'd never been complete. Without her, he'd never know completion.

Her body opened to his, accepting him as if made for him only. The movements were older than time itself, but they'd never felt so new. And the fulfillment, when it came, was like nothing he'd ever known before. It wasn't only a fulfillment of body, it went deep into his soul, cleansing him, making him whole.

Chapter Twelve

Jack came awake slowly, aware that he'd slept deeply, dreamlessly. He shifted against the pillows, reluctant to open his eyes. He wanted to linger in the limbo between sleep and waking. As he breathed deeply his nostrils were teased by a delicate scent, a soft floral with overtones of sandalwood. He rolled over, his arm reaching out, seeking, but the bed was empty.

He opened his eyes and a sense of loss drifted over him. Sheri was gone. He didn't need to look for her. After last night, he could sense her absence as easily as her presence. He was back in his own bedroom at home, the old house in the mountains once more hundreds of miles away. Her clothes were gone; his had been neatly folded and set on a chair. All that remained was the lingering scent of her on his skin, and even that was fading in the morning light.

Jack pulled himself up, propped his elbows on his bent knees and buried his head in his hands. What had happened last night? It had all seemed so clear-cut, so obvious. The feel of her in his arms, in his bed, had seemed inevitable, preordained.

He hadn't thought of anything but the need that had burned in his gut. He hadn't thought of duty or commitment or responsibility. Most of all, he hadn't thought of Eleanor.

"Dammit!" He jerked back the covers and stood up. Striding into the bathroom, he twisted the shower on with vicious force, then stepped under the scalding water, as if the heat could burn away the guilt he felt.

Eleanor. How could he have forgotten his engagement? He'd never pretended to be madly in love with her, but at least she had the right to expect fidelity. And he hadn't even managed that.

And Sheri. He leaned against the cool tile, letting the hot water pound on his back. What was Sheri thinking right now? Did she have regrets? She'd been so soft in his arms, yielding but not passive. There'd been passion in her touch, a need as great as his own.

He groaned as his body reacted to the memories. God, he was worse than a randy teenager. He wrenched the controls, gasping when ice-cold water poured over his overheated skin. At this rate he was going to give himself a heart attack. At least then he wouldn't have to worry about dealing with the consequences of his actions.

Jack toweled dry and dressed for work without paying any attention to what he was doing. His instincts told him he should find Sheri, talk to her. But what would he say? He didn't know how he felt, didn't know what she would want to hear. And there was Eleanor to consider. Although, having already slept with another woman, he supposed that simply talking to her was no great crime.

Still, shouldn't he talk to Eleanor first? And what was he going to say to her? He groaned, his fingers fumbling with a navy silk tie. He was supposed to see Eleanor to-night...some dinner party they were attending as a couple. How was he going to face her? And what was Sheri going to think?

A headache nagged at his temples. What had happened to his neatly ordered life? Where had it gotten off track?

Nothing was turning out as he'd planned. Nothing was going as he'd expected.

He couldn't talk to Sheri until he had a chance to think things through. Besides, she must feel the same, or she wouldn't have stolen out of his bed. Feeling like the lowest worm on earth, Jack grabbed his briefcase and all but fled the house.

SHERI STOOD BACK from the window, watching the Jag back out of the drive. Even from this distance she could sense Jack's confusion. Or was it her own? The car sped out of sight and she turned away from the window, her fingers twisting in her hair, her expression troubled.

When she'd slipped from the bed this morning, she'd told herself it was for Jack's sake, to give him time. But she had to be honest with herself and admit that she was the one who'd needed time. Time to come to terms with the changes in herself, time to wonder how Jack was going to feel about last night.

She wandered outside, seeking the quiet peace of the rose garden. She lifted a hand to Melvin, who was carefully nipping faded blossoms, but she didn't seek out his company.

Had last night been wrong? Denial rose inside. Surely something that felt so good, so right, couldn't be wrong. Her expression softened, her eyes warm with memories. She felt as if she'd been half-alive until now. All that had come before faded into insignificance.

And yet she'd lost something. She reached out to touch a rosebud, exerting all her willpower. The petals unfolded slowly, reluctantly. Sheri's hand dropped to her side, her fingers trembling. She'd known the price she'd have to pay for loving. She was no longer part of either world. She'd sacrificed most, if not all her powers for one night in Jack's arms.

And she'd do it again, she thought fiercely. For those few hours, she'd been complete in a way she'd never known before. If that was all she ever had, it was surely worth any price. And to have Jack's love— She hardly dared even dream of that.

How did he feel about her?

JACK COULDN'T HAVE answered that question to save his soul. The only thing he knew for sure was that he didn't know how he felt. He wasn't sure if that was a significant advance over knowing nothing at all, but at least it was something.

Work sat unattended on his desk while he stared out the window, his thoughts so tangled he couldn't even begin to sort them out.

On the one hand, there was Eleanor. Sophisticated, elegant, a product of his world, a world he understood. She'd make a wonderful hostess, a good companion, a helpmate in the true sense of the word. And he could give her the security and stability she wanted. She'd be an asset to his career, a good mother to their children and she wouldn't leave him in a perpetual state of confusion.

And then there was Sheri. His face softened. How could he possibly describe Sheri? Sweet, giving, full of light. She'd never understand his career, never give a socially important party. She'd bring home stray people and stray animals and expect him to help them. She'd turn his life upside down without even knowing it. He didn't even know if they could have children.

Good God! What was he thinking of? He turned away from the window he was looking out of and glared at a potted palm. He was acting as though it were a matter of choosing between the two of them. As though, if he didn't marry Eleanor, he and Sheri might—

"It's a ridiculous idea," he muttered to the palm. "She isn't even human." But she'd felt very human in his arms last night. "Besides, it's arrogant to think like that. I don't even know if she'd have me. And after last night, I can almost guarantee that Eleanor won't. And would it be fair to her even if she did?" His scowl deepened.

"I don't love her. Not that I love Sheri," he added hastily. "I care for her, but I can't be in love with her. I *won't* be in love with her." The words seemed to echo hollowly in the office and Jack was grateful when there was a quick knock on the door. A distraction was just what he needed right now.

"Come in."

But Tina was already in, poking her head around the door. "Your secretary said you might be busy, but I knew you wouldn't be too busy to see me."

"You knew that, did you?" Jack grinned affectionately. "What if I said I *was* too busy?"

"You'd be lying," Tina told him cheerfully, stepping into the office and shutting the door behind her. She was wearing jeans and a green top so bright Jack put a hand over his eyes.

"Is that thing legal? It's enough to cause traffic accidents."

"Of course it's legal. Besides, it reflects my mood."

Jack's brows rose. He perched on the edge of his desk, watching as his sister sat down in a chair, then bounced to her feet again. "Well, this is certainly a change. You've been drooping around the house for days now."

She turned to look at him, her face wreathed in smiles. "I have the best news."

"I thought you and Mother were going to be in Santa Barbara another day."

"We came home early," she told him, impatient with details.

"How was the trip?" he asked, just for the pleasure of watching her turn, full of impatience.

"Jack! Do you want to hear my news or not?"

"We-l-l." He dragged the word out, backing up when she took a threatening step toward him. He laughed. "Okay, what's the news?"

"Mother has agreed to let me go for my master's. She's going to give me the money from my trust fund." The words tumbled over themselves, so tangled they were almost incoherent.

"She did? You mean she ignored my advice?"

"Jack!" She threatened him with her purse and Jack ducked, laughing.

"Okay, okay. I'm really happy for you, brat." He held out his arms and she threw herself into them, hugging him exuberantly.

"Can you believe it? I was just about to give up hope."

"So what changed her mind?" Jack's smile lingered as he watched her pace the office, too excited to sit still for even an instant.

"Well, I suppose it was Sheri, in a way."

"Sheri?" Jack's smile faded, his eyes growing watchful. "Sheri talked with Mother?"

"No. But she and I talked, and she told me I should tell Mother about Mark."

"Mark? The guy with the dolphins?"

"How did you know? Oh, Sheri must have told you. Oh, Jack, he really is wonderful, and I think you'll like him. Sheri was right. I was an idiot not to tell you and Mother about him months ago. She said I was underestimating you."

Jack remembered his initial reaction when Sheri had told him about the man in Tina's life. Luckily Tina was too absorbed in her story to notice the guilty flush that rose in his face.

"Yes, well, I suppose it's understandable," he muttered uncomfortably.

"Sheri said that all Mother cared about was seeing me happy. So I told her all about Mark. She was a little hesitant at first, but when I told her how wonderful he was, she said she didn't care if he had fins himself as long as he made me happy. How could I have been so wrong? Really, Jack, I don't think she'd have cared if I'd told her he was a practicing warlock and carried a magic wand."

Jack coughed uneasily.

"So, has she met this marvelous man?"

"No, but he's coming to dinner next week. You'll be there, won't you? And I want Sheri to be there, too. After all, if she hadn't been so sure that Mother would accept Mark, I might not have told her. And we'd still be fighting."

Jack listened to her rattle on. From her description, Mark seemed to be a cross between Jacques Cousteau and Robert Redford. He was relieved that everything had turned out so well, but he couldn't help a mild feeling of pique.

He'd been talking himself blue in the face for almost six months, trying to convince his mother to release Tina's trust fund. He'd finally come to the conclusion he was going to have to give her the money himself, which would have caused considerable hostility on his mother's part.

In a matter of weeks, Sheri had managed to turn the whole situation around so that everyone was delighted. It would have been some consolation if she'd had to use magic to accomplish it, but she hadn't. Still, the important thing was that the problem had been resolved. He wasn't going to quibble over the means.

His good humor was stretched a little thin when his mother came to visit him midafternoon. It wasn't enough that he hadn't managed to get any work done. It wasn't enough that he felt like a total cad every time he thought of his fiancée. It wasn't enough that thinking of Sheri left him completely confused.

His own mother applied the coup de grace when she visited later in the day. He was delighted, of course, that she'd decided to open her own needlework shop, pleased that she felt it was time she put her skills to work. He'd been telling her that for years. And it certainly didn't bother him at all that she attributed her change of heart to Sheri's suggestion that it was almost a duty not to hide talent like hers away.

No, he didn't mind a bit. He smiled and told his mother he was sure the bank could arrange a business loan. He'd see to it personally that she got their very best business advisor to help her set up shop. The smile didn't last past seeing her out the door, however.

"Hell and damnation!" He shoved his hands into his pockets and stalked to the window, glaring out at the cloudless blue sky.

In the space of a few short weeks he'd lost control of his life. It was all sliding out from under him. Everything he'd worked for, planned for. So what if he'd begun to have doubts that he even wanted what he'd planned. It should have been his choice that it had all changed. Where had he lost control? Was it the first time he'd kissed Sheri? When he'd found out she was a genie? The moment he'd met her? Or did it go even farther back?

He'd leaped at the opportunity to check out his uncle's house, desperate for an excuse to leave L.A. Had things been slipping away from him even then? So he'd started to sense that some changes were necessary. But he hadn't wanted to make them all at once, with no control over their direction.

By the time he got home, the headache that had nagged at him all day was pounding in his temples. A last-minute emergency had kept him at the office late. Eleanor was due to arrive in half an hour. He didn't know what he was going to say to her—didn't even know what he *wanted* to say. And he needed to talk to Sheri, though he had no idea what he was going to say to her, either.

He pushed open the front door, rubbing the back of his neck. When had life gotten so complicated? He didn't have to look far for an answer. Sheri was in the living room, a slightly mangled needlepoint canvas in her lap. Jack doubted if she'd done much stitching, any more than he'd done much work.

She looked up and their eyes met for an instant before they both looked away. Seeing her brought memories flooding back. The way she'd melted against him, the sweet taste of her mouth, the delicate scent that lingered in his mind. His first instinct was to go to her. Everything had felt right with her in his arms. But Jack hadn't built his life on his instincts. He'd built it by thinking things out clearly, logically, making decisions based on facts. How did you apply logic to someone who couldn't even exist in a logical equation?

He thrust his fingers through his hair, feeling an irrational surge of annoyance. Everything had been so much easier before she'd popped into his life on a cloud of smoke. He cleared his throat.

"Sheri."

"Jack."

She watched him, her eyes reflecting the same uncertainty he felt. Just where did they go from here? Jack was damned if he knew.

He went to the bar and poured himself a stiff scotch before turning to face her again. Did she have to look so damn beautiful?

"How are you?" *Brilliant, Jack. Absolutely brilliant. Why don't you ask her if she'd like to do lunch next week?*

"I'm fine," she said softly. "How are you?"

"Fine. Just fine." *Sure, if you don't count budding insanity as a problem.*

Silence stretched again. Jack was vividly aware of Eleanor's impending arrival. He needed to say something about that. *Gee, I realize that we spent last night making passionate love to each other and that we need to talk. But my fiancée is going to be here any minute, so let me check my calendar to see when I can fit you in.*

Sheri reached up and twined her fingers in her hair. Jack remembered the feel of that hair in his hands, draped over his chest. He swallowed a groan and a large gulp of scotch. Maybe if he kept talking he wouldn't keep remembering.

"Tina came to see me today." His voice was a little too loud, he knew, the tone overly hearty.

"Did she?"

If Sheri was puzzled by the choice of topic, he couldn't tell it.

"That's nice."

"Wasn't it. Did you know that my mother has decided to release Tina's trust fund so she can stay in college?"

"No." She smiled, the first natural expression he'd seen. "That's wonderful. Tina must be very happy."

"Ecstatic," Jack agreed, staring into his drink. "Absolutely ecstatic." He looked up suddenly, pinning her with a cool gray stare. "She seems to feel she has you to thank."

"Me?" She shook her head. "I don't know why."

"She says you're the one who convinced her to talk to Mother."

"I suggested she do so, but I didn't do anything more than that."

"Well, it was apparently enough." Jack heard the edge in his voice and took a deep breath. He felt as if he were boiling inside. All the guilt and frustration was churning. "And this afternoon Mother came to see me."

"Did she?" Sheri tilted her head, sensing his volatile mood but uncertain of its origin.

"It seems she's decided to open up a shop specializing in needlepoint."

"That's good, isn't it?" she said hesitantly.

"It's great. I've been trying to talk her into something like that for years. But it seems that you just suggested she shouldn't waste her talents, and presto change-o, she decides it's the thing to do."

"Are you angry with me, Jack? Should I not have spoken to Tina or your mother?"

"Hell, no, talk away." He swallowed the last of his drink and set the glass down with a thump. "You've done a great job of fixing up their lives. I'm delighted."

"I didn't really do anything. I just helped them to see what they wanted. They had to make the decisions themselves."

"Don't apologize. I think it's great." He bit the words off, struggling against the irrational anger he felt. He wanted to quarrel. He needed to quarrel with her. She was so bloody perfect. Didn't she ever get angry?

"Since you're so good at this sort of thing, why haven't you helped me to see what I really want?"

"You are a man who needs to find his own way."

The quiet answer did nothing to soothe his mood. "Tell me what it is I want," he demanded. He leaned back against the bar, gripping its edge with his hands. "Tell me what's wrong with my life. What do I need to be happy?"

"Those are things only you can know."

"No, no. You did a great job with my family. Don't tell me you don't have some theories on where I'm going wrong." He waved one hand. "Tell me what you think."

"Jack, I—"

"Don't beat around the bush about it. What if I make it a wish? Don't you owe me another wish? You know we've never really discussed the details of this whole arrangement. What do I need to change in my life? Tell me."

Sheri's eyes dropped from his. "You know as well as I do."

"Tell me."

"You've chosen an easy path," she said softly. "You're doing what's expected of you, not what you want to do."

"And that's an easy path?" he asked incredulously.

"You're not taking any chances with your life." She looked up, catching him with that clear blue gaze. "You're doing what's safe. And yes, for you, that is easier."

Jack stared at her, feeling her words sink into him with the impact of blows. He wanted to deny what she was saying, but he couldn't. There was too much truth in it. In a few short sentences, she'd made him face things he'd been avoiding for years.

The rage that had been eating at him for months was suddenly white hot and uncontrollable.

"Keep your damned magic nose out of my business," he said hoarsely. "And keep it out of my family's business." He saw her eyes widen at his tone, but he was too angry to soften it.

"Jack, I did not mean—"

"I don't care what you meant. You pop into my life and you turn everything upside down. And then you start poking your nose into things that don't concern you. Well, you may be able to tidy up other people's lives, but leave mine alone. I've been managing just fine without you."

He started for the door, but stopped halfway there. "Eleanor is going to be here in a few minutes. We're going out to dinner." He said it quite deliberately, wanting to get a reaction from her. Anger, hatred, reproach, something that would justify his anger, something that would satisfy his need to quarrel with her.

Hurt flared in her eyes the instant before she lowered them.

Jack's rage flared higher. "Well, aren't you going to say something?"

"What would you like me to say?"

The simple question had no answer.

"Aren't you going to tell me I'm a cad, say that I owe you better than this after last night?"

She looked up at him, her eyes clear and shining, hiding nothing. "You don't owe me anything because of last night. I don't expect anything from you."

"Dammit!"

She jumped as the curse exploded out of him.

He stalked over to her, his eyes fierce as he stopped in front of her. "Why the hell *don't* you expect something from me? Do you always have to be so bloody self-sacrificing?"

She stared at him, her eyes wide. He turned away from that look, his rage flaring higher still. Everything had been going just fine without her.

The clock in the hall struck eight, interrupting him. "Look, Eleanor is going to be here any minute. We need to talk, but not tonight."

Sheri nodded without looking up. Jack rubbed the back of his neck. He wanted to say something more, wanted to tell her he was sorry. But he couldn't get the words out. With a muttered curse, he left the room.

Sheri watched him go. There was an ache in her chest that made breathing difficult. She lowered her eyes to the canvas in her lap, only then noticing that it was twisted in her hands. Her fingers shook as she smoothed it out.

She'd never seen Jack so angry. But there'd been pain beneath the anger and that was what lingered in her mind. Was she the cause of his pain? That was the last thing she'd wanted. Was he angry because of last night? Did he feel they'd done something wrong? The thought deepened the ache in her chest. How could something that had been so right, so inevitable, possibly be wrong?

But Jack didn't necessarily share her feelings. Maybe it hadn't been as wonderful for him. Could humans share that kind of physical closeness without feeling the kind of soul-deep connection she'd felt last night? Was that what it had been to Jack? He couldn't have been so tender if she hadn't meant something to him. Yet it didn't have to be more than friendship.

Sheri pressed a hand to her chest, trying to soothe the pain lodged there. She'd let herself hope for so much, too much. Maybe she'd been dreaming of something Jack couldn't give her. Not because of his engagement, but because of what she was. Sometimes she almost forgot how far apart their worlds really were. Maybe Jack couldn't forget.

The doorbell rang, interrupting the endless circle of her thoughts. She got up, setting aside the hopelessly twisted canvas. It was a good thing Glynis was going to have a shop to occupy herself, because Sheri's lack of progress with a needle and yarn was enough to send the woman into the depths of despair.

"Hello, Eleanor." She stepped back to let the other woman enter, then shut the door and followed Eleanor into the living room, wondering if she should feel self-conscious. If she'd thought for even a moment that Eleanor loved Jack, then perhaps she'd feel guilty over last night.

Eleanor stopped near the fireplace, shrugging off the light cape that covered her slim gray dress. "Is Jack here?"

"He's upstairs changing. I'm sure he won't be long. If you'd like, I could make you a drink."

"No, thank you." Eleanor tugged off her gloves, her expression uneasy.

"How is the dog?" Sheri asked.

"He's fine." Eleanor's mouth softened in a faint smile. "He's getting a bit spoiled, I'm afraid. I rather think I may keep him."

There was a hint of defiance in the announcement but Sheri smiled, pleased. "That's wonderful. He really did seem to be a very nice dog."

"Yes, he is." The smile faded.

Sheri was at a loss. Since Eleanor remained standing, Sheri moved over to the bar, leaning against it as she'd so often seen Jack do. "I'm sure Jack won't be much longer," she offered, thinking that perhaps the other woman was getting annoyed with the delay.

"Actually, I'm rather glad we have a few moments alone."

"You are?" Sheri asked, surprised.

"Yes." Eleanor drew a deep breath, her fingers tightening on the soft kid gloves she held. "There's something I've been wanting to say to you."

"All right." Sheri gave her an encouraging smile.

Eleanor hesitated, wondering at her own motives. But she'd started now, and it really did need to be said. "I wouldn't mention this if it weren't for my concern for Jack. A concern I'm sure you share."

"Is there something wrong with Jack?"

"No. At least, nothing serious. That is, nothing that can't be dealt with." *Get to the point,* she told herself, annoyed with the way she was beating around the bush.

She drew in a deep breath and reminded herself that she wasn't doing this out of selfish motives. "You see, people are beginning to talk."

"About what?"

Sheri's bewilderment was obvious and Eleanor felt a stab of irritation at being forced to explain what should be obvious. Why wasn't anything as it should be with this woman?

"They're talking about you and Jack. The fact that the two of you are living in the same house has raised a few eyebrows. Naturally, *I* don't think there's anything going on, but there are those who do." She paused, but Sheri didn't say anything, only continued to watch her with those big blue eyes.

Eleanor jerked her gloves through her fingers. "I wouldn't say anything it if weren't for the fact that, as a banker, Jack really can't afford to be gossiped about. His reputation is very important."

"You mean people think that Jack and I are—" she hesitated, searching for the words "—more than friends, and because you and he are engaged, they think Jack is a bad person?"

"Well, not a bad person exactly," Eleanor said. Dammit, why couldn't the woman just understand these things the way everyone else did? Why did she have to look so worried and confused? "I mean, it's not just the engagement, though that's part of it. Even if we weren't engaged, it wouldn't be a good idea for people to think that you and Jack were— Well, that you were having an affair. I'm sure you understand what I mean," she finished hastily, sorry she'd even brought the subject up.

"No, I don't. Please tell me what you mean. I want to understand."

"Well, I—" Eleanor felt as if she'd somehow gotten in over her head. She'd thought that a polite warning would be enough to protect her engagement. She'd make a few comments, Sheri would get the point and it would all be over, nice and civilized. She wished Jack would come down and put an end to this. But there was no sign of him, and Sheri was looking at her, waiting for her to continue.

"Well, I just mean that you're hardly the type of woman who gets involved with a banker. I don't mean to say there's anything wrong with that," she added quickly. "I suppose that a banker's wife needs to be rather dull and conventional. Like I am."

Sheri didn't smile at the mild humor and Eleanor cleared her throat, continuing uneasily. "You're more the bohemian type. Bankers can't really afford to be bohemian."

Sheri stared at her. "You mean, my being here could cause Jack harm?"

"No, no. Not harm precisely." How had the conversation gotten so completely out of control? "I just think that some people—stuffy people—might be concerned about your relationship with Jack." She stopped, drawing a shallow breath. "Don't you think it's awfully hot in here?"

Sheri didn't seem to hear her. She smoothed her hands over the skirt she was wearing, her expression sober. "Thank you for telling me this, Eleanor. Please excuse me." She didn't wait to hear Eleanor's mumbled reply, but walked quickly across the room.

Eleanor watched her go, her hands knotted around her gloves. What had she done? She felt as if she'd just struck something totally defenseless. She started forward. "Sheri, wait."

But the only response was the quiet click of the front door. She sank into a chair, tossing the abused gloves on an end table. She'd only been doing what she had to to protect her engagement, to protect Jack. She hadn't said anything that wasn't true. It wasn't as if she'd set out to hurt the woman.

Why didn't the justification make her feel any better?

SHERI WALKED BLINDLY. Her direction didn't matter. She just had to keep moving. Everything had gone wrong. She should never have come here. Nothing but trouble had resulted from her presence. She'd made Jack unhappy, when all she'd wanted was for him to be happy. The idea that her presence could cause him trouble cut deep.

Eleanor's motives were a little tangled. Sheri was not such a fool that she didn't see that. But there had been a ring of truth to the woman's words. People might think less of Jack because of his association with her. She bit her lip to hold back a sob.

Her pace increased until she was almost running. Trying to outrun her own thoughts. But they were relentless. It was her fault. She'd been so sure that his uncle was right, that she could help Jack. How could she have been so arrogant? Jack didn't need her. He'd never needed her. He'd be better off without her, better if she'd never entered his life.

Jack had been so angry with her. He'd known that she was causing him trouble and he hadn't told her. That was why he'd been so angry. She was such a fool, a stupid little fool. And she'd lost everything. She belonged nowhere. She should have known she couldn't step out of her world into his. She dashed a trembling hand across her eyes, feeling the dampness of tears.

As if tears could return any of what she'd lost. She stepped blindly off the curb. She had nothing. No future. No life.

Nothing.

Chapter Thirteen

Jack turned away from the mirror, his hand going to his throat. He suddenly felt as if he were choking. He tugged at his tie, his chest aching. Something was wrong. Something was horribly wrong. He drew a shuddering breath, trying to steady his pulse. This was absurd. Nothing was wrong except that he'd made a total ass of himself.

He'd flown off the handle with Sheri. He tugged at his tie again. *Sheri. There's something wrong with Sheri.* He was halfway to the door before he caught himself, slowing his footsteps to a normal pace. This was ridiculous. There was nothing wrong with Sheri except that he'd hurt her. He'd go downstairs and apologize calmly, like an adult.

But he found himself hurrying downstairs, his heart beating too fast. He couldn't explain the urgency he felt. He had to talk to Sheri. Explain to her how wrong he'd been to take his frustrations out on her. He hadn't meant to hurt her. That was the last thing in the world he wanted. She meant too much to him. He had to assure her that it was all going to work out. He'd make it work out.

He took the last two stairs in one long stride, his heart pounding with anxiety. He had to talk to her before it was too late. Too late? He stopped in the hall, drawing in a deep breath. Why would it be too late? He pushed his fingers through his hair, trying to pinpoint the source of his urgency. He had to explain, to tell her— Tell her what?

He shook his head, once more trying to slow his pulse. He had to talk to Sheri, but there was no reason it had to be this instant. The feeling lingered, driving him into the living room.

"Sheri—" He stopped as Eleanor rose from a chair, her faultlessly made-up face arranged in a faultless smile of greeting. "Eleanor." The name came out on a flat note and he tried again, going forward to kiss her cheek. "Eleanor." There wasn't much more enthusiasm the second time and his eyes were already searching the room. "Where's Sheri?"

Pique flashed in Eleanor's eyes, and her mouth tightened.

"She went out."

"Out?" Jack looked at the dark windows, fear clutching at his throat. "Out where?"

"She didn't say. We really should be on our way, Jack. We're running a trifle late."

"Didn't she say anything? It's dark out."

"I'm sure she realized it was dark out. I don't know what you're worried about. She's a big girl."

Eleanor reached for her cape, but Jack was still staring at the darkness. "It's not like her to just wander off without saying something," he muttered. He turned suddenly, and his eyes caught Eleanor's. She was unable to prevent the flush that rose in her cheeks, and Jack's eyes darkened to storm gray.

"What did you say to her?"

"I don't know what you mean." She looked away.

"You said something to her. I want to know what it was."

"Really, Jack, you're making a ridiculous fuss over this. Jack!" she said on a startled note as he stepped forward and grabbed her arm with ungentle fingers, his eyes burning into hers.

"What did you say to her?" he demanded.

"I—I didn't say anything," she stammered, half-frightened by the look in his eyes.

"Tell me." He shook her arm slightly. The cool voice of reason suggested he was overreacting. It was swallowed in the choking feeling of disaster that threatened to overwhelm him.

"I only said what needed to be said," she defended herself.

"Tell me, dammit."

"I told her that people were beginning to talk. Well, they are. And I told her that it wasn't going to be good for your reputation if she stayed here, that a banker had to be very circumspect."

Jack released her arm, turning away with a gesture of disgust. Eleanor rubbed her arm, staring at his back.

"How could you hurt her like that?" His voice was low, rough with anger. "She's never hurt anyone in her life."

"I didn't mean to hurt her," Eleanor told him, unaware of the pleading note that had entered her voice. "I didn't say anything that wasn't true, Jack. People *are* beginning to comment on your relationship."

He spun, pinning her with a fierce look. "I don't give a damn what people are saying. That's something you probably can't understand. All I care about is Sheri." He stopped, struck by his own words. "All I care about is Sheri," he repeated, letting the truth sink in.

"Don't you think that's a rather awkward thing to be telling me," she asked stiffly. "I *am* your fiancée."

"You don't love me." He looked at her as if seeing her clearly for the first time. "You never have."

"That's not true."

"And I've never loved you," he continued, overriding her feeble words. "We never pretended otherwise. We were safe for each other and convenient. I thought it was enough, but it's not."

"Jack—"

"No. It's the truth and you know it."

She stared at him, her face paper white. "What are you going to do?"

"I'm going to find Sheri. I have to talk to her." The wonder of finally realizing his true feelings was swept aside by a growing fear. He couldn't define the source, but he didn't doubt its validity. Something was wrong. Terribly wrong. "I've got to find her."

He was halfway to the door before he realized the futility of his action. She could be anywhere. Remembering their impromptu journey the night before, she could literally be anywhere in the world by now. He stopped and turned back into the living room. Eleanor stood near the fireplace, but Jack was oblivious of her.

Something had happened to Sheri. He knew it beyond a shadow of a doubt. She needed him and he didn't have the slightest idea of how to find her.

He tugged aside the curtains, staring out the window as if the answer might lie in the darkness outside.

"I'm sure she's all right."

"Shut up, Eleanor." The words were without heat. His anger hadn't really been for her, anyway. It had been for himself. For his own blind stupidity. Sheri hadn't run away because of anything Eleanor had said. She'd left because she thought he didn't want her. And for that, he had no one but himself to blame.

He turned away from the window with an abrupt movement that made Eleanor jump. "I'm going to look for her."

"I'll go with you."

"No."

The flat refusal didn't have an effect. She followed him out the door, swinging the cape over her shoulders.

"I'm going with you."

Jack whirled so quickly she almost walked into him. "*If* I find Sheri and *if* she's all right, I don't want you with me."

Eleanor swallowed hard at the blunt words, but she set her chin, meeting him eye to eye. "*When* you find her and nothing is wrong, I want to know it. After all, you seem to think it's my fault she left. I have a right to know that she's all right."

Jack spun away from her with a growl of impatience. He didn't have time to argue. Let Eleanor do as she liked. All he cared about now was finding Sheri, telling her what a fool he'd been.

As it happened, finding her was not hard. Turning right at the end of the block, Jack felt as if his heart had stopped. The eye-searing flash of red lights shattered the darkness. This was what he'd feared, what he'd expected.

Beside him, Eleanor was silent as he pulled the car to a halt at the curb and flung open the door. A small crowd had gathered at one corner, staring at the spot of activity in the normally quiet neighborhood. Jack hurried past, barely aware of their existence.

A policewoman moved to block his advance, but she wasn't quick enough. Jack stopped next to the small cluster of white-coated men who knelt in the street. Someone reached for something, shifting out of the way.

Jack knew he would never forget the picture he saw. Sheri's hair drifted across the pavement, a delicate cloud of white gold. The red lights flashed across her face, throwing a garish imitation of life into her waxen features. One hand lay across her chest, the fingers, lax, lifeless.

"Get back now."

The policewoman had to take hold of Jack's arm to get his attention. The paramedic shifted, blocking Jack's view of Sheri's still figure.

The officer tugged on Jack's arm again. "Please move back, sir."

"She's a friend of mine." He turned blindly toward her.

"You can't do her any good by getting in the way," she told him with professional sympathy. "Move back onto the sidewalk."

Jack backed away, recognizing the truth in her words. He wanted nothing more than to push them all out of the way and take Sheri in his arms, but that wasn't the way to help her. He stumbled up onto the curb, his eyes still on the tableau in the street.

"Are you Jack?" a thin voice asked at his elbow.

He turned reluctantly, and stared down at the old woman. He didn't recognize her, was sure he'd never met her, but she seemed to know who he was.

"I'm Jack Ryan."

"She was always talking about you. I'm Mrs. O'Leary." When Jack didn't appear to recognize the name, she clarified, "Sheri helps me with my garden two or three times a week. I'm sure she's mentioned it."

"I . . . yes, of course." Sheri hadn't mentioned it, but, then, he hadn't asked. Pain sliced through him. He should have spent more time with her and less time trying to deny his feelings. He'd been such a stupid, stupid fool. He hoped to God he'd have a chance to make it up to her.

"It's a tragedy. A lovely girl like her." Mrs. O'Leary shook her head.

"What happened? Do you know what happened?"

"Saw the whole thing. My eyes are just as good as they were when I was twenty," she told him proudly.

"What happened?"

"I was sitting on the porch, enjoying the night air. It's nice this time of year, you know. Saw her go tearing by like the hounds of Hell were right on her heels. Seemed real upset. I called her name, but she didn't hear me. Guess she didn't hear the car, either. She stepped right off the curb in front of it. He tried to brake but..." She shook her head.

Jack closed his eyes, seeing it all just as if he'd witnessed it himself. The car, the girl caught in the flare of headlights.

"Sir, they're taking your friend to the hospital."

He opened his eyes to see the policewoman standing in front of him. Behind her, they were loading a stretcher into the ambulance.

Mrs. O'Leary's reedy voice followed after him as he moved toward the Jag. "You be sure and let me know how she goes on."

Eleanor said nothing on the short ride to the hospital. She huddled in her seat, the cape drawn around her as if she were chilled. Jack hardly remembered her presence.

They reached the hospital just moments after the ambulance, but Jack had only a glimpse of the stretcher as Sheri was rushed through the door. He strode into the emergency room, hating the cold clinical scent of it.

During the short drive from home, his mind had been filled with remembrances of Sheri: laughing in the sunlight; her eyes full of concern over the plight of Melvin and his family; the innocent sensuality with which she'd come to his bed. He could lose it all. And there was no one to blame but himself. His own blind stupidity could cause him to lose the most precious thing he'd ever known.

"There was a young woman just brought in." He hovered over the admitting desk.

The woman behind it looked up, her eyes full of professional compassion. "Her name?"

"Sheri. Sheri Jones."

"The young woman who was struck by the car."

"Yes," he managed hoarsely. "Is she all right? Where is she?"

"Are you a relative?"

"She doesn't have any relatives. I'm a close friend."

"She's with the doctor now. I'm afraid I don't have any information about her condition. If you'll take a seat, the doctor will speak with you as soon as he can." She gestured to a narrow waiting room and returned her attention to the paperwork in front of her.

Jack stood there, his mind a blank. Sheri was lying somewhere, behind one of those closed doors, alone and hurt. Eleanor took his arm and he followed her automatically as she led him to the waiting room.

"I'm going to see if I can find your mother. This is her bridge night, isn't it?"

Jack nodded. He didn't care whom she called. He didn't care about anything but Sheri. Was she badly hurt? He kept seeing her lying so still and pale on the street. What if she— He cut the thought off. She was going to be all right. She *had* to be.

He was staring out the window, when he heard the door open. He spun around, but it was only Eleanor. He didn't bother to hide his disappointment.

Eleanor didn't feel any offense, however. She handed him a coffee and he took it, though she wasn't sure he was aware of it in his hand.

The waiting room was empty but for the two of them. Eleanor sat on one of the padded benches, staring at a painting on the wall. The soft golden fields seemed inappropriate in this place so full of fear. Jack continued to stare out the window, his shoulders tense.

When the door opened, Eleanor looked up, relief flooding her features as Roger walked in. Jack turned, looking beyond his friend, hoping to see a white coat. Seeing that Roger was alone, he turned back to the window without a sound.

"Any word?" Roger asked Eleanor, since it was clear Jack wasn't going to be talking.

"No." She shook her head.

Roger glanced at Jack and then sat down in the chair next to her. "Have they told you what happened?" he asked quietly.

"It was a hit-and-run. I don't think Jack knows any more than that." She smoothed the folded length of her cape, her fingers trembling. "I don't think he even knows I'm here."

Roger reached out and caught her hand in his, his expression tender. "It's going to be all right." He gave her fingers a reassuring squeeze before getting up and moving over to Jack.

"What happened?"

Jack glanced at him. He had to make an obvious effort to focus his attention on Roger. "She stepped in front of a car. It was only a couple of blocks from home. She was upset, not paying attention."

There was a sharp sound and he looked down to see that he'd crushed the cup Eleanor had given him. Lukewarm coffee poured over his hand and dripped onto the floor. Roger took the remains of the cup from him and tossed it in a trash can before handing him a handkerchief.

"Anything else?"

"They called the paramedics. She didn't have any ID. She never carried a purse. She should have carried a purse, even if she didn't need it." That point bothered him. He rubbed his hand across his forehead, momentarily lost in thought.

"How did you find out?" Roger asked gently, leading Jack back to the present.

"I was looking for her. I knew something was wrong. I could feel it. There was an old woman there. Sheri had been going to see her a couple of times a week, helping her in the garden. She talked about me. I didn't even know she was doing something like that. I should have known. I should have asked."

"It's going to be all right, Jack. Sheri's stronger than she looks. Besides, she's probably got some pretty strong powers of recovery in that bag of tricks. It's going to take more than a car to get her down."

"Then why is it taking so long?" Jack asked fiercely. "Why haven't they come to tell us she's all right? Why hasn't she come out herself."

Roger couldn't answer. He put his hand on Jack's shoulder, offering support. The door opened again, this time yielding the white coat they'd all been longing to see.

"How is she?" Jack covered the distance between him and the doctor in two long strides. "Is she all right?"

The doctor was young, with a shock of thick black hair and blue eyes that looked as if they were accustomed to laughter. But there was no laughter in them now.

"Your friend is still unconscious."

"Is that bad?" Jack demanded.

"We don't really know yet. There isn't an obvious reason for her continued unconsciousness. We'll be running some tests."

"She has a head injury?" Roger asked, his expression as anxious as Jack's.

"Not that we've found," the doctor admitted. "Actually, we can't find any sign of injury. She doesn't even have a bruise. If it wasn't for the fact that we have witnesses to her being struck by a car, we wouldn't have any idea what was wrong with her."

"No sign of injury?" Eleanor questioned. "Isn't that rather odd?"

"Miraculous might be a better word."

"If she wasn't hurt, then why is she unconscious?" Jack asked.

"We don't know yet. We've done a blood workup and there's no sign of drugs or alcohol."

"I could have told you that." Jack was furious they'd even had to check.

The doctor lifted one hand in a soothing gesture. "It's pretty routine these days, especially in a case like this. With no obvious injuries, we had to check."

"So what you're telling me is that you haven't the slightest idea why she's unconscious," Jack said.

"More or less. Her body has had quite a shock. There could be injuries we haven't found yet. As I told you, we're going to run some tests. We should know more when the results of those are in, which won't be before morning. I'd suggest you go home, but I don't think you'd pay any attention."

Jack didn't answer. He didn't have to. The set of his jaw made it clear that nothing short of a military escort would get him to leave. The doctor sighed. With a promise to let them know if there was any change, he left them alone.

It was left to Roger to break the silence. "Well, that doesn't sound too bad," he said, his tone too hearty. "Sheri will probably wake up in an hour or so with nothing but a nasty headache to show for this."

Jack's expression didn't change.

Eleanor put her hand on his arm. "I'm sure Roger is right, Jack. She's going to be fine."

Jack didn't even glance at her as he turned away, returning to his silent vigil by the window.

Roger and Eleanor looked at each other, uncertain in the face of the wall Jack was erecting between himself and the rest of the world.

"I'm sure she's going to be all right," Eleanor said uneasily.

"Sure she will," Roger agreed. "By tomorrow morning, we'll all be laughing with her about this."

BUT SHERI WASN'T LAUGHING with anyone the next morning. She was still unconscious and the doctors were beginning to worry. Roger took Eleanor home in the wee hours of the morning, returning just after dawn with a change of clothing for his friend. Jack took it with a word of thanks.

In the men's room, he shrugged out of his dinner jacket. It seemed as if centuries had gone by since he'd put it on. He changed into the jeans and cotton shirt Roger had brought, stuffing his dinner clothes into the satchel. Splashing water on his face, he tried to drive the grit from his eyes.

As he entered the waiting room, his eyes sought Roger. "Any news?"

Roger shook his head slowly, his expression somber. It didn't take a medical degree to know that the longer Sheri remained unconscious, the greater the reason for concern.

It was midmorning before a doctor came to talk to them. She didn't say much that her colleague of the night before hadn't said. They still didn't know why Sheri was unconscious. They had ordered more extensive tests, in hopes that they could find the source of the problem.

Jack listened to everything the woman said, absorbing the implications behind the actual words.

"Can I see her?"

"I don't see why not." Dr. Jeffries nodded, her eyes taking in the pallor of Jack's skin beneath the dark shadow of beard. "But you have to promise me you'll get some rest afterward." She lifted her hand, stilling his protest. "I don't need another patient."

"I'm not leaving."

There was no arguing with that flat tone. The doctor didn't even try. "I'm sure we can find someplace for you to stretch out. Now if you'd like to see your friend, I'm going that way. I can show you to her room."

Roger caught Jack's arm when he moved to follow the doctor. "Tell her I'm here."

Jack nodded. "I will."

Stepping into Sheri's room, Jack was struck by the stillness. It was more than just the physical quiet. There was something more. It gradually sank in that what he was sensing was Sheri's absence. He'd never consciously realized how life filled a room when she was in it. But that feeling was missing here.

He let the door shut behind him and reluctantly approached the bed. Once he actually saw her lying there, it wouldn't be possible to pretend that this was a mistake of some sort, that Sheri was safe at home. It would be real then.

He stopped next to the bed and looked down at her. She was so pale and still. Not the woman he knew at all. Her hair was spread over the pillow, framing her face. Her lashes created dark shadows on her ashen cheeks.

"Sheri?" He picked up her hand. Her skin felt cool to the touch. Her fingers were lax in his. It was as if he were touching a shell—the mind that should have been occupying it was elsewhere.

"Sheri? Sweetheart, wake up." He patted her hand gently, but there was no response. "You have to wake up. I have so much I need to tell you.

"Roger is here. He's worried about you, too. You know, the doctors don't know what's wrong with you, so I know you could wake up if you wanted to. But you've got to fight, Sheri. You've got to fight. Sheri?''

She didn't move, in fact, she seemed barely to breathe. He might have been talking to himself. And he had a sudden, terrible premonition that it was always going to be this way, that he'd never hear her voice or see her laugh again.

''Please.'' The one word was all he could get out past the choking feeling in his throat. He gripped her hand as if he could will her to wake up with the force of his need.

He had no idea how long he'd been standing there, Sheri's unresponsive hand in his, when Dr. Jeffries entered the room.

''Are you still here?'' She clucked her tongue in annoyance. ''You're not going to do her any good if you collapse.''

''I'm all right.'' Jack didn't look up as she stopped beside him.

Dr. Jeffries took Sheri's hand from Jack's, checking the pulse automatically. ''Did she respond at all?''

Jack shook his head slowly. ''Nothing. I can't lose her.''

''Well, we're going to do our best to see that you don't,'' she told him briskly. ''I want you to get some sleep now.''

''I'm not leaving her.''

''We're going to be taking her for some tests in a few minutes and you can't come along, so you might as well sleep.'' She took his arm, leading him out the door, ignoring his mumbled protest.

He stumbled into the bed she showed him, and was nearly asleep before his head hit the pillow. But his sleep was troubled, haunted by nightmare images of glaring headlights that bore down on him. He could hear the scream of brakes, smell the burning rubber and then, just when it was inevitable that the lights would strike him, the whole sequence would start over again.

Jack woke suddenly, sitting up in bed, panicked and breathless. Sweat beaded on his forehead and his chest heaved with the effort of breathing. Rubbing one hand over his face, he sought to swallow the panic that threatened to smother him.

If something had changed with Sheri, he knew someone would have woken him. He didn't draw a steady breath until he found a nurse who told him there had been no change.

The pattern repeated itself many times in the days that followed. Jack's life centered on the hospital, and all his concentration was on Sheri. He spoke to people when they came to visit, but five minutes after they were gone, he couldn't remember what he'd said. His mother and Tina visited every day. Eleanor came often, her eyes haunted.

It was almost a week before it occurred to Jack to wonder why Eleanor was so concerned. It wasn't hard to come up with an answer. She felt guilty. Her words had sent Sheri out into the darkness. Or so she thought.

"Eleanor." She jumped, looking up from the magazine she'd been staring at.

Jack sat down next to her. It was an effort to focus on anything but Sheri, but it wasn't fair to let Eleanor continue to suffer. Sheri wouldn't want that.

"Is there any change?" Her anxious fingers creased the magazine.

"No." The answer hurt every time he gave it. He rubbed his hand over his jaw, grimacing at the rasp of several days' beard. He knew from the brief glimpses he got of himself in the men's room mirror that there was little of the respectable banker about him these days. Unshaven, his clothes creased from sleeping in them more often than not, he was hardly the Jack Ryan he had been. What would Sheri think if she saw him now? Most likely she'd laugh and tell him he looked like a pirate.

Eleanor shifted beside him, her slim fingers folding and unfolding the magazine. Jack forced the image of Sheri, her eyes sparkling in a smile, from his mind.

"I'm sorry," he told Eleanor. "My concentration isn't all it should be right now."

"That's okay. You've got a lot on your mind."

"I think you do, too. More than you should have."

"I don't know what you mean." Her eyes flickered to his and then away.

"You think you're responsible for Sheri's accident."

She winced at the blunt statement, her hands trembling. "I should never have said those things to her," she said.

Her voice was so low, Jack had to strain to hear it. "No, you shouldn't have. But that's not what upset her so. At least that's not the bulk of it. It was my fault. We quarreled before you got there. Or maybe it would be more accurate to say that *I* quarreled. I don't think Sheri knows how to quarrel." He stopped, thrusting his fingers through his hair, his eyes dull with pain.

"She told me some things I didn't want to hear. I lost my temper and said some hurtful things to her. I was a fool," he admitted bitterly. "I hope I get a chance to tell her how much of a fool."

"You will. You have to keep believing that." Eleanor touched his hand tentatively.

Jack noticed that his ring no longer rested on her finger and he took her hand in his, running his thumb over the faint mark at the base of her third finger. "We'd never have made it work, you know." Eleanor's hand rested in his more comfortably now than it ever had.

"I know," she said.

Jack released her hand and stood up. The momentary distraction was slipping and his thoughts were returning to Sheri. Nothing else could hold his attention for long.

Eleanor clenched her hands as she watched him leave the waiting room. He'd looked so lost, shattered. His heart and soul were wrapped up in the still figure who lay down the hall. If she died— She bit her lip against the sob that welled up in her throat, but it was not to be denied.

Roger found her hunched in the chair, her face buried in her hands, shoulders shaking with sobs. He crossed the room in an instant, sitting next to her, his heart pounding with fear.

"Eleanor. My God, what's happened? Is it Sheri?"

"No, it's me." She looked up at him, her eyes red rimmed with tears. "I'm an awful person."

He reached out and took her in his arms. "You're not an awful person. What happened?"

"Jack." The one word broke on a sob.

Roger tightened his arms around her. "Jack is in a lot of pain right now. I wouldn't take anything he said too seriously."

"He told me it wasn't my fault. But it was. I shouldn't have said those things."

"Shouldn't have said what things?"

It took several minutes to get the story out of her. She sobbed it into his shirtfront, her voice thick with tears. Roger listened, his heart aching for her pain.

"I had no right to say those things to her. She'd never done anything to me. How could I be so cruel? And now she's going to die and it's my fault."

"She's not going to die." He shook her lightly for emphasis, his hands gentle on her shoulders. "And the accident wasn't your fault."

"That's what Jack told me. I don't know how he can even stand the sight of me," she wailed. "He's not even mad at me." She looked up at him, heartbreak in her eyes. "I'm not a very good person, Roger."

Her hair was a mess. Her eyes were swollen from crying. Her nose was red, her skin blotched. Roger had never seen her look more beautiful in his life. His mouth quirked in a tender smile as he reached up to brush the hair from her forehead.

"I'm not too great myself. Maybe between the two of us we could work on it. Okay?"

Eleanor's breath caught and her eyes widened. There was a gentle promise in his eyes. A promise she hardly dared to believe. But she wanted to believe it. She wanted it desperately. She clutched his shirt.

"Yes. Oh, yes."

"SHERI? Sheri, it's Roger." There was no response and Roger stepped closer to the bed, reaching down to take her hand, shocked by the lifelessness he felt. It had been over a week and there'd been not a flicker of life.

Looking at her, it was almost impossible to believe that she merely slept, but there was a transparency to her features, a fragility in the stillness of her form. Roger had the feeling that if he glanced away, she might disappear, simply wink out of existence. He held her hand tighter.

"Sheri, you can't do this to Jack. He's not going to get through this one. If you love him, you can't leave him like this."

There was no response and Roger stared at her, feeling helplessness slip over him like a dark tide. He'd never seen Jack this way. He moved, he answered when spoken to, but he was one of the walking wounded, and there was a look in his eyes that was frightening to see.

"Sheri, you've just got to wake up." He tried a brisk tone. "You were right about Eleanor and me. She's not engaged to Jack anymore and I think we're going to work things out. If you'll just wake up, you can say 'I told you so' as much as you like. Sheri?'' He leaned closer, seeking some sign of life, however subtle.

But there was nothing. If it hadn't been for the barely perceptible rise and fall of her chest, he would have believed that she'd already gone beyond reach.

"Ah, Sheri, wake up, honey."

"Do you think she hears?"

Roger started at the sound of Jack's voice, turning to look at him. He was a far cry from the man he'd known for almost twenty years. His clothes were creased, his face unshaven, his eyes bloodshot from lack of rest. He hadn't left the hospital since Sheri had been brought in and his skin held the pallor of someone who'd been too long out of the sun.

"I don't know," Roger said at last, releasing Sheri's hand as Jack stepped beside the bed.

"Sometimes I think she has to be able to hear me. And then I think I'm crazy." He reached out, stroking a lock of hair from her forehead.

Roger glanced away from Jack's face, feeling as if the look in his eyes was something too intense, too private for another to see. "I guess it helps to think she can hear us," he offered.

"If she can hear me, why doesn't she respond?"

"I . . . Jack, you've got to face the fact that maybe she *can't* respond." Roger said the words as gently as he could, prepared for the wild denial that sprang into Jack's eyes.

"No!" Jack said. "No," he repeated more quietly, utter determination in his face. "I won't believe that. I *can't*." He looked at Sheri, then lifted his eyes to Roger's. "I don't know what I'll do if she—" He broke off, unable to complete the sentence.

Roger didn't know what to say. There was no comfort he could offer Jack. No comfort anyone could offer. He reached out and grasped his friend's shoulder, offering silent support.

THE MORE TIME that passed, the more the doctors shook their heads and expressed complete bafflement. There was no sign of injury, no reason Sheri shouldn't wake up, yet she continued to sleep, growing paler and more wraithlike with each passing hour until she seemed to be nothing but a thin husk lying in the hospital bed.

With every day, Jack's helpless rage grew, bubbling inside him. Sleep became a distant memory. Every moment was spent at Sheri's bedside. He was terrified to leave her for even a moment, afraid she might lose her frail grip on this world—his world. The world she'd wanted so desperately to be a part of.

He pressed his forehead against the metal rail that bordered her bed, remembering how she'd talked of learning to be human. Why hadn't he told her then that it was hardly something she should wish for? Why hadn't he told her that she was perfect as she was? He'd been so caught up in petty concerns that he hadn't offered her the reassurance she'd needed.

He didn't deserve her. He knew that now. And if she'd only open her eyes, he'd set her free, though it would be like tearing his heart out. He'd give anything, his very life, if only she'd smile at him one more time.

JACK PACED back and forth in the waiting room. His mother and Tina sat in one corner, their eyes on him, saying nothing, their hands linked for support. Roger leaned against the window, staring out into the parking lot. Eleanor sat quietly, her hands in her lap, staring at nothing in particular.

There was an unspoken sense that some crisis point was near. They'd all gathered here, waiting. Outside, the sun blazed down with a heat that hinted at what summer would bring. To those inside, it might as well have been pouring rain.

"You know, she really was learning to needlepoint." Glynis broke the silence. "I'm sure she could have been quite good if she'd just had a few more lessons."

"She was reading a book about Einstein," Tina offered, her usual vibrance muted by the circumstances and surroundings. "I don't think she understood any of the formulas, but she told me he seemed like a nice man."

"She's the one who gave me Lucky," Eleanor said to no one in particular. "She told me animals could sense someone with a kind heart." Her voice cracked on the last words and she bent her head, fumbling for a handkerchief.

"She really brought an extra sparkle to the house. And no one understood the garden quite like—"

"Stop it!" Jack barked the words, his voice hoarse.

Startled, they all looked at him.

"Just stop it! You're all talking about her like she's dead."

"Jack, they didn't mean—" Roger stepped away from the window, his voice soothing.

"I know you all think she's going to die," Jack said furiously. "But you're wrong. She's going to get well. I'm not going to let her die. She can't die. God, she can't." His voice broke on the words and he spun on one heel, stalking out of the room before anyone could say another word.

"I didn't mean to imply—" Glynis broke off, her eyes showing her distress.

"Jack knows that, Glynis," Roger told her. "He's just a little ragged. We're all a little ragged."

Just then the door of the waiting room opened again. But it wasn't Jack returning. It was Dr. Jeffries, her comfortably middle-aged face holding out little promise of good news. She looked around the small gathering.

"Is there a change?" Roger asked, voicing the question on all their minds.

She shook her head slowly. "Not the change we've all been hoping for. I saw Mr. Ryan leaving the hospital." She stopped, drawing in a deep breath. "It might be a good idea if he were here. She just seems to be fading away. It can't be much longer now. I'm sorry."

There was a long, still moment when no one spoke, no one looked at anyone else. It was what they'd all been expecting, and yet, now that the moment was at hand, they were totally unprepared.

"I'll go find Jack," Roger muttered, pushing past the doctor.

JACK STALKED OUT of the hospital, blind to his surroundings. It wasn't right. It wasn't right. The phrase repeated itself in his head, echoing over and over again. No matter how far or how fast he walked, he couldn't escape it.

A sharp tug on his shirt brought him to a halt. He jerked loose from the thorn that had snagged in the fabric. Blinking, he looked around, realizing that he was standing in the middle of a small rose garden. Around him, roses blazed in half a dozen different colors. Their perfume hung in the warm air, heavy and sweet.

He reached out to touch a delicate blossom the color of sweet butter. Sheri loved roses. His hand shook as he stroked the velvety surface of the petals. His mouth twisted in a half smile as he remembered his mother's garden ablaze with flowers weeks too soon.

It wasn't right. He blinked against the burning in his eyes. They should have had a chance to share many gardens together. There were so many things he wanted to do with her, so many things he wanted to say to her. He wanted a chance to tell her that he loved her. They should have had more time, all the time in the world.

"Jack." He didn't turn toward Roger's voice, but stared blindly at a rosebud the color of a gentle sunrise.

"Look, I know I snapped in there. I'll apologize when this is all over. I guess I'm running on a ragged edge, but when Sheri wakes up—" His voice broke and the rosebud seemed to blur. He drew a deep breath. "When she wakes up, things will get back to normal."

"Jack, Dr. Jeffries came in after you left."

Jack spun, his eyes pinning Roger with a look of desperate hope. "What is it? Is there a change? I knew I shouldn't have left her."

Roger caught his arm, stopping his headlong rush back to the hospital.

"Jack, Dr. Jeffries says that Sheri is fading away. She says...she says that it probably won't be long until... until..." He couldn't finish the sentence. He looked away from the dawning realization in his friend's eyes.

"No." Jack murmured the word. "No. I won't let it happen. I can't." He looked around the rose garden dazedly. "I don't know what I'd do without her."

"Jack, I... I'm sorry." The words seemed worthless, but it was all he could say.

"You know, she wanted to be human," Jack said to no one in particular. "She wanted to fit in my world. My world." He laughed roughly. "My world is what's destroyed her. My God, how could I be so blind?" He slapped at one of the rosebushes, oblivious of the thorn that caught his palm, tearing at the skin.

"It's my fault she's lying in there. It's all my fault."

"Jack, it's not your fault. There was an accident. It could have happened to anyone."

"To anyone, yes. But not to Sheri. She should have been able to avoid it. Didn't it ever occur to you to wonder why she didn't avoid it?"

"No one can avoid every accident. Not unless you're a wizard or—" Roger broke off, realizing what he was saying.

"Or a genie," Jack finished bitterly.

"I hadn't thought of that. What happened? Why didn't she just disappear when she saw the car?"

"Because of me."

"Don't be an idiot. Sheri might have been hurt, but she'd never let herself get hit by a car."

"She didn't *let* herself get hit. She couldn't prevent it. She told me once, only I didn't listen. I was too bloody selfish to think about what was happening."

"Told you what?"

"I asked her if genies ever fell in love," Jack said softly, remembering another rose garden, another time. "And she said that they did, but that it wasn't like a human falling in love. She said that they lost most of their powers." He snapped a rosebud off, staring blindly at the delicate shape. "They lose most of their powers," he repeated as much to himself as to Roger. "I should have thought . . . But I didn't. I only worried about what was happening to me. Not about what it could do to her."

"Jack, you're not making any sense."

"Don't you see? She didn't get out of the way of that car because she *couldn't*. She didn't have her powers anymore because she loved me. She loved me. And now she's going to die."

He watched understanding come into Roger's eyes, before looking away. Since the accident he'd lived with the knowledge that Sheri's love for him might be the cause of her death. It ate into him with the bite of acid—a burning pain he'd live with the rest of his life.

He looked at the rosebud he held, remembering how Sheri had loved roses. How was he going to go on without her? Pain emptied his mind of thought. Softly, as if drifting on the perfumed air, Sheri's voice slipped into his mind.

"Love is something we are, not just something we feel. A human dies of a broken heart only on the inside. For us it's more than that."

And Dr. Jeffries's voice. *"She just seems to be fading away."*

Something struggled to life in his mind, something so delicate he hardly dared label it hope. *Love.* Sheri had believed in that. *"It won't be long,"* Dr. Jeffries's voice reminded him. There was so little time. Was it possible?

He pushed past Roger, unaware of the other man's presence. It was a foolish hope, his desperation showing in the fact that he even dared consider it.

There was a nurse in Sheri's room, but Jack didn't see her. He ran to the bed and took Sheri's cold hand in his, the forgotten rosebud caught between his palm and hers. He could see the change in just the short time since he'd left her. She was so pale, her skin almost translucent.

"Sheri. Sheri, I love you. I didn't tell you before because I was a fool. You've got to come back, sweetheart. I love you."

He waited, hardly drawing a breath, but there was no response. Behind him, Roger stepped silently into the room. He didn't know what had sent Jack rushing back here, but he wanted to be present in case his friend needed him.

"Sheri." Jack made his voice more commanding, no longer pleading but demanding. "Sheri, you've got to come back."

"Mr. Ryan, please keep your voice down."

Jack didn't even turn to look at the nurse. All his attention was focused on Sheri, all his will.

"Sheri, you have to come back. I didn't get my third wish."

"Mr. Ryan, lower your voice."

The nurse's scandalized tone was no more than an annoying noise. Roger reached out, silencing her with a hand on her arm. He thought he could guess what was going through Jack's mind, through his heart. He was unashamed of the tears that burned in his eyes as he watched his friend's last desperate efforts.

"Sheri, I want my third wish. You owe me that."

There was no response from the still figure on the bed, no life in the hand that lay slack in his.

"Sheri?" His voice cracked on the name. "Oh, God, please don't leave me alone. I can't make it without you. Please. You owe me that third wish. You can't go without giving me that much. I'll let you go after that, but I want that wish. It was part of the deal. Remember?"

His voice fluctuated between demand and pleading. Still no response, and Jack seemed to shrink in on himself, his shoulders hunching like those of a very old man.

"Please. Please don't leave me alone," he said brokenly.

Roger started forward, unable to bear the agony in his friend's voice. The nurse didn't move, understanding that this was an intensely private moment. Roger was halfway to the bed, when he stopped as if he'd run into a wall.

He heard Jack's breath catch and knew he hadn't imagined the flicker of movement.

Jack leaned forward, his eyes intent. Surely her lashes had moved. "Sheri." He kept the edge of demand in his voice.

Her lashes flickered again and Jack's fingers tightened over hers.

"I want that last wish. You promised me that."

Her lashes lifted slowly, as if carrying a heavy weight. She looked at him, her eyes a faded blue, so little of her left in them that Jack felt a terrible fear. What if it was too late?

"You promised," he told her firmly, gripping her hand as if he could hold her there with his strength alone.

She took a shallow breath and moistened her lips. "I have . . . nothing to give you."

The whisper was so low, he had to bend close to hear it. "I only have one wish," he persisted.

"Mr. Ryan!"

"I have nothing to give," she repeated, the dim awareness fading from her gaze.

Her eyes started to drift shut and Jack's hand tightened fiercely.

"You can give me this. You have to give me this."

She moistened her lips again, the effort clear. "What do you wish?"

"I want you to love me as much as I love you."

She stared at him for a moment and then her eyes fell shut.

"Sheri!" Jack's voice held raw panic. Had he been wrong? For seemingly endless moments there was no movement and he tasted the bitterness of loss.

But then her lashes moved again, lifting slowly. The faded blue seemed a little darker, a little brighter.

"I love you, Sheri. I love you more than life itself. You've got to come back to me. We'll raise horses or sail around the world or fly to the moon. It doesn't matter as long as we're together. I want you to love me. That's my last wish. The last command I'll give you."

Her fingers shifted in his, curling over the rosebud. Jack's hand closed over hers. He had to lean over to hear her words, but they settled into his heart.

"You don't have to wish for what you already have."

He took a deep breath, feeling the tightness ease in his chest. Roger drew a deep breath, aware that his cheeks were damp. It was going to be all right. Against all the odds, it was going to be all right.

"I love you." Jack bent to kiss her, knowing he could never say it too much. She'd taught him how to dream again and she'd taught him that magic was real. Together they'd learn about love.

And ever afterward, the nurse would tell the story of how the rosebud unfurled before her eyes until it was a magnificent golden bloom, the color of sunshine and promises.

Have You Ever Wondered If You Could Write A Harlequin Novel?

Here's great news—Harlequin is offering a series of cassette tapes to help you do just that. Written by Harlequin editors, these tapes give practical advice on how to make your characters—and your story—come alive. There's a tape for each contemporary romance series Harlequin publishes.

Mail order only

All sales final
